SO MANY BABIES

Four heart-tugging stories about the littlest matchmakers—as they find their way through the Buttonwood Baby Clinic and into a family's welcoming arms!

THE BABY LEGACY by Pamela Toth
Special Edition #1299 On sale January 2000

When an anonymous sperm donor tries to withdraw his "contribution," he learns a beautiful woman is eight months pregnant—with *his* child!

WHO'S THAT BABY? by Diana Whitney
Special Edition #1305 On sale February 2000

A handsome Native American lawyer finds a baby on his doorstep—and more than he bargains for with an irresistible pediatrician who has more than medicine on her mind!

MILLIONAIRE'S INSTANT BABY
by Allison Leigh
Special Edition #1312 On sale March 2000

Pretend to be married to a millionaire "husband"? It seemed an easy way for this struggling single mom to earn a trust fund for her newborn. But she never thought she'd fall for her make-believe spouse....

MAKE WAY FOR BABIES! by Laurie Paige
Special Edition #1317 On sale April 2000

All she needed was a helping hand with her infant twins—until her former brother-in-law stepped up to play "daddy"—and stepped right into her heart.

Dear Reader,

Happy 20th Anniversary, Silhouette! And Happy Valentine's Day to all! There are so many ways to celebrate…starting with six spectacular novels this month from Special Edition.

Reader favorite Joan Elliott Pickart concludes Silhouette's exciting cross-line continuity ROYALLY WED with *Man…Mercenary… Monarch*, in which a beautiful woman challenges a long-lost prince to give up his loner ways.

In *Dr. Mom and the Millionaire*, Christine Flynn's latest contribution to the popular series PRESCRIPTION: MARRIAGE, a marriage-shy tycoon suddenly experiences a sizzling attraction—to his gorgeous doctor! And don't miss the next SO MANY BABIES—in *Who's That Baby?* by Diana Whitney, an infant girl is left on a Native American attorney's doorstep, and he turns to a lovely pediatrician for help.…

Next is Lois Faye Dyer's riveting *Cattleman's Courtship*, in which a brooding, hard-hearted rancher is undeniably drawn to a chaste, sophisticated lady. And in Sharon De Vita's provocative family saga, THE BLACKWELL BROTHERS, tempers—and passions— flare when a handsome Apache man offers *The Marriage Basket* to a captivating city gal.

Finally, you'll be swept up in the drama of Trisha Alexander's *Falling for an Older Man,* another tale in the CALLAHANS & KIN series, when an unexpected night of passion leaves Sheila Callahan with a nine-month secret.

So, curl up with a Special Edition novel and celebrate this Valentine's Day with thoughts of love and happy dreams of forever!

Happy reading,

Karen Taylor Richman,
Senior Editor

Please address questions and book requests to:
Silhouette Reader Service
U.S.: 3010 Walden Ave., P.O. Box 1325, Buffalo, NY 14269
Canadian: P.O. Box 609, Fort Erie, Ont. L2A 5X3

DIANA WHITNEY
WHO'S THAT BABY?

SPECIAL EDITION®

Published by Silhouette Books

America's Publisher of Contemporary Romance

To Mona, David and all their beautiful babies.

Special thanks and acknowledgment are given to Diana Whitney for her contribution to the So Many Babies series.

SILHOUETTE BOOKS

ISBN 0-373-24305-7

WHO'S THAT BABY?

Copyright © 2000 by Harlequin Books S.A.

Visit us at www.romance.net

Printed in U.S.A.

Books by Diana Whitney

Silhouette Special Edition

Cast a Tall Shadow #508
Yesterday's Child #559
One Lost Winter #644
Child of the Storm #702
The Secret #874
*The Adventurer #934
*The Avenger #984
*The Reformer #1019
†Daddy of the House #1052
†Barefoot Bride #1073
†A Hero's Child #1090
‡Baby on His Doorstep #1165
‡Baby in His Cradle #1176
*††I Now Pronounce You Mom
  & Dad* #1261
††The Fatherhood Factor #1276
Who's That Baby? #1305

*The Blackthorn Brotherhood
†Parenthood
‡Stork Express
††For the Children

Silhouette Romance

O'Brian's Daughter #673
A Liberated Man #703
Scout's Honor #745
The Last Bachelor #874
One Man's Vow #940
One Man's Promise #1307
††A Dad of His Own #1392

Silhouette Intimate Moments

Still Married #491
Midnight Stranger #530
Scarlet Whispers #603

Silhouette Shadows

The Raven Master #31

Silhouette Books

36 Hours
Ooh Baby, Baby

DIANA WHITNEY

A three-time Romance Writers of America RITA Award finalist, *Romantic Times Magazine* Reviewers' Choice nominee and finalist for Colorado Romance Writers' Award of Excellence, Diana Whitney has published more than two dozen romance and suspense novels since her first Silhouette title in 1989. A popular speaker, Diana has conducted writing workshops, and has published several articles on the craft of fiction writing for various trade magazines and newsletters. She is a member of Authors Guild, Novelists, Inc., Published Authors Network and Romance Writers of America. She and her husband live in rural Northern California with a beloved menagerie of furred creatures, domestic and wild. She loves to hear from readers. You can write to her c/o Silhouette Books, 300 East 42nd Street, 6th Floor, New York, NY 10017.

IT'S OUR 20th ANNIVERSARY!
We'll be celebrating all year,
continuing with these fabulous titles,
on sale in February 2000.

Special Edition

 #1303 Man...Mercenary...Monarch
Joan Elliott Pickart

 #1304 Dr. Mom and the Millionaire
Christine Flynn

 #1305 Who's That Baby?
Diana Whitney

#1306 Cattleman's Courtship
Lois Faye Dyer

 #1307 The Marriage Basket
Sharon De Vita

 #1308 Falling for an Older Man
Trisha Alexander

Intimate Moments

 #985 The Wildes of Wyoming—Chance
Ruth Langan

 #986 Wild Ways
Naomi Horton

 #987 Mistaken Identity
Merline Lovelace

#988 Family on the Run
Margaret Watson

 #989 On Dangerous Ground
Maggie Price

#990 Catch Me If You Can
Nina Bruhns

Romance

 **#1426 Waiting for the Wedding**
Carla Cassidy

#1427 Bringing Up Babies
Susan Meier

#1428 The Family Diamond
Moyra Tarling

 **#1429 Simon Says...Marry Me!**
Myrna Mackenzie

#1430 The Double Heart Ranch
Leanna Wilson

#1431 If the Ring Fits...
Melissa McClone

Desire

 #1273 A Bride for Jackson Powers
Dixie Browning

#1274 Sheikh's Temptation
Alexandra Sellers

 #1275 The Daddy Salute
Maureen Child

#1276 Husband for Keeps
Kate Little

#1277 The Magnificent M.D.
Carol Grace

#1278 Jesse Hawk: Brave Father
Sheri WhiteFeather

Chapter One

The moment he turned on the light, he saw the limp orange lump floating in the fishbowl. It had been that kind of a day.

The loss pained him. He'd told Spence he didn't have time for a pet, even one that required no more than a bowl of water and a daily dose of food flakes. His gregarious law partner had insisted that everyone needed something to care for, even a stoic isolationist like Johnny Winterhawk.

Johnny had capitulated, accepted the finned creature despite misgivings. Living things didn't do well in his company. The last such offering had been a vigorous pothos plant presented by Rose McBride, administrator of the Buttonwood Baby Clinic, in appreciation for having discovered and stricken a particularly onerous clause from the clinic's lease agreement.

Johnny had been pleased by the handsome little plant. He'd placed it on a sunlit windowsill and watered it religiously every morning. Within weeks, the shiny green leaves faded to mushy yellow. Now yet another life force had shriveled in Johnny's clearly inept hands.

Sighing, he removed the deceased fish and carried it into the bathroom for disposal. "Rest in peace, little fellow." He pulled the handle. With a whoosh and a swirl, the tiny creature disappeared.

A prick of real remorse startled him. It was only a fish, after all, although he'd been oddly fond of it, and had rather enjoyed watching the creature snap up the food flakes poured into its bowl each day. Not that he'd been emotionally attached to it, of course. Johnny knew better than that. Nothing in this world was permanent. Not plants, not fish, not people.

Especially not people.

Still, he'd put forth serious effort to provide what the little fish had needed, just as he'd made a serious effort to care for the plant. He always made a serious effort. It was never enough.

Perhaps the Creator was displeased. Johnny's grandfather would have commanded a four-day fast, along with communion into the dreamworld, a place where spirits of earth, sun and sky might bestow spiritual awakening to those who'd broken their spiritual harmony with the earth.

To Grandfather, all living things were one, and all knowledge was bestowed by ancestral whispers to those who had the courage to listen.

Johnny respected that philosophy. He simply had a different approach—easy come, easy go. Not particularly profound, but it worked. And it kept him sane.

Returning to his nightly routine, Johnny poured his usual nightcap—two fingers of amber whiskey served in an etched-crystal brandy snifter—then he methodically turned on both the stereo and the television, cranking the volume until every square foot of the expansive house vibrated with sound. A glance at a gold-and-diamond watch worth more than his grandfather had earned in a year confirmed that it was barely 10:00 p.m. The night was young.

He settled at the table, opened a fat, triangular valise stuffed with documents and went to work.

An hour later, he'd finished his first drink and poured himself another when the doorbell jangled above the din from the stereo and television. He pushed away from the table, swearing under his breath. No visitors announcing themselves an hour before midnight brought good news. The last time it had been this late, he'd found a sheepish neighbor on the doorstep, reeling drunk and slurring apologies for having flattened Johnny's mailbox.

Johnny hadn't cared about the mailbox. He had, however, been furious that the intoxicated fool had gotten behind the wheel of a car, and Johnny had said so. Explicitly.

There had also been a late-night prank that resulted in half the neighborhood being draped with toilet paper, and an unpleasant visit by the doddering widow from down the street, who'd been served with a small-claims-court summons and had actually scolded him for working late, thus forcing her to stay up past her bedtime for the free legal advice to which she felt utterly entitled.

Steeling himself, Johnny strode to the door, prepared for a drunken neighbor, a mountain of toilet paper or a wild-eyed widow clutching a summons. He was, in fact, prepared for just about anything. Anything, that is, except a wailing infant with a note pinned to its blanket.

It really had been that kind of day.

Stifling a yawn, Claire Davis stuffed her stethoscope in the pocket of her lab coat and had nearly made her escape when she heard the desk phone ring.

Nurse Jansen intercepted the call. "Buttonwood Baby Clinic. How may I help you?"

Claire dodged the nurses' station and slipped into the doctors' lounge. She was so tired she could have slept standing up. Her back ached, her eyes burned and her contact lenses felt as if they'd been fused to her eyeballs with Super Glue.

If she hadn't been such a sucker for a panicky new mom who couldn't tell the difference between scarlet fever and prickly heat, she'd have been home by now lounging in a hot bubble bath and preparing to sleep through her first day off in a week. Instead, she'd spent the past two hours soothing a frantic Mrs. Martinez, and explaining that a newborn really didn't need three layers of clothing in an overheated room.

Now Claire leaned against the cool metal locker, weary to the bone. The bubbles beckoned. She could practically smell the steam, feel the sensual slither of silky soap caressing her skin. The image lent momentary buoyance, bestowing enough energy for her to exchange her lab coat for a warm sweater and the lumpy canvas backpack that served as a portable communications center, research facility, office and purse.

The lounge door creaked open. Claire heaved a sigh, spoke without turning around. "Unless it's an emergency, just page whoever is on call. I'm officially off duty."

"You've been officially off duty since five this afternoon," came the cheery feminine reply. "That didn't keep you from coming back in to see the Martinez baby."

"Personal patients get personal perks."

"Then you may want to take this call."

A teasing lilt to Nurse Jeri Jansen's voice made Claire glance over her shoulder. "Is it one of my patients?"

The young woman sported a taunting grin and a gleam of sheer mischief in her huge hazel eyes. "Nope."

"Is it an emergency?"

"It doesn't seem to be."

"Doesn't seem to be?"

"It's a little difficult to tell. All the caller says is that he wishes to speak with a physician." Jeri lowered her voice, which quivered with a peculiar hint of amusement. "I heard a baby fussing in the background."

If curiosity hadn't taken so much energy, Claire might have been intrigued by the gleam in the young nurse's eye and the sparkle in her voice. She cast a weary glance at the marker board to see whose name had been written in for the evening calls. "Page Dr. Parker. He's great with fussy babies."

Jeri's grin widened. "Are you sure you don't want to take this call yourself?"

"I'm positive." Closing the locker, Claire shouldered her backpack, dug out her car keys and displayed them with a provocative jangle. "My bubble bath awaits."

"Ah, a bubble bath, is it?" Jeri sidestepped neatly as Claire exited the lounge. "Well, no one can say you haven't earned it," she called as Claire hurried down the hallway toward the elevator. "Don't worry about a thing. You just enjoy your evening, and have a nice day off tomorrow."

A prick of guilt slowed Claire's progress. Frowning, she glanced over her shoulder just as Jeri returned to the phone at the nurses' station.

The nurse grinned, winked, mouthed "Good night" before picking up the receiver.

Claire responded with a nod and a smile, then poked the elevator call button before she changed her mind. She could already feel those fragrant bubbles massaging her aching body.

Jeri's voice filtered down the hallway. "I'm sorry to have kept you waiting, Mr. Winterhawk—"

Claire went rigid. *Mr. Winterhawk?*

"I'm afraid we don't have a pediatrician available at the moment. However, I'd be happy to take a message and have Dr. Parker return your call."

The remainder of Nurse Jansen's voice floated around Claire in a fog. All she could think about were the images spinning through her mind. Obsidian eyes, shoulders to die for, lips so sensual that the merest curve of a smile turned her knees to water and melted her heart like warm butter.

She spun on her heel, her pulse pounding, to make eye contact with the nurse whose gaze twinkled with amusement. "I understand, Mr. Winterhawk. I will impress upon Dr. Parker the urgency of your situation."

It was him, the one man on earth who possessed a mystical power to turn a no-nonsense, professional pediatrician into a quivering mass of longing with no more than a quiet gaze, a stoic glance in her direction.

The moment Claire leaped forward, Jeri crooned into the receiver. "Oh, wait a moment. I do believe Dr. Davis is now free to assist you." With that, Jeri pushed the hold button, uttered a slightly maniacal laugh and held out the receiver.

Claire snatched it out of her hand, stupidly found herself smoothing her hair. Few things on earth were more enticing to Claire Davis than a hot bubble bath. Johnny Winterhawk was one of them.

He loomed in the doorway, not a tall man but a powerful one, bronze and obsidian, copper and jet, so male that every ounce of moisture evaporated from Claire's mouth and the icy night air steamed against her heated skin.

"Good evening, Mr. Davis. I'm Dr. Winterhawk." At his blank stare, her smile stuck to her cheeks as if stapled. "I mean, I'm Dr. Davis. You're Mr. Winterhawk. Of course, you already know that." Was that a giggle? Claire felt dizzy. She'd giggled, actually tittered like an idiot schoolgirl. "I mean you know who you are. You certainly don't know who I am. Except that I've just told you—"

Dear Lord, please strike me mute.

"—or at least, I've just tried to tell you, but it seems as if my tongue has a mind of its own this evening...." Another giggle.

This was not acceptable, not acceptable at all.

Claire snapped her mouth shut, felt her lips curve into what must have appeared to be a demented grimace. She felt like a raving lunatic, but he was so close, so very close. Close enough to smell him, to see the gleam of bewilderment in eyes so intensely dark that a woman could get lost in them. Close enough to observe sparkling drops of milky moisture on his cheek, damp blotches on his pin-striped shirt, a puff of snowy powder marring his perfectly scissored black hair.

"Thank you for coming, Doctor." His voice was resolute, but a quiver of tension caught her attention. She regarded him more analytically now, mustering enough lucidity to recognize veiled panic in his eyes. "I know what an imposition this is, but under the circumstances—"

A thin wail emanated from inside the room, barely audible beyond the cacophony of television and radio noise also blaring from inside the house. The fragile cry instantly snapped Claire into physician mode. She straightened, glancing past the impressive man to the interior of a surprisingly lush home. He'd barely stepped aside to allow her access when she pushed past him, following the sound to a tiny infant nested in a blanket-padded car seat that had been placed on a dining-room table amid a clutter of documents and legal briefs.

With her attention completely attuned to the child, the din of music and television chatter grated on her last nerve.

"For heaven's sake, turn off the television," Claire muttered. "If I had to listen to that racket for more than five seconds, I'd cry, too."

Johnny leaped forward to silence the television. A moment later, the music ceased, and a semblance of blessed silence settled over the house, broken only by the pitiful sobs of the fussing infant.

Claire set her knapsack on a chair and scooped the

unhappy baby into her arms. The baby stiffened normally at the movement, flailing little arms that seemed strong, well developed, normally coordinated. "There, there, precious, what seems to be the trouble, hmm?" The baby sobbed, bobbled its little head against her shoulder to gaze up with eyes as dark as those of the man who watched anxiously.

"She's been crying for over an hour," he said. "I found some powdered formula...." His gaze slipped to a diaper bag that had been opened, its contents strewn about the sofa as if eviscerated in a panic. "I tried to feed her."

Claire smiled, wiping the remnants of the meal from the infant's feathery black hair. Crusted formula was splotched on the baby's face, and her pajamas were saturated, as well. "Looks like she's wearing most of it." She angled an amused glance in his direction. "Or perhaps you are."

He blinked, glanced down at his own stained shirt. "I have no experience with children."

"Too bad they don't come with instructions, isn't it?" Rubbing gentle circles on the baby's back, Claire glanced around the luxurious room. The ambience surprised her. It was modern, sparkling clean, a tapestry of warm earth tones and shining crystal that seemed as far removed from the inner soul of this man as did the Ivy League clothing in which he wrapped himself.

On a bookcase, nested between modern crystal and a stack of worn leather volumes, was an odd bowl of murky water with a thick coating of muck on the gravel. There was also a glass display case containing a pair of small beaded moccasins and what appeared to be a tanned-hide pouch of some kind. In the foyer, she'd noticed an embroidered replica of the Southern Ute tribal flag, lovingly framed and displayed in a place of honor. The home was a collage of the old, the new and the peculiar, as much a dichotomy as the man himself.

Perhaps that was what had always fascinated her about Johnny Winterhawk—the incongruity of what she saw in him versus what he displayed to the world.

Of course, it was all just a fantasy, the safety of worship from afar. Claire had been smitten by the handsome lawyer the moment she'd laid eyes on him. In the two years Claire had worked at the Buttonwood Baby Clinic, they'd passed in the hallways, exchanged an occasional nod of greeting. Claire had sighed, shivered and had sweet dreams for a week after such encounters. They'd never officially met until tonight.

The infant bobbled in her arms, capturing her full attention. "I'd like to examine her. May I use the table?"

Johnny blinked, then rushed forward to gather papers from the table. He jammed them into a worn leather valise, fat at the bottom and narrow at the top, with a strap clasp and rolled leather handles darkened with the patina of constant use. It rather reminded her of an old-fashioned physician's bag.

Johnny glanced around, retrieved a small receiving blanket from a wad of items that had apparently been dumped from the diaper bag and spread it across the polished oak surface. "I was afraid to remove her out from the car seat," he murmured. "She seems quite fragile."

"Babies are tougher than they look," Claire assured him. She placed the infant on the blanket and began to undress her carefully, angling a glance at the staunchly distraught man hovering nearby. "Tell me again how you happened to be, er, baby-sitting this evening?"

He paled slightly. "It's a rather delicate matter."

"Is it?" Resting her palm on the baby's tummy, Claire used her free hand to unsnap her case and retrieve her stethoscope. "Physicians are a discreet breed. I'll take your secrets to my grave."

He hiked a dark brow, whether in shock or anger she couldn't tell. "Are you mocking me?"

"I'm teasing you." She smiled, surprised herself by absently patting his arm. Her fingers tingled at the touch. He was firmer than she'd imagined, his muscles rigid beneath the smooth fabric of his expensive dress shirt.

Licking her lips, she focused her attention back to her tiny patient. "You're clearly upset by whatever has happened here tonight. I was trying to break the tension. I meant no offense."

"Of course not." He sighed, pinched the bridge of his nose. When he glanced up, the confusion in his eyes touched her. "It's just that this is...quite personal."

She considered that. "So I've gathered. Since you've requested my assistance, and since the well-being of an infant is at stake, I'm obliged to ask certain questions, and frankly you are quite obliged to answer them."

A flush crawled up his throat. He coughed, glanced away. "My apologies, Dr. Davis. You've gone out of your way to be helpful, and I've repaid you poorly."

Her heart fluttered. He was without a doubt the most perfect man God had ever created. Claire wondered if he was aware of that. "A nice cup of coffee would go a long way in paying my bill. You could use some yourself." She issued a pointed nod toward a brandy snifter of amber liquid on the wet bar, remnants of the nightcap he'd mentioned on the telephone and ostensibly the reason he refused to drive the infant to the clinic. Claire had admired that about him. She also had an aversion to operating a vehicle after having imbibed even a moderate amount of alcohol.

"Coffee. Of course. How thoughtless of me not to have offered." Clearly frustrated, he brushed his hand along the side of his head, spreading a new smear of powder across his ebony hair.

"Graying at the temples is a good look for you," she said cheerily. Removing the baby's pajamas, she grimaced at the wafting aroma. "I presume you didn't get around to a diaper change."

"Diaper?" He blinked as if unfamiliar with the word. Comprehension dawned slowly. "Diapers," he repeated, seeming horrified at his oversight. "It didn't occur to me...." His voice trailed off as he gazed helplessly from the red-faced, kicking infant on the table to the crystalized powder coating his hand.

Claire wondered how much of the formula had actually gotten into the bottle the indomitable Mr. Winterhawk had gamely prepared. She had to hand it to him; he'd certainly given it the old college try.

An irked squeak brought her attention back to the infant, who kicked her fat legs wildly and flailed a tiny fist against her tummy. Claire's heart felt as if it had been squeezed. Babies were her business. She'd seen hundreds of them, all beautiful, all adorable.

There was something special about this black-eyed, button-nosed babe, something almost mythical and chilling. It was as if this tiny infant had the power of a magus, the eyes of an old soul trapped in a newborn body. She felt a kinship to the child, an instant bonding so sudden and forceful that her own body vibrated with it.

She brushed her knuckles across the silky soft baby cheek. "What is her name?"

Johnny yanked at his collar, skewing his tie to the side. "Lucy."

"Lucy," Claire crooned. "A beautiful name for a beautiful girl." At that moment, Claire fell utterly and completely in love with this precious infant. It wasn't professional. It wasn't even rational. But it was nonetheless real. And it would change the course of her life forever.

The coffee dripped quietly, its fragrance wafting through the kitchen to mingle with the peculiar aroma of warm milk and sweet powder. Johnny slumped against the counter, willed his trembling knees to stay the course. From his vantage point, he could see through the open door into the dining room where a lovely Titian-haired doctor nurtured the now content infant with heartrending tenderness.

Claire Davis. So that was her name. It was a good name—strong, independent, yet delicate and feminine, like the woman who wore it.

Johnny remembered her from the clinic. She was not a woman one could easily forget. He vividly recalled the first time he'd seen her. While idly glancing out the glass door of Rose McBride's office, he'd been surprised to discover a gorgeous redhead in a lab coat staring back at him. She'd blushed prettily, walked into a counter and dropped an armful of charts on the floor.

Johnny had been fascinated by the wreath of color circling her porcelain complexion, the dazzling impact of her embarrassed glow as a nurse bent to assist her. She'd angled a glance at him, seen him staring at her, then flushed to a bright fuchsia, scooped up the strewn folders and fled.

From that moment on, he'd searched for the beautiful redhead every time he'd gone to the clinic, and made it a point to study her when she wasn't looking. Now she was here, in his home, with light from his dining-room chandelier dancing in her hair with the sparkling hues of warm sherry in sunlight.

Every nuance was alluring, every smile, every dimple, every twist of auburn brow, every whisper from moist, full lips. Few women were natural beauties, but this one was. Her blue eyes were large, round, exquisitely framed with thick dark lashes that didn't appear to have been coated with black goo that so many women seemed obliged to paint on themselves. A pale smattering of freckles shone golden across otherwise alabaster skin untinted by makeup. Her brows were pale, neatly plucked, but otherwise natural.

Yes, she was pleasing to the eye. But it was her manner that held Johnny's rapt attention, the radiance as she whispered to her tiny patient, the expertise with which her slender fingers caressed and stroked and gently probed. Professionalism was evident in every movement, efficiency in every touch. She turned the child competently, positioned the stethoscope around the small, bare back.

Johnny flinched at how easily she'd managed to

unwrap the infant that he had been too cowardly even to remove from the car seat.

Claire Davis. Here. In his home. Holding both his past and his future in her very competent hands. He wondered if he could trust her with either.

Then realized that he had no choice.

Claire set her coffee cup aside and reread the note Johnny had shown her.

Please take care of Lucy. I have faith in you.
                                              Samantha.

She swallowed hard, handed the note back to him. "This was pinned to her blanket?"

Johnny nodded, sat heavily in a plush lounge chair across from the sofa where Claire held the sleeping infant.

"May I assume that you are familiar with this Samantha person?" Although Claire had meant the question to be kind, Johnny flinched at the inference. Evasive banter was a waste of time even when performed as a courtesy, so she cut to the chase. "Is Lucy your daughter?"

His Adam's apple bobbed. "I presume so."

"Presume?"

His shoulders squared slightly, increasing their impressive width. A powerful man, she noted, with an extraordinarily well-muscled upper body that provided a potent contrast to provocatively slim hips and lean legs that probably weren't as long as they appeared. "Samantha and I were involved during the time the child was apparently conceived," he said simply. "Since she has seen fit to bring Lucy to me, I must presume that the child is mine."

Claire nodded. The infant was gorgeous, with dark skin, high cheekbones and exquisitely crafted Native American bone structure that mirrored her father's. "She looks like you."

Johnny's gaze softened. "She looks more like her mother, actually. Samantha's eyes are the same almond shape, and she has the same round little nose that always seemed like God had put it there as an afterthought—" He bit off the words, as if realizing that they had revealed more intimacy than intended. When he spoke again, his voice was firm, his eyes guarded. "I don't understand what has happened here tonight. If Samantha had required my assistance, all she had to do was ask. There was no reason for such…clandestine measures."

The bewilderment and pain in his eyes struck Claire with unexpected force. "I can only imagine how unsettling it must be to suddenly discover you have a child." Not to mention having that child dropped on the doorstep like the morning paper. A wave of anger surged through her chest, forcing her to take several calming breaths. "Have you contacted the authorities?"

The suggestion clearly shocked him. "Of course not." He licked his lips, then stood so quickly that the massive lounge chair vibrated. "I won't pretend to understand Samantha's motives here, but I do know her to be a loving, honorable woman who would never willingly cause pain to a living thing. There has obviously been a misunderstanding."

"Of course," Claire murmured.

"This is merely temporary. Samantha will clear everything up as soon as she returns."

"And when will that be?"

His jaw dropped only for a moment before he tightened it with a stoic clench. "Soon."

"I'm certain you're right." Claire wasn't certain at all. A woman who'd leave a child on a doorstep didn't seem to be sending a message that she'd be back anytime soon, but Claire would rather gnaw her own arm off at the elbow than to say that aloud.

Judging by the confusion and hurt in Johnny's eyes, he clearly wasn't willing to accept that a woman he'd once cared about deeply, a woman who had betrayed him by having kept his child secret, would have betrayed him again by abandoning that child, perhaps as she'd once abandoned him.

Claire couldn't comprehend how any woman could leave a man like Johnny Winterhawk or this precious infant who had so deeply etched a groove in Claire's own heart.

Gazing down at the sleeping child on her lap, she was drawn to stroke the baby's silky scalp, catching fluid strands of short ebony hair between her fingers and smiling as baby lips twitched. A glimmering bubble appeared at the corner of her slack little mouth.

A twinge of real pain twisted Claire's heart at the realization that this precious, innocent child had been betrayed by the one person on earth she'd trusted to love her, nurture her, care for her always. To Claire, maternal desertion was the most heinous of crimes. She could not, would not allow Lucy's mother the same benefit of doubt that Johnny was plainly willing to offer.

In fact, she did not like this Samantha person one

bit. It took every ounce of control not to reveal the extent of her anger to the man ~~who was desperately~~ trying to excuse the inexcusable.

"Samantha is a good woman," Johnny said suddenly.

Claire felt herself flush, wondering if he could also read minds. Still, she couldn't bring herself to agree with him. "She must have had her reasons, although I won't pretend that I can conceive of a single one that excuses the choice she has made." Reluctantly shifting the sleeping babe back to the car seat, Claire stood. "However, Lucy appears to be well nourished, normally developed and in good health. You should probably bring her into the clinic tomorrow for a more thorough examination and a few tests."

Johnny stiffened as if he'd been shot. "I can't do that."

"Why not?"

"I have appointments in the morning."

"The clinic opens at 6:00 a.m."

"I'll be at my office by then and I won't be home until ten at night. I have a law practice to run." His brows rose into a ridiculously pompous arch that she might have found amusing if fatigue hadn't sucked the humor right out of her.

"I wouldn't know anything about hard work and long hours. I'm just a doctor." She scooped up her bag, tossed her sweater over her arm. "As for the baby, just toss her into the car seat on your way out in the morning. I'm sure she'll be fine on her own for a good fifteen or sixteen hours."

Pained comprehension dawned, etching itself in every line of his handsome face. The long-term consequences of fatherhood had no doubt just occurred to him. "Oh, my God."

Now it was Claire's turn to arch a brow. "Exactly."

He dropped into the chair, ashen. When he slumped forward with his elbows on his knees, she thought he'd fainted. After a long moment, he spoke without looking up, his authoritarian tone having softened to an almost palpable panic. "What am I going to do?"

Claire could practically feel his terror, his confusion, his abject misery. For some odd reason, it touched her as if it were her own. She set her knapsack down, and knelt beside him. "You're going to do what you have to do," she said gently, "to take care of your daughter."

"I don't know how."

"I'll teach you."

He shook his head. "That would be too much to ask. Besides, this is just—"

"I know, I know, it's just temporary." She sighed, sat back on her heels. "Temporary or not, a baby needs full-time care and attention. Which is not to say that you have to let your career go to hell in a handbasket. You'll have to make some adjustments, true, but nothing you can't handle."

He raised his head, angled a doleful glance. "How do you know what I can and cannot handle."

"I'm a good guesser." Her teasing wink got a small smile out of him. Very small, but very potent. An army of goose bumps slipped down her spine at even the hint of his smile. "Besides, lots of parents have to work, which is why there are places like the Buttonwood Child Care Center."

"Child care?" He brightened, as if the thought of

such a wondrous place hadn't occurred to him. "Of course."

She stood. "Joy Rollings runs the center. I'll give her a call first thing in the morning, and tell her to expect you."

Gratitude in his eyes turned to panic so quickly she barely had time to react before he shot from the chair and clutched both of her hands in one of his powerful palms. "Tomorrow? What about tonight?"

"The center is open from 6:00 a.m. to 6:00 p.m."

"But I can't possibly... I mean, I nearly drowned her with a bottle. What if I drop her? What if...?" He shook his head. "No, no, that is not acceptable, not acceptable at all."

Claire's empathy cooled as quickly as it had evolved. "In that case, your options are limited." She unsnapped her case, retrieved a card from a pouch and handed it to him. "Call this number. All your problems will be solved."

He stared at it blankly for only a moment, then every trace of color drained from his face as his feigned bluster melted before her very eyes. "The state welfare agency?"

"They'll send someone out to pick up the child, and you can wash your hands of the problem once and for all." Claire knew her tone was cold. She meant it to be. "Oh, you'll have to send a pesky check once in a while. Oddly enough, the state expects parents to support their children with money even if they're unwilling to support them in any other way, but hey—" she gave his back a chummy slap "—a fancy high-priced lawyer like yourself shouldn't care about a few paltry dollars, particularly if it alleviates that handsome legal mind of yours from dealing with unimportant details, such as changing diapers and mixing baby formula. Sound like a fair trade?''

Most of the color had returned to his face, and his eyes had gone completely black. ''Involving the authorities could result in charges being filed against Samantha.''

''True, but that's not your problem, is it? I mean, once the state gets its paternalistic paws on baby Lucy, she might end up in foster care, bounced from hither and yon until her poor baby psyche has been permanently damaged. As long as it doesn't interfere in your law practice, what do you care?''

He flinched again, but to his credit never broke eye contact with her. ''Touché, Dr. Davis, your point is well taken.''

''Oh, call me Claire. After all—'' she elbowed him playfully ''—I know all your secrets now, so it seems a bit highfalutin to stand on formalities, don't you think?''

''You don't know all my secrets, Claire.'' He smiled, not a full-blown smile, exactly, but much more well formed than his prior effort. The effect was devastating. ''At least, not yet.''

Chapter Two

Late-night shadows scattered along the sidewalk, pooling in between amber shafts of illumination from porch lights that dotted the Eastridge apartment complex. Shifting the precious bundle in her arms, Claire managed to position her key in the lock and elbow the light switch as she stepped inside a room filled with lush house plants and unlit scented candles.

"Welcome to my humble abode," she murmured to the bright-eyed infant. "I know, I know, it's been a busy night for such a tiny girl, hasn't it? But it's been a busy night for your daddy, too, and I think he needs a few hours to get himself together. Discovering that one is a father can be a bit disconcerting, even for the strong, silent type."

Lucy seemed intrigued by the one-sided conversation, which gave Claire yet another opportunity to convince herself that the impulsive decision to bring

Lucy home with her was based more on sound logic than emotional whim. It was reasonable, she told herself, to give a stunned man time to gather his thoughts, rearrange his schedule and make room in his life for a child whose existence had been completely unknown to him.

"No, sugar-bug, your daddy hasn't rejected you. He's just upset because that's how men get when they lose control over their lives."

Lucy widened her eyes. Claire's heart melted. Her daddy hadn't rejected her, but her mother had.

A clench of fury tightened Claire's chest. Despite Johnny's gallant defense, Claire disliked Lucy's mother intensely. She told herself that she wasn't being fair, that she was prejudging the woman without the slightest understanding of what tragedy might have warranted such desperate measures.

But in Claire's mind, there could be no excuse to give away one's child.

She shrugged the diaper bag off her shoulder, carried the cooing infant into her bedroom. Because she couldn't help herself, she hugged Lucy close, brushed her cheek against her soft little scalp. A tear burned, clouding her contact lens.

"Don't you worry, little one. You have people who love you, who will take care of you always."

Lucy looked up, blinked and burped. For some reason, that tickled Claire immensely. "I swear, you are the sweetest baby I've ever seen in my life. Trust me, I've seen more than my share of sweet babies."

Claire laid the infant in the middle of her bed. At two months old, Lucy was just learning to arch her little body, and might be able to turn over, so Claire placed a couple of pillows on each side of the child to keep her safe.

"We're going to have a lovely time, you and I."

Bright baby eyes blinked up, struggling to focus on Claire's movements as she slipped off her skirt and blouse and tossed them over a nearby chair.

"Tomorrow morning we'll go shopping," Claire told the infant. "Your wardrobe leaves a bit to be desired, don't you think?" She shimmied into a frumpy but practical flannel nightgown, traded her dried-out contacts for a pair of gold-rimmed eyeglasses and stretched out on the bed beside the squirming infant. "Red would be a smashing color on you. Something in gingham, maybe, with a few well-placed ruffles. Nothing garish, of course. All in the best of taste." She finger combed the peculiar thatch of dark baby hair, unsuccessfully attempted to curl the straight strand around her finger. "Maybe we can find one of those adorable elastic head bows. You'll be so beautiful your daddy will be putty in your tiny hands."

Lucy cooed, whacked her tummy. Claire's heart gave a lurch, and her biological clock suddenly issued an irresistible tick. All her life, Claire had wanted children, had simply presumed that someday she'd have them. She'd always wanted to be a doctor, too. It had never occurred to her that the two longings would be incompatible.

Never until now.

It hit Claire with sudden clarity that she was thirty-two years old, single and sliding toward the middle of her life without having ever looked up from her first goal long enough to realize that she may have jeopardized the second.

She'd worked hard to get where she was today. There had been little time for relationships, and those few she'd attempted had been less than satisfactory. Most men had expected sex. Claire had not been inclined to offer that. She'd possessed the same urges as any woman, of course, but had been leery of committing herself either physically or emotionally ever since her best friend had become pregnant in high school. Giving in to those urges, she'd decided, was not for her, not until her life was in order and her future assured.

So Claire had thrown herself into her work, and she'd waited for the right time, the right man, the ring on her finger. Well, her finger was still bare, and she'd yet to experience lovemaking. Now she wondered what it would be like to be held by Johnny Winterhawk, to be loved by him, to have borne him this beautiful child.

The image made her shiver with delight. It was fantasy, of course. Claire had her secret yearnings, but she was above all a pragmatist. She understood that about herself, just as she understood that simply having children could never be enough for her. She wanted a family, a real family, with two loving parents who would cherish each other as much as they cherished the issue of their union, the precious lives they had created.

It was that lack of intimacy, of love and family, that left a nagging void deep inside, a cold emptiness in a place she never searched too carefully.

Tonight that void had suddenly become full and vibrant, throbbing with a sensation that had first exploded when Johnny Winterhawk stared into her eyes, and had settled into sweet reality when she'd gazed upon Lucy's precious little face.

This is merely temporary. Johnny's words echoed in her mind.

Claire sighed. "This is dangerous territory," she murmured. "I can't afford to fall in love with you, sweetie." Even as she spoke, she knew it was too late.

Two years ago, Claire had come to Buttonwood looking for something indefinable, something she hadn't even recognized. Now she finally understood why she was here, why she'd plucked one particular professional-opportunity flyer off a Cincinnati hospital bulletin board at the end of her residency and found herself in the one place on earth where she'd instinctively known that her destiny awaited her.

Now she'd found that destiny.

In the dark, innocent eyes of this beautiful abandoned babe, she saw the reflection of another discarded child, one who had grown up loved and cared for yet had never escaped the secret heartache of having been given away by her birth parents.

Claire saw herself in Lucy. Perhaps that's why the pain of this infant's abandonment sliced so deeply into her own heart.

A scrap of pink fabric peeked from beneath the sofa. Johnny scooped it up, spread the tiny shirt in his palm. His chest constricted with a peculiar ache. He had a daughter. He had a child.

Dear God, how had this happened? How could he not have known?

"Samantha," he murmured. "Why?"

In a wave of emotion, he crushed the shirt in his

fist, pressed the soft cotton to his throat. A sweet scent wafted up, powdery and cloying. Silence suffocated him, a loneliness in the gut as sharp as a blade. He turned on the television, cranking the volume up, then hit the stereo switch as he paced. Noise flooded the house, shaking the walls. Good noise. Distracting noise. Music drowned out the wail of a used-car salesman, weather reports mingled with the stilted dialogue of old movies, headline news segued from the cheery jingle of a cereal commercial.

Night surrounded him. Fatigue weakened his muscles, but sleep was the enemy, a place haunted by secret loneliness and memories he couldn't control. Emotions could be bottled during the chaos of waking hours; pain could be ignored through the focus of work.

Work was Johnny's life, had always been his life, first to achieve the success that was so important to him, and later to keep him from dwelling on past failures or acknowledging the emptiness of a heart betrayed too often.

Now that heart was in jeopardy again.

The image of his precious daughter floated through his mind. Everyone Johnny had ever loved had been lost to him. His parents, his wife, even the woman who had borne him a child. Love was temporary; people were temporary.

Fatherhood was forever.

The concept gave him chills, made his palms sweat. Johnny had never allowed himself to think in such permanent terms before. Now he must, for no matter when Samantha returned or why she had left in the first place, his life would never be the same.

Part of him whispered that was a good thing. But another part, the largest part, was absolutely terrified.

Myra Bierbaum glanced up from the word-processing keyboard, arched a raspy brow above her tortoise-framed spectacles and eyed Johnny's fatigued features a bit too acutely for comfort. "Tough night?"

"No worse than usual." Avoiding his office manager's knowing gaze, Johnny absently flipped through the stack of messages she handed him. "Call the ranch-association president, and see if you can reschedule the monthly meeting until next Tuesday, then cancel my afternoon appointments and clear my evening schedule for the rest of the week."

"You got it, boss." Matronly, motherly and totally irreverent, Myra cocked a knowing eye. "Dare I hope you had a hot date last night, and have finally been convinced that there's more to life than striking option clauses from corporate personnel contracts?"

"See if Spence can take over the school-board meeting tonight. If he can't, contact the district administrator and have the busing contracts postponed to next month's agenda."

"Blonde, brunette or redhead?"

Johnny refused to make eye contact or lend credence to the woman's prying. He loved Myra to death, but she drove him nuts. She was a busybody, of course, but so was just about everyone else in Buttonwood. Gossip was the town's official pastime, which was why Johnny took such pain to keep his personal life personal.

The woman grunted. "You need a life. All work and no play makes Johnny a dull boy."

"It also makes Johnny your employer."

"In name only." She yawned hugely, allowing her glasses to slip from her wrinkled nose and bounce on a garish pearl chain at her bosom. "You and Spence couldn't survive without me."

"We wouldn't even try." He sorted the phone messages with practiced efficiency. "You can handle this one. Give this to this week's law clerk to check precedents and give me a list of citations for court next week." He flipped through the rest of the stack, trashing several, pocketing one, delegating the rest with succinct instructions.

At the end of the routine, he spun on his heel, took two steps toward his large, sunlit office at the end of the hall before hesitating. He spoke without looking. "And Myra, get Hank Miller on the phone for me."

He heard the squeak of her swivel chair, the soft intake of breath. When she spoke, the sting had evaporated from her voice. "I knew it, knew the minute I laid eyes on you this morning that something was wrong."

Myra uttered a concerned cluck. He recognized without looking that she'd probably pursed her lips while squeezing her thick hands together the way she did when she was worried about him. She was always worried about him, it seemed. Much as he tried to discourage that, he nonetheless loved her for it.

Squaring his shoulders, he forced an even glance over his shoulder. "Nothing is wrong, Myra. I simply have business to discuss with the sheriff, business that is mine and mine alone. Are we clear on that?"

A prick of regret stung him as he noted the sorrow in her eyes. She nodded briefly, forcefully enough to vibrate the poodle pelt of graying curls on her scalp.

He would have turned away, but she extended a hand. The pleading gesture stopped him, forced him to meet her empathetic gaze.

"You can't keep people from caring about you, Johnny."

He studied her, softened his voice with a smile. "I can try."

With that, he strode into his office and closed the door. Ten minutes later, the intercom buzzed as Myra announced that Hank was on line one.

Johnny took a deep breath, pressed the button. "Hank, how's it going?"

"Can't complain," came the jovial reply. "Had me a real lively time at the steak house over on the highway last night. There was a pair of twin beauties there from out of town that couldn't keep their hands off me. Had to flip a coin just to keep the both of them happy! Now if you'd have been along, I wouldn't had to wear myself into such a frazzle."

Johnny smiled, pinched the bridge of his nose. Hank enjoyed bachelorhood to the fullest, and was always trying to entice Johnny into joining his tom-catting forays into the local singles' scene. "My loss, Hank. I'm sure you took up the slack."

"Did my best, and that's a fact." A hiss of air filtered over the line, as if Hank had heaved a sigh. "So what's going on, Johnny? Myra sounded like a woman who'd just scraped her favorite cat off the pavement. You got problems?"

"No, no problems." He spoke quickly, too quickly. Puffing his cheeks, he exhaled slowly, forced himself to lean back in his chair. "Actually, I just need a favor."

"Name it."

"Do you remember Samantha Cloud?"

"Sure do. Pretty woman, ran off to Albuquerque a year or so back with that ne'er-do-well boyfriend of hers."

Johnny flinched. "Yes, well, I need to find her, and I was wondering if you could do a little checking for me." A nerve-racking silence followed. Johnny felt compelled to break it. "Just a few discreet inquiries… off the record."

There was a rustling sound, as if Hank had shifted to peruse papers on his desk. "Sure, I can do that." More rustling was followed by the unmistakable rasp of a throat being cleared. "Don't want to tell me what this is about, do you?"

The office door cracked open, startling Johnny. He glanced up to see his partner, Spence McBride, peering into the room. He motioned Spence inside, and completed his conversation with Hank. "Not at the moment. Let me know what you find out."

"Will do," Hank said.

Johnny cradled the receiver as Spence settled into the guest chair across his desk, a half-eaten sandwich in his hand. He kicked one lean ankle over his knee and sucked mustard from his fingers. "Myra's worried about you."

"Myra's always worried about someone. Worry is what she does."

"Yep, she's good at it, too." Spence licked his lips, took another bite of his breakfast.

Johnny nearly gagged at the sight of it. "Good Lord, what is in that thing?"

"This?" Wide-eyed, Spence gazed at the huge conglomeration, yet another of his famously atrocious sandwich fetishes that were the talk of the office.

"This is my newest specialty," he said proudly. "Sardine, banana, mashed avocados and sliced kiwi fruit on a garlic-onion bagel. All the major food groups. The perfect meal."

"You're a sick man."

"Perversity is its own reward." He smacked his lips. "So why are you hunting for Samantha?"

Apparently, he'd overheard more of the conversation than Johnny had hoped. He managed a noncommittal shrug. "That's my business."

Spence quirked a brow. "Guess you just have a hankering to get that old heart broken again, huh?"

"Samantha never broke my heart."

"Oh, that's right. It was your ex-wife who broke your heart. Samantha just laid the pieces out and stomped them a little flatter."

With some effort, Johnny unclenched his jaw, dug a familiar agenda packet out of his in basket. "I need you to take over the school-board meeting tonight."

"Sure, no problem." Spence popped the final bite of sandwich in his mouth, wiping his hands on the napkin as he chewed. He retrieved the agenda, gave it a halfhearted glance, then tossed it aside. "If you don't tell me what's going on with Samantha, you leave me no choice but to turn Myra loose. Once that old bloodhound gets the scent, there won't be any stopping her. Whatever you're trying to hide will be all over town before sundown."

Johnny closed his eyes, swallowed a surge of panic. "It'll be all over town by noon, I imagine. I'm meeting Claire at the child-care center after lunch."

"Claire?" Spence perked up. "Who's Claire?"

"Claire Davis. She's on the pediatric staff at the clinic."

Spence nodded as if that made sense. He leaned forward, propping his elbows on his knees, and he waited. There was no sense in putting it off. If Johnny trusted anyone in this town, it was Spence McBride. They'd known each other in high school, although they hadn't been close back then. They'd become good friends since Spence returned to Buttonwood a few months ago and brought his ranch-law expertise to Johnny's law firm.

Yes, Johnny trusted Spence as much as he was capable of trusting any human being. Even if he didn't, there wasn't much point in keeping a secret that would be all over town by the end of the day. Buttonwood would be buzzing about the mysterious dark-eyed baby that Johnny Winterhawk was caring for. Speculation would run rampant.

Most of it would be true.

"So," Spence prodded, "are you going to tell me why you're looking for Samantha?"

Johnny sighed. "Because I want to find out why she left our child on my doorstep last night."

Whatever Spence had been expecting to hear, that obviously wasn't it. If he hadn't already finished his sandwich, he probably would have choked on it. As it was, his face turned beet-red, his breath caught in his throat and his jaw drooped like a broken gate on a rusty hinge while Johnny methodically related grisly details.

Spence wiped his forehead, visibly shaken. "You've got a kid," he muttered. "Wow. Better you than me."

"Thanks for the support."

"Cripes, what are you going to do?"

Johnny wished he knew. Still, he heard himself uttering the same mantra he'd repeated last night. "It's temporary. Samantha will be back any time now."

He'd almost begun to believe it, until the phone rang.

"Hope you're sitting down," Hank said. "You're not going to like this."

It was nap time at the Buttonwood Child Care Center, although one wouldn't have noticed from the chorus of tiny voices, grunts and fusses emanating from the cheery sleep room. Colorful mats were arranged in neat rows on the clean, carpeted floor, some topped by thumb-sucking toddlers dozing drowsily, some supporting youngsters who kicked, rolled, sang and hummed with dogged determination to keep their eyes open to the bitter end.

Three women hovered among the throng, offering drinks of water, tucking thin covers over wriggling bodies, then moving into the infant room to check sleeping babies in their cribs.

Across the room, Joy Rollings waved. "I'll be right with you, Claire."

"Take your time," Claire called back. Johnny wouldn't arrive for another thirty minutes or so. "I'm early."

A wail from the baby room captured the day-care owner's attention. As Joy went to check on the source of the displeased cry, Claire shifted Lucy in her arms, and went to wait in the deserted play area.

The moment Claire entered the sunlit room strewn with bright toys and tiny, child-size furnishings, she spotted the lonely figure at the far end of the playroom. "Rachel?"

Startled, Nurse Rachel Arquette spun around, absently cupping one hand around her bulging belly. Her eyes widened in surprise. She offered a thin smile of greeting. "Dr. Davis, how nice to see you."

Claire lifted Lucy against her shoulder, and picked her way through the clutter of discarded toys. "You look wonderful," she said, although the woman actually looked fatigued and terribly sad. "How are you feeling?"

As if reading the worry in Claire's eyes, Rachel forced a brighter smile. "I'm fine, just fine. Thank you for asking."

A lot of people had been asking about Rachel Arquette lately. More specifically, they'd been asking about the mysterious father of Rachel's child. Speculation had been creative, widespread and not always kind. The latest grist for the gossip mill had been the constant attention heaped upon Rachel by Dr. Dennis Reid, the clinic's pompous and controlling chief of staff.

Anyone with half a brain could see that Reid had designs on Rachel, and Claire suspected him as the source of the rumor that he was in fact the father of her unborn child. It was possible, Claire supposed, although Dennis Reid certainly didn't seem to be Rachel's type.

Actually, Reid didn't seem to be anyone's type. He was universally disliked by the nursing staff for his arrogance and high-handed manner, and held in relatively low regard by clinic physicians for basically the same reasons. Still, he was Claire's boss, so she was careful to keep her opinions to herself.

Meanwhile, Rachel had refused to respond to the growing curiosity about her child's father by becoming sadder and more withdrawn each time Claire had seen her.

"I've been hoping you'd attend our Lamaze classes," Claire said.

Rachel glanced away. "I'm a nurse. I already know how to breathe."

The reply was issued softly, without rancor. Claire's heart went out to her. Instinctively, she touched the woman's thin shoulder. "There's more to the classes than perfunctory exercises, hon. We support each other, share our joys, our worries. We're a family."

A shimmer of moisture brightened Rachel's eyes. She took a shaky breath, clamped her lips into a tight smile and focused on the wriggling infant in Claire's arms. Her lips loosened; her breath slid out all at once. "Ohh, who do we have here?"

A ridiculous pride puffed Claire's chest as she shifted the infant to allow Rachel access. "This is Lucy. I'm watching her for a friend. Isn't she beautiful?"

"She is precious," Rachel whispered, stroking a tiny hand with her fingertip. "I just love babies."

Claire hiked a brow, aimed a pointed look at Rachel's pregnant tummy. "Under the circumstances, I'm glad to hear that."

A bubble of genuine laughter from Rachel warmed Claire's heart, but it lasted only a moment before the sadness returned to Rachel's eyes. She circled a protective palm over her stomach. "I can't wait for my son to be born. He's all I have now."

Claire hesitated. "Rachel—"

"Goodness, look at the time." She stepped back,

averting her gaze, her body language pulling back into herself. "It's been lovely seeing you again."

As she brushed past, Claire spun around, managed to touch her wrist, stopping her. Rachel met her gaze slowly, sadly.

"Here," Claire said, fumbling in the pocket of her blazer with her free hand to retrieve one of her business cards. "Take this. My home phone is on the back, and so is my pager number." She pressed the card into Rachel's cool palm. "Call me anytime, for any reason."

Rachel stared at the card, bit her lip and nodded silently. A sparkle of moisture slipped down one cheek.

"I care," Claire whispered as Rachel reached the doorway.

The woman paused, her shoulders quivering. She glanced back, seemingly choked by emotion. A moment later, she slipped through the opening and was gone.

Claire sighed, lowered herself into a sunny yellow plastic chair. "With so many people in the world, why is it that so many of them are lonely?" The baby gurgled, and bobbed her head sideways as if following the sound of Claire's voice.

"Ah, but you mustn't worry, sweet girl. There will always be enough love for you. I promise you that."

It didn't occur to Claire to question the peculiar affirmation. In some faraway part of her mind, she understood that she was in no position to promise this child anything, that she was merely a temporary caretaker and that their time together would be all too fleeting. She understood that, although dwelling on it would have been too painful. She felt blessed to have these moments with Lucy, and she wasn't about to waste them on the realities of what was to come.

Claire carefully laid Lucy on her lap, tucking her in the dip between her own thighs. "Do you know how lucky you are to have such a wonderful daddy?"

The baby's head swung around. A fat tongue poked out, wrapped in baby bubbles.

"Yes, you most certainly are a lucky girl. I never knew my real daddy. Odd how one can so desperately miss a person one has never met."

As she spoke, Claire unwrapped the thin receiving blanket to once again inspect each tiny leg and count the sweet button toes. "Why, there they are again! One, two, three..." She gave an exaggerated gasp, hiking her eyebrows. "Ten of them! Imagine that!"

Lucy grinned. Or perhaps she just had gas. It didn't matter, because Claire couldn't have been more delighted as Lucy kicked her fat legs and flailed her tiny fists. With the sweet heaviness of the warm, wriggling body, the powdery fragrance, the fresh scent of laundered cotton and gentle oils, Claire was surrounded by the auras of motherhood—a soft ache in the chest that made her feel more whole, more alive than she could ever remember.

Layer by layer, Claire removed fabric, examined the soft, round belly, the reddened skin beneath her little armpits, the perfect fold of a baby ear, the delicate quiver of a fleshy little throat. Every inch was perfect. Every inch.

It was a silly thing, she supposed, this compulsion to constantly reassess the infant. She couldn't explain the joy it gave her to touch this precious baby, to smooth the soft cotton shirt, caress each delicate baby finger.

Such dark little eyes, so intense, so wise. "You mustn't worry, precious. Your daddy won't let anything bad happen to you. And neither will I," she whispered. "Neither will I."

As Claire bent forward to kiss the infant's silky cheek, a tingle slipped down her spine. She straightened slowly in the small chair, instinctively knowing before she gazed toward the doorway what she would see.

Johnny Winterhawk stood there, hovering just inside the room with an expression of awe and wonder that moved her to the marrow.

His powerful form filled the doorway, shoulders seeming even more broad by the fit of a dark, tailored business suit that hugged him like a supple second skin. From his perfectly groomed ebony hair to the tips of his gleaming Italian shoes, he exuded grace, power, control. And danger.

Danger for any woman whose heart raced at the sight of him, whose blood steamed in his presence, whose breath backed up in her throat until she feared her lungs might explode.

Most women looked twice at Johnny Winterhawk. Most women sighed, exchanged a yearning glance, silently wondered what ripple of bone and sinew lay hidden beneath the elegant, tailored cloth. He was masculine perfection, a walking wonder of sheer sensuality silently raging behind a wall of civility. He was magnificent. He was vital. He was gorgeous. Claire wanted to rip his clothes off.

"Hi." She cleared the horrifying squeak from her voice, and tried again. "You're early."

"Am I?"

"A little."

His gaze slipped to the infant in her lap. His eyes glowed softly, with wonder. "You're so good with her."

"It's easy to be good with her. She's such a good baby." Managing to take in enough air to clear the cobwebs from her brain, Claire gave the blanket a quick wrap and lifted the infant to her shoulder.

As she started to stand, Johnny took two massive strides and cupped his palm around her elbow, assisting her. A spark from his touch shot into her shoulder.

She swayed briefly, then stood. Her knees did not buckle. But they wanted to. "So..." She sucked a breath, offered a bright smile. "Are you ready to take over your daddy duties?"

"I—" His gaze darted, his lips thinned. "I wonder if I might impose upon you a bit longer."

"Of course." A rush of relief startled her, although the steely glint in his eye gave her pause. "Is something wrong?"

He ignored the question. "Lucy will be spending more time in my care than I had originally anticipated. I would appreciate some, ah, instruction. If it wouldn't be too much trouble," he added quickly.

"No trouble at all. Lesson number one, holding the baby." Before he could protest, Claire placed Lucy in his arms, nearly laughing out loud at his horrified expression as he shrugged up his shoulders and hunched forward, awkwardly cradling the baby as if she were a porcelain football.

His eyes rolled frantically, his skin paled and beads of moisture traced his upper lip. "She's so fragile," he whispered. "I can barely feel her."

"You're doing fine." The terror in his eyes was

perversely endearing. Claire decided one just had to love a man who took fatherhood so seriously. "Lesson number two, we've already touched upon. Babies are tougher than they look. They don't break easily, nor do they bounce, so try not to drop her."

His head snapped up. He looked as if he might faint.

"Now, on to lesson number three." Claire shouldered the diaper bag, dug her car keys out of her pocket and dangled them in front of his stunned face. "Shopping!"

Johnny groaned.

Chapter Three

"You have to snap that whatchamacallit into the doohickey, and tighten tension on some kind of switch lever." Claire turned the instruction sheet over, scratched her head. "That's if you want to use the portable crib function. If you want to transform it into a playpen, you're supposed to loosen the lever, unsnap the whatchamacallit and twist the doohickey into the thingamajig. I think."

"Huh?" Shifting one segment of the mesh-sided portable crib under his arm, Johnny hoisted himself on one knee, grunted as he rapped his elbow on the coffee table.

Claire turned the instruction sheet over, angled a sympathetic glance. "It's a little crowded in here." The observation was unnecessary, since the formerly immaculate living room was cluttered with mounds of stuffed shopping bags, tiny garments, toys, crib mobiles, baby supplies, a stroller still in its packing carton and one "handy-dandy all-in-one nursery"— a bewildering assortment of tubes, pads and mesh panels that could supposedly shift from crib to play-pen to changing table with the merest flick of a finger.

Johnny frowned, inspected his elbow. "It would be easier to replicate the space shuttle out of bottle caps. Why would someone engineer this kind of monstrosity for an infant?"

"It's not for the child—it's for the parent." Smiling, Claire glanced around the once tidy room. A screwdriver poked out of an expensive silk-flower arrangement on the polished oak coffee table. A pair of needle-nose pliers sagged against the breast pocket of Johnny's expensive monogrammed dress shirt. The handle of a claw hammer stuck from between tapestry sofa cushions. "Some Christmas Eve in the future, you'll have to assemble a tricycle in the dark using nothing but a pair of fingernail clippers and the tooth-pick from your holiday martini. This is good practice."

For a moment, Claire actually thought he was blushing. His gaze lowered, his lips curved into a half smile that did peculiar things to her insides. Clearly, he was getting used to the idea of fatherhood, but he was also still shaken by it. His smile dissipated as quickly as it had appeared. He squared his shoulders, rearranged his features into an unreadable mask.

Without responding to Claire's teasing comment, he returned his attention to the assemblage problem, moving his lips as he worked as if giving himself silent support for the effort.

Claire watched him greedily, fascinated by every nuance of expression, every hint of frown or smile.

There was something vulnerable about his struggle with the unfamiliar equipment, a nervous determination in his effort that was exquisitely touching. His collar yawned open, his tie was askew and his sleeves were rolled up to expose muscular forearms dusted by a smattering of dark hair. As cool and confident as he'd been in his formal business attire, he was now charmingly befuddled, sitting cross-legged on the floor amid a nest of packing material, cardboard and bubble wrap.

Lying beside her on the sofa, Lucy yawned hugely and stuffed a baby fist in her mouth. "Someone is getting sleepy," Claire said. "I think your daughter has given up hope of having a nap in her brand-new crib."

"Have faith," Johnny muttered. Squatting on one knee, he bent to inspect a bewildering array of template holes stamped on the metal frame. "Wait a minute, I think I know what this is for...." He grunted, snapped a spring-loaded steel arm into one of the openings, grasped the tubular mesh-side frames and hauled the unit upright. With a click, a shudder, a whoosh, the little crib stood firm and sturdy amid the chaos.

Johnny grinned in triumph. Claire's heart gave a lurch. She licked her dry lips. "Congratulations. You've passed the first test of fatherhood, crib construction." He looked so inordinately pleased with himself that Claire couldn't keep from laughing. "Now all we have to do is move it into the nursery and tuck Lucy in for a nice quiet nap."

"The spare room is at the far end of the hall." He grabbed a bulging shopping bag and began to root through the contents. "I wouldn't be able to hear her."

"Most babies sleep better in a quiet room. Besides, you shouldn't have to turn your living room into a nursery."

He grunted, retrieved a package of crib sheets from the bag. "It's only temporary."

Claire considered that. "You've purchased a lot of permanent stuff for a temporary situation."

He shrugged, struggled to extract the linens from their packaging. "The child needs these things no matter where she is."

"She needs a solid-silver hairbrush?"

He looked stung. "She has hair."

"Yes, she does indeed."

"Grooming is important."

Claire couldn't argue that. "And three separate crib mobiles?"

"The saleswoman said that infants need visual stimulation."

"And the computer that teaches ABC's?"

"Educational toys give a child a better start in life."

"She can barely lift her head, Johnny." Claire bit her lip, so amused by his adorable sulk that she feared she'd laugh out loud. "And what on earth is she going to do with two dozen stuffed animals? Not to mention the fact that you bought her so many frilly dresses, she'd have to be changed four times a day just to wear them all before she outgrows them."

"Proper clothing is important to a child's self-esteem."

Something in his eyes alerted Claire that Johnny might have been speaking more from experience than parroting the salesperson's pitch. She regarded him thoughtfully. "I guess you weren't born rich, were you?"

The question seemed to unnerve him. "I was not a ragged little Indian kid scuffing barefoot through the reservation in feathers and a torn loincloth, if that's what you mean."

She hiked a brow. "A little touchy, are we?"

He sighed, allowing his shoulders to roll forward. "Sorry. Guess I do get a bit defensive about the stereotype of my heritage. Actually, my parents struggled when I was quite young, but by the time I was in school, they were middle-class suburbanites, just like your own family."

"What do you know about my family?"

He blinked up from the drape of balloon-and-bow fabric he'd finally extracted from the package. "Nothing, I suppose. I just presumed—" A slow flush crawled up his throat. His smile was a little sheepish. "Touché. I guess we all fall into the stereotype trap."

Her heart fluttered. "It's only a trap if we can't find the way out."

Johnny studied her as if seeing her for the first time. A smile spread slowly, sensually, lighting his face from within. "How did you get so wise?"

"It just soaks into my head with the auburn hair rinse."

"So that beautiful copper tone isn't natural?"

"It would be more natural if I left those pesky gray sprouts in it." To her horror, she giggled. "I cannot believe that I have just entrusted you with my most solemn personal secret."

He laughed then, a genuine guffaw from the solar plexus that vibrated down her spine like a sensual massage. She'd never heard him laugh before. It nearly undid her. "Attorney-client privilege," he said, clearly amused. "Your secret is safe with me."

Returning his attention to the packaged crib sheet, he frowned, tore at the plastic wrap and muttered under his breath.

Claire plucked the item from his hand, removed the packaging and handed it back. Johnny held the limp cotton fabric studded with tiny balloon-and-bow stencils as if he'd never seen a fitted sheet before.

"I take it you have maid service?"

He glanced up, startled. "Certainly."

"Ah. In that case, you are clearly inexperienced in the fine art of bed making. Allow me to demonstrate." She took the sheet, gave it a shake. "These cupped corners are molded to fit around the crib pad, like so."

Johnny leaned over her shoulder, watching. His scent surrounded her like soft arms, musky and sweet, an aching combination of aromatic body wash, grooming fragrance and pure man.

Her fingers trembled. She cleared her throat. "First you tuck one side over the mattress, left and right, then you smooth it over the crib pad and tuck in the far side, like so."

"Amazing. It fits perfectly."

If he'd smelled any better, Claire wouldn't have been able to resist taking a nip out of his throat. "We also have these cute little blanket clips—" she rooted through a shopping bag to retrieve the package "—which fit through the mesh walls, clip to the blanket and keep the baby from kicking the blanket off."

His eyes lit. "An excellent idea."

"Didn't you purchase a new crib blanket?"

"Yes, several." He stepped over a mount of torn plastic wrap to retrieve yet another shopping bag, from which he extracted a soft, fleecy blanket embroidered with tiny sheep. "Do you think she'd prefer the yellow or the pink? I think there's a white one, as well...."

"Yellow is fine." Her fingers brushed his arm as she took the blanket from him. She moistened her lips, waited for the tingling to subside, then fastened the blanket clips and stepped back to view her handiwork.

From the corner of her eye, she saw Johnny struggling with a mass of wires and colorful butterflies. While clamping the crib mobile on the tubular frame, he angled a defensive glance in her direction, as if daring her to criticize the extravagance. "This one is also a music box. You wind it up, and the butterfly wings flap. It should be quite interesting for her to watch."

She smiled. "Indeed."

A muscle jittered at the curve of his jaw. "I do have a responsibility to make her life as comfortable as possible for the time that we are together."

Claire's smile faded. "She's your daughter, Johnny. You'll be spending time together for the rest of your lives."

The subtle tilt of a brow was the only indication he'd heard her. "Perhaps the star-collage mobile would be more appropriate for an infant of her age."

To give herself a moment for thought, Claire busied herself clearing some of the packing materials from the floor. There was something going on here, something Johnny wasn't telling her. On the one hand, he insisted that he was merely caring for the child temporarily, until her mother returned. If that were the case, why had he spent hundreds of dollars on infant equipment for a weekend of baby-sitting?

There was only one way to find out, Claire decided. The direct approach. She glanced up, saw him tightening the mobile clamp on the crib frame. "When is Samantha returning, Johnny?"

His fingers paused in their task, but only for a moment. "Soon."

"When?"

"I don't know."

"But you know more than you did last night, don't you?" When he didn't reply, she dumped an armful of trash by the front door, then circled the diminutive, net-sided portable crib to confront him. "You made some phone calls this morning, didn't you? You know something."

He studied a small purple-and-pink butterfly, rubbing a gleaming plastic wing between his thumb and forefinger. "I know that when Samantha does return, she'll need help to care for Lucy properly."

"And you plan to give her that help?"

"Of course."

"By retaining custody of Lucy?"

Startled, he glanced at Claire, then averted his gaze. "I'm not qualified to care for a child." His gaze settled on the bowl of murky water that Claire presumed had once been occupied by an unfortunate and now defunct creature of the finned persuasion. "I will, however, see that Samantha has assistance from those who are qualified."

"You're making this all sound very mysterious."

The pain in his eyes shocked her. He raked his fingers through his hair, took a step backward and sat heavily in his lounge chair. "I spoke with Hank Miller this morning."

"The sheriff?"

He nodded. "Hank placed a few discreet phone calls to friends in the Albuquerque police department. It seems that Samantha's boyfriend, one Rodney F. Frye, is well-known to them. He was arrested for burglary last week. Sam bailed him out. He didn't show up for the arraignment."

Claire's heart sank. "He skipped bail?"

"Apparently." Johnny rubbed his forehead. "Hank used credit-card slips to track them as far as Montana. It appears they're heading to Canada."

Claire sat slowly on the sofa beside the dozing infant. "If that's true, it doesn't seem Samantha is planning on returning any time soon."

Johnny shrugged. "Samantha is not a bad person, but she is an emotionally frail one. She left Lucy with me out of love for her, not because she believed the child would be an inconvenience."

"That's an assumption on your part." Claire flinched at the roughness of her own tone, but couldn't suppress her anger at this woman. "So when she shows up, you're simply going to hand Lucy back to her?"

The allegation clearly annoyed him. "Of course not. I will, however, see that Lucy has the best professional care available, and that Samantha receives the help and counseling she needs until she's able to be a proper mother to our child." Johnny studied Claire intently, extended a pleading hand. "You don't understand what Samantha has been through. She's had a difficult life—"

"So that makes it all right for her to choose a fe-

lonious lover over the well-being of her own child?''
Unable to contain herself, Claire stood quickly, spun
away from the man who was regarding her with unnerving acuity. ''A child is not a puppy to be bounced
from owner to owner every time it's too much trouble! No matter how loving a caretaker you purchase
for Lucy, no matter how luxurious her surroundings
or how many expensive stuffed animals you buy her,
that little girl will never forget that her own mother
abandoned her. She'll live with that for the rest of her
life, Johnny, the rest of her natural life. How can you
defend that? How can you defend a woman who
would do that to her own child?''

Johnny regarded her, his dark, intense eyes boring
straight into the very core of her. ''You seem to be
taking this rather personally.''

Claire wiped the moisture from her eye, angry with
herself for having revealed too much. ''I take child
neglect personally. Everyone should.''

He said nothing for a moment, simply leaned back
in the chair and studied her in silence. Claire felt her
skin heat. She absently smoothed her chambray shirt,
rearranged the covers around the sleeping infant on
the cushion beside her.

''Tell me about yourself, Claire.'' It was a command, issued softly but in the tone of a man used to
having his requests honored without question.

Sharing personal information didn't come easily to
Claire. ''There's not much to tell. I grew up like you
did, with middle-class parents who worked hard and
loved me the best they could. I went to college, became a doctor, settled in Buttonwood and am happy
with my life.''

''Are you really?''

"Am I really what?"

"Happy with your life."

"Yes."

"And your parents, do you miss them?"

"We talk on the phone every week, but yes, I miss them." She angled a glance. "Are you close to your parents?"

"No."

When he said nothing further, she prodded him gently. "Do they live nearby?"

"My father is dead. My mother lives in California with her new husband."

"Oh." She fidgeted with the corner of the baby blanket. "How old were you when your mother remarried?"

Clearly, the conversation had shifted into forbidden territory. Johnny responded, but with a gruffness that brooked no further discussion. "I was twelve. She walked out on my father and me, so when it comes to mothers abandoning their children, I have some small experience with that."

Claire nodded, was shocked by the unexpected sound of her own small voice whispering from a place she hadn't explored in a very long time. "I do, too." She paused a beat, gathered her courage to share something that few people knew about her, something she rarely discussed because it was too personal, too painful. "I never knew my birth parents. My mother gave me to an orphanage when I was Lucy's age. No one knows who my father was. I was lucky enough to have been adopted by dear, loving people who gave me everything I ever needed in life. Everything except—" her voice broke "—except the knowledge of who I really am and where I come from."

"That's important to you?"

"Yes." She sniffed, dabbed the wetness on her cheek with the back of her hand. "It will be important to Lucy, too."

"Samantha has not abandoned Lucy."

"Hasn't she?"

His jaw clenched, his fingers tightened into a white-knuckled fist. "No, she hasn't. She wouldn't."

Tears welled in Claire's eyes, blurring her vision, stinging her lids. She gazed over her shoulder, unable to quell the trembling in her limbs. "You must have loved her very much," she whispered, and was stunned by the pain that thought evoked. "You must love her still."

Johnny went ashen. He swallowed hard, glanced from the sleeping infant on the sofa to Claire, then back again. "I never loved Samantha," he said quietly. "Nor did she love me."

Whatever Claire had expected to hear, that wasn't it.

Johnny inhaled deeply, leaned back in the lounge chair and covered his eyes with his hand. "Samantha and I had been friends since childhood. I ran into her again shortly after my divorce."

"I didn't know you'd been married."

He shrugged. "My ex-wife's father owned the Phoenix law firm where I'd planned to spend a long and lucrative career. We had a whirlwind courtship, after which I was determined to lavish her with every imaginable luxury. Unfortunately, that took a great deal of my time."

"She felt neglected?"

"Yes. So I bought two tickets to the Bahamas, and came home early one afternoon with them to surprise her.'' He plucked a piece of packing material off his slacks, studied it as if it were a small nugget. ''She was surprised, all right. So was the guy in bed with her.''

''Oh, Lord.'' Claire sat heavily on the sofa. ''I'm so sorry, Johnny.''

''Don't be. It was for the best.'' He flicked the tiny piece of plastic away, brushed his palms together. ''I moved back to Buttonwood, started my own practice and the rest is history.''

''That's when you and Samantha, er, began your relationship?''

Pursing his lips, he furrowed his brow. ''I wouldn't call it a relationship, exactly, but she'd just experienced yet another emotional breakup with the volatile Mr. Frye, so we were both alone, miserable and in need of comfort. There were no promises made, no pretense of anything beyond what it was—the sharing of two friends who needed each other.''

He sighed, lowered his hand and leaned forward, propping his forearms on his knees. ''Both of us understood that what we shared would be temporary. I wasn't looking for permanence, and Sam had already spent years in a turbulent relationship in which estrangements were as routine as the sunrise, and nearly as frequent. I suppose I shouldn't have been shocked when I returned from work one evening to find her closet empty except for a note saying she and Frye had reconciled yet again and they were moving to Albuquerque. Apparently, he has family in the area.''

''You say you shouldn't have been shocked, but it sounds to me as if it took you by surprise.''

He considered that. ''Yes, I suppose it did. I'd tried to show Samantha that she deserved better treatment, that she was entitled to respect both for herself and from others.'' Heaving a sigh, he rubbed his palms on his thighs. "I'd thought Samantha had grown emotionally during our time together. I was disappointed to learn otherwise.''

"It wasn't your fault, Johnny."

When he looked up, the pain in his eyes broke her heart. "Then whose fault was it?"

"She was an adult, able to make her own choices in life."

"Emotionally, Samantha was a child. Our rebound relationship—" he swallowed hard, glanced away "—in retrospect, I realize it was selfish of me, a way to alleviate my own loneliness without commitment. It didn't help Samantha. In the end, it might have caused her irreparable harm." He studied the sleeping infant, his eyes softening. "If only I'd known…"

Leaning forward, Claire reached across the coffee table, and laid her palm on his hand. "You know now," she whispered.

"Yes. I know now."

A soothing heat transferred from his warm skin into the river of her pulse. Their eyes met, held. Silence surrounded them, yet Claire felt a song thrumming through her blood. The insight Johnny Winterhawk had offered into his past had touched her deeply. More than that, it had opened her heart to the gentleness in him, the honor ingrained in his spirit. He was too kind, too compassionate to realize that Samantha had used him as much as he'd used her. In fact, Claire suspected that Johnny had given much more to the relationship than he'd ever received.

She suspected that he had always done so, yet wouldn't confess to that. She also suspected that he had indeed loved Samantha, and loved her still. Not that he'd ever confess to that, either. Johnny Winterhawk was a man who denied his feelings, feelings that ran so deep and so true that they were as much a part of him as the bone and sinew of his body.

He was, she realized, a man of compassion and tenderness, of false bravado and hidden pain. He was a strong man, a tender man, a man for whom failure was not an option, and insecurity a mortal sin. He was stoic and vulnerable, fragile and fierce.

And he was the most fascinating man she had ever known.

"Claire!" Panic surged, his knees nearly buckled. "Claire, I can't— She won't hold still. I'm going to drown her!" A shriek, a squeak. Legs churned, water splashed. Johnny felt faint. *"Claire!"*

Claire peeked in the kitchen door, folding a fluffy towel. "You're doing fine."

"She has water on her face! Oh, God. She's blinking. It got into her eyes, Claire, into her *eyes!*"

"Eyeballs are waterproof." Claire sauntered with a maddening lack of speed. "A few splashed drops are not going to melt her, Johnny. She's enjoying herself."

Frantic, he shifted his grip beneath the wet, wriggling body. "She's as slippery as a peeled grape. There must be a better way to do this."

"Such as?"

"Can't she be dry-cleaned or something?"

She shrugged. "I suppose you could try vacuuming her."

He angled a disgusted glance. "You think this is funny, don't you?"

"Oh, yes."

Her delighted grin sent an army of goose bumps down his spine.

"Actually, I haven't had this much fun since the class bully fainted in postmortem pathology and I won the coin toss to practice my suturing technique. I've always regretted allowing my classmates to talk me out of embroidering my initials on his chin while the big lug was still unconscious."

He couldn't help but smile. Claire Davis had brought a breath of fresh air into his life, a mixture of compassionate wisdom and irreverent humor that had kept him sane during the past three days. "Remind me never to tick you off."

"I'm quite harmless."

"You are a lot of things, Claire Davis. Harmless is not one of them."

Her eyes darkened, cool blue irises thinning to a glowing azure ring around pupils expanded by sensual interest. "That's the nicest thing anyone has ever said to me."

A flutter worked its way through his chest as he studied her. She was an exquisite woman, with delicate features, creamy skin scattered with golden sundrops and lips always curved in the hint of a smile, as if she understood a joke no one else could quite fathom.

A slip of wet skin against his forearm shot his blood pressure up ten points and refocused his attention on the splashing infant in the sink. He began to hyperventilate, gasping for breath. "Here…take her."

"Nope." Infuriatingly, she stepped back, draped the folded towel over her arm. "You can't learn what you won't try."

"I can't even keep a damned fish alive," he blurted. "Please, Claire. I'll change diapers, I'll brush hair, I'll even risk poisoning the poor child by trying to feed her—"

He sucked a breath as Claire suddenly stepped forward to lay a soft hand on his arm.

"You're trembling," she said softly. Her gaze settled on his face, probing him with unnerving intensity. "You're really frightened, aren't you?"

His knees nearly gave way. All he could say was, "I killed the goldfish."

She wasn't smiling now, not even the hint of humor. Her eyes were wide, knowing, filled with compassion. "I'll stay here with you."

Part of him was relieved. The other part was chagrined to realize that she was not going to take over. He licked his lips, stared down at the glimmering twist of torso, the happily flailing baby limbs. Lucy blinked up, dark eyes bright and glowing. Bubbles gathered at her pursed baby lips. Her legs churned. Water splashed into her own face, causing her to gasp, stiffen and emit a peculiar gurgling squeak of pleasure.

Johnny took a deep breath. "She looks clean to me."

"Have you washed her hair?" Apparently, the distraught look on his face spoke volumes, because Claire smiled gently, reached for a squeeze bottle on the counter. "You hold the bottle in your free hand, use your thumb to flip up the lid. Squeeze a small amount of liquid onto her scalp, thusly." She demonstrated. "Now massage it into a foam…easy, now, remember what I told you about the soft spot at the top of her little skull."

The memory made him queasy. Imagine, an area of an infant's head where the only thing between a tiny brain and disaster was a covering of silky soft skin and hair. His stomach lurched. He sucked another breath, struggled to do as he'd been asked. Lucy responded to the soaping of her little head by uttering a trill of pleasure. Johnny felt himself smile in response.

"She likes that," Claire said.

"Yes, she seems to."

"Now use the washcloth to rinse off the soap. Let her head lie back a little...that's good...now the water will run backward, out of her face."

Claire's voice calmed him, soothed him, gave him enough confidence to complete the bathing chore, after which he wrapped the infant in a bath towel and carried her into the living room.

"That wasn't so bad, was it?" Claire asked.

"Only slightly worse than being tied to railroad tracks and seeing the headlamp of an oncoming train."

She laughed. "Well, look on the bright side. You don't have to do it again until tomorrow."

He angled a withering look. "Tomorrow, we'll try the vacuum."

She chuckled, flopped on the sofa and watched with undisguised amusement as Johnny struggled to stuff one wriggling infant into a pair of tiny flannel pajamas. When he'd finished, he glanced up proudly. "Not bad, eh?"

"Not bad at all." Something in her evil grin gave him pause. "When do you plan to put the diaper on?"

"Diaper?" He glanced down in horror just in time

to see the wet stain darken the tiny pj's and spread
over the previously clean crib sheet. "Damn."

"A daddy's work is never done." Smiling, Claire
stood, leaned over the crib. As she reached down to
stroke Lucy's cheek, her eyes took on an ethereal
glow. "You're such a lucky little girl," she whispered, "to have a daddy who takes such good care
of you."

A lump wedged in Johnny's throat. He understood
why Claire identified so deeply with Lucy, and he
recognized her kinship with a child abandoned by her
mother just as Claire herself had once been abandoned. Johnny was touched by that, probably because
he could relate to it himself. The scars of his own
mother's rejection still burned in his heart. Over the
years, she'd tried to maintain contact with him, but
Johnny had refused. If she hadn't loved him enough
to stay, he'd seen no reason to love her back. Like
everything else in Johnny's life, love had always been
temporary.

It was the way of things.

Claire loaded the final bowl into the dishwasher.
She'd made soup for their supper that evening, and
had even been motivated to whip up homemade bis-
cuits. Odd, she thought, how comfortable she'd become in Johnny Winterhawk's home. In the three
days since Lucy had appeared on Johnny's doorstep,
Claire had barely been away except to sleep and rush
back for the next round of parenthood lessons.

Now she knew Johnny's home as well as she knew
her own. There was a sense of belonging here that
was mysterious, almost frightening, yet exhilarating
beyond anything she'd experienced.

Claire had never been a woman to worry about her own place in the world. She'd simply accepted life on its own terms, facing each day and each challenge as a precious gift. Until she'd walked into Johnny's life, until she'd gazed into Lucy's wise little face, Claire had never thought about what tomorrow would bring. Now she could barely think of anything else.

Closing the dishwasher door, she set the timer, wiped her hands on a towel and moved toward the doorway. The living room was darkened, with only a soft light from a corner lamp as illumination. Johnny still refused to move the baby's crib into the spare room down the hall. She suspected that he actually slept in the living room now. Presuming, of course, that he slept at all. He looked terribly tired. She was concerned about him.

A shadow caught her eye, the silhouette of Johnny leaning over the crib. He murmured something—she couldn't hear what—and reached downward. A flicker of movement from beneath the crib blanket made him laugh. "What a grip," he whispered. "You're a strong girl, aren't you?"

As Claire watched, he extracted his finger from the baby's grasp, then gently brushed his knuckle along her cheek. It was the sweetest thing Claire had ever seen in her life.

Johnny straightened abruptly, as if suddenly aware of Claire's presence in the room. Feigning an impassive expression, he squared his shoulders, clasped his hands behind his back. "She doesn't appear to be sleepy."

"If you want to hold her for a while, it's all right."

"I was simply making certain she was breathing properly."

"Of course."

It was sad, Claire thought, the way he tried to cover his emotions. Earlier she'd seen him brush a kiss on her tiny cheek. When he'd spotted Claire watching him, he'd become flustered, made an excuse about the baby's skin feeling warm. Instinctively, she realized that he was concerned about becoming too attached to the infant. That was the saddest thing of all, the fear that he was destined to lose anyone he allowed himself to love.

Claire rubbed her upper arms, glanced around the familiar room. "I guess it's time for me to go. I'm on duty again tomorrow."

A flash of panic flared in his eyes. "It's still early. Would you like a drink? Some wine, perhaps, or a cocktail?"

She laughed. "I'm wise to your schemes. You get a glass of wine into me, then you won't allow me to drive home."

He smiled. "It worked last night."

"Yes." She shivered at the memory of cuddling up in Johnny's bed, smelling his scent on the sheets, knowing he was just beyond the door. "But it won't work tonight, I'm afraid."

Rubbing the back of his neck, he walked around the crib, gazed out one of the sparkling bay windows toward a sliver of moonlight in the sky. "I know I'm being selfish. For three days, you've put your entire life on hold for my benefit. You must think me terribly ungrateful."

"No." She walked toward him. They met by a polished sideboard filled with crystal and porcelain and tribal treasures of his childhood. They were so close she could feel the heat from his body. Her palms itched to touch him. "I've loved every minute."

A muscle in his jaw twitched. He wanted to say something. Claire knew it, felt it. She held her breath. "Claire...?"

The phone rang, a jangling blast that nearly stopped her heart. Johnny swore, spun around and dashed to answer it before the noise frightened the baby. He snatched up the receiver, barked a gruff greeting while Claire was still trying to catch her own breath. An unhappy wail from the crib drew her attention.

"There, there," she murmured, lifting the crying infant to her shoulder. "Noisy old telephone. You just tell me all about it."

Lucy sniffed, bobbled her head backward. Her lip quivered, and her eyes glowed with tears. Claire reached into the crib for the pacifier, which Lucy accepted with greedy sucking noises.

"That's better, isn't it, sweetie? Nothing more comforting than a yummy hunk of suckable plastic."

The baby's eyelids drooped sleepily. Claire hugged her a moment longer, then laid her back into the crib. When she straightened, Johnny was standing there. He looked as if he'd been shot.

"What's wrong?"

He opened his mouth, closed it again, then stumbled to the sofa and sat down, dipping his head forward.

Claire sat beside him. "Johnny, tell me. Who was on the phone?"

"It was Hank." He drew a ragged breath. "They've found Samantha's car in a ravine north of Kalispell, Montana. It went off the road, crashed into a tree...." His voice sagged, dissipated.

Icy fingers of fear clamped around her spine.

Johnny rubbed his palms over his face. His shoulders quivered. When he dropped his hands, he stared directly into Claire's eyes with exquisite sorrow. "They're dead, Claire. Both of them."

"Oh, Johnny, I'm so sorry."

His mouth trembled, his jaw clenched. He searched her eyes with questions she couldn't answer, with pain no man should endure. There was nothing more to say, nothing that could be said. Claire slipped her arms around his broad shoulders, pressed his face to her breast and held him while he cried.

She stayed with him all night, caressing him, comforting him as he paced the living room, allowing him to scream and to sob and to curse the heavens that would allow such tragedy. Then she sat with him on the sofa, gathered him in her arms as if he were her own and rocked him as he drifted into a stunned, silent sleep.

Claire did not sleep. As night drifted slowly into morning, she watched the pink blush of dawn slip from the horizon. The quiet decision had already been made. Her life had already been changed. Forever.

Chapter Four

"I have to cancel lunch today, Megan." Claire shifted the phone to her shoulder, clamped it under her chin to free her hands. She flipped through the chart of one of her favorite patients, a cheery youngster who tolerated frequent ear infections with courage most adults would be unable to muster.

Megan's disappointed groan filtered through the phone line. "You're not working through lunch again, are you? Honestly, Claire, you have to take time for yourself once in a while."

"Nope, not working. Johnny and I are taking Lucy for a walk in the park. According to Joy Rollings at the day-care center, Johnny calls so often to check on Lucy that it's disrupting their schedule."

"Sounds as if the intrepid Mr. Winterhawk is taking fatherhood seriously."

"That's an understatement." Claire laid the patient

chart on the counter long enough to accept a medication order handed her by duty nurse, Nell Hastings, whose twinkling eyes seemed to mirror Claire's own jovial mood. She acknowledged Nell with a smile, read the order and scrawled a signature.

After the hefty nurse rumbled away, Claire returned her attention to Megan Malone Duncan, her very best friend and confidante since they'd met when Megan enrolled in Claire's Lamaze class. "The truth is that Johnny takes fatherhood too seriously, if that's possible."

"No man can take fatherhood too seriously. Maybe I should have Mac chat with him?" Pride in her husband seeped into Megan's voice, along with a wistful sigh that made Claire laugh aloud.

"I thought married women were supposed to take their husbands for granted," Claire said.

Megan smiled, too, but only for a moment. When she spoke again, her tone was serious, thoughtful. "Honestly, Claire, I'm so happy, sometimes it scares me. I have everything—a beautiful son, the finest husband God ever set on this earth, all that I've ever dreamed of. Sometimes I just stand by Tyler's crib watching him sleep, and I can't stop the tears. He's so perfect, so precious."

Claire felt as if her heart had been squeezed. "I know," Claire whispered. And she did know. She felt the same way when she gazed into Lucy's exquisite little face. "I'm so happy for you. You deserve every wonderful thing life has to offer."

"So do you, hon." Her voice softened, was edged by worry. "You know, this entire thing with Johnny's daughter showing up on his door, and him calling you of all people... well, it's almost eerie, don't you think?"

A peculiar tingle slipped down Claire's spine. "What do you mean?"

There was a muted scratch on the other end of the line, like the scrape of chair legs on a wooden floor. "I mean, you've had a crush on this man since the first time you've laid eyes on him. Two years and you haven't said more than 'good morning' to each other. Then out of the blue, the clinic phone rings and suddenly you're the center of Johnny Winterhawk's life. Doesn't that strike you as almost...prophetic?"

It did, but Claire wasn't about to jinx her good fortune by acknowledging that. "It's pure happenstance." She hesitated as Nurse Hastings returned to the station, waiting until the motherly woman had gathered her charts and left before resuming the conversation with Megan. "Johnny is going through a difficult time right now. He needs a friend."

"Well, he's found a good one in you. I ought to know."

"You're biased."

"Yes, I am." The smile faded from her voice. "The loss of Lucy's mother must have been hard on him."

"It's been awful," Claire said. "After the accident, he tried to contact Samantha's parents, only to discover that her mother died last year of pneumonia, and her father had a heart attack a couple of months later. Since Samantha had no siblings, that means the entire maternal side of Lucy's family simply doesn't exist anymore. Johnny had to take care of all the arrangements. There were only three of us at the memorial service. It was so sad."

"Poor Johnny." Megan issued a shuddering sound. "Poor Lucy. It will be difficult for her, growing up without a mom."

"Yes," Claire murmured, surprised by a sharp stab of pain of empathy. She'd never gotten over not knowing her own birth mother, although she'd been truly blessed by a wise and loving adoptive mom whom Claire cherished beyond measure. "At least Lucy has her father."

"Yes, she has her father." After a silent moment, Megan heaved a long-suffering sigh. Papers rattled on the other end of the phone line, as if she was flipping through her personal calendar. "So lunch today is off. How about dinner tonight? Mac will be home early, so he can take care of Tyler. We deserve a girls' night out."

"Perfect." Claire jotted a note on the back of a prescription blank, tucked it in the pocket of her lab coat just as Nurse Hastings reappeared to signal that the patient in room three was ready for examination. "I'll meet you at Millie's diner, six o'clock," she murmured, then hung up and hurried down the hallway to check on little Donny Banks's most recent ear infection.

"Look, Lucy, a squirrel!"

Claire's excitement was contagious, wringing a smile from Johnny as he watched her turn the stroller toward the huge pine tree where a fat gray squirrel scurried in search of edible goodies. The rodent swished its fluffy tail, sat up on its haunches and stared at the bench where two large humans, and one very small one, stared back.

"I think it likes you," Claire whispered to the

blinking infant. She lifted one of the baby's hands, waving it toward the curious animal. "Say hi to the squirrel, sweetie." Lucy gurgled. Claire laughed. "Close enough."

Johnny wasn't interested in a fuzzy-tailed rodent. He was, however, utterly enamored by the glowing woman beside him, a woman whose breathless laughter affected him like a swift punch to the gut. She was without doubt the most genuine person he'd ever met, a woman of boundless joy and sincere compassion who seemed to read his every thought as if it were her own. She was also bonded to Lucy. Even an emotionally reclusive sap like himself could have seen through a blindfold how deeply Claire loved the child, which made Johnny's decision even more difficult.

She slanted a glance at him. "You look like hell. Did you get any sleep at all last night?"

"Some."

"Did Lucy have a bad night?"

"No, she only woke up once." He rubbed his eyelids, let his breath slide out on a sigh. "I managed to give her a bottle without drowning her, then she went back to sleep."

"Sounds like you've got this daddy business under control."

"Yeah."

The bitter edge on his voice made her flinch. He glanced away, flexing his fingers into a loose fist, acutely aware that she was regarding him with a peculiar mix of curiosity and disapproval. Ordinarily, Johnny couldn't have cared less whether his decisions met with agreement or not. The opinions of others had never swayed him, or even affected him. Claire was different. He didn't know why, but even a mild hint of reproach in her gaze was enough to cause distress.

That distress would increase tenfold when she learned of the difficult conclusion he'd come to last night.

"What is it, Johnny? What's wrong?"

"Wrong?" He blinked, coughed, feigned interest in the fluttering flight of an errant butterfly. Despite his best intention to the contrary, sarcasm sharpened his tone. "What could possibly be wrong?"

He felt Claire stiffen in surprise, knew without looking that she was studying him quizzically. He wanted to explain, wanted to control the emotional flood gathering inside his chest, but seemed helpless to do so.

The realization that his daughter's fate was in his own incompetent hands had shaken him to the core. All the terror, the anger, the wrath at an unfeeling universe that had allowed a young woman to die and left a beautiful child motherless, all the secret fury knotted deep inside him burst forth with a harshness that shocked even himself.

Teeth gritted, throat tight, the words rumbled out on a snarl. "Here I am, a man who has never willingly accepted responsibility for another living soul, who can't even keep a damned fish alive, and I'm suddenly in charge of the life, health and happiness of a totally helpless, utterly dependent miniature human being. That's what's wrong, Claire. It's more than wrong—it's criminally negligent."

A glint of worry flashed in Claire's eyes, disappearing with the next blink. "Life is filled with challenges, Johnny. We either accept them and learn the lessons they teach, or we stagnate in a puddle of our own fear."

He studied her a moment, then averted his gaze. "Reality can't be changed simply because we wish it to be. Facts are facts."

The subtle swish of fabric alerted him that she'd shifted beside him. A sweet scent brushed over him, along with a soothing warmth radiating along his right shoulder. He knew without looking that she'd laid her hand on the back of the bench, and that her fingers were resting mere inches from his arm. "What facts are we discussing here, Johnny?"

A lump wedged in his throat. He turned his head, coughed it away. "It's one thing to care for an infant for a few days, or even a few weeks. It's quite another to raise a child to adulthood."

When she spoke, her voice was tense, wary. "I've worked with hundreds of new parents over the years. All of them were frightened, awed by the responsibility of having brought a new life into the world. Such qualms are normal, a manifestation of respect such a commitment requires." She paused a beat. "You cringed at the word *commitment*."

"Did I?" He knew that he had. "Must be a guy thing."

He chanced a look to see if she was smiling. She wasn't. "You aren't alone in this, Johnny. You have friends, people who will help you."

"It isn't me who needs help. It's Lucy." Johnny was fascinated by her eyes, one moment as clear and guileless as the gaze of a child, the next filled with the infinite wisdom of an ageless sage. "Every child deserves a stable, two-parent home. I can't give her that, Claire, can't give her what she needs. There isn't a judge in the land who wouldn't agree with that.''

For a moment, she stared blankly, as if the ramification of what he'd just said had eluded her. ''You are her father.''

''Not in the eyes of the law. At least, not yet.'' Crushed by the horrified comprehension dawning in her gaze, Johnny concentrated on studying a thin cloud stretched along the horizon. ''Even with blood tests to back up my paternity, without having my name on the birth certificate I'd have to petition the court for legal custody.''

''A technicality.''

''It's a big technicality. The precedents I've researched indicate that most judges are reluctant to grant such custody to a single man, particularly one who works long hours and knows nothing about children in the first place. Lucy would spend more time in day care than with me. That's not fair for her.''

''What are…you trying to say?''

The catch in her voice broke his heart. He closed his eyes, tightened the fist on his lap. He would have answered if he could.

''You're not going to give up custody of Lucy.'' It was not a question; it was a statement of fact issued with such force that each word struck like a punch to his chest. ''You are not going to reject this beautiful child, and force her to grow up with the pain of having been abandoned by both of her parents.''

''Foster care makes sense, Claire. Lucy will have a stable family, a real home life with both a mother and father who have the experience to raise a child properly.''

For some reason, Johnny was desperate to make

Claire understand. When he turned toward her, his heart nearly stopped. She was white as death, her bright eyes glimmering with moisture, her lush lips quivering with emotion.

"A child is not a pet," she whispered. "You can't simply give her away because she's an inconvenience."

"She's not an inconvenience!" Oddly enough, Johnny meant that with all his heart. "I will always be a part of my daughter's life. I'll fight tooth and nail for the most generous visitation the court will allow, and I'll spend every precious minute I'm given with her."

He reached for Claire's hand. She pulled it away. "How terribly stoic of you."

That stung. A gurgle from the stroller captured his attention. Lucy was staring up at him as if she'd understood every word. Pain ripped through him with shocking force. He loved his child, loved her so much that the sheer strength of emotion terrified him. At that moment, he wanted to grab his precious baby, to wrap her in his arms, to fight the world to keep her safe and happy.

But he didn't know how to do that. "Lucy's welfare is all that counts, Claire. I have to see that she has everything she needs in this life. If I can't give her that, I have to find people who can."

Claire's freckles stood out like golden raisins in a bowl of cream. Her lips moved a moment before sound emerged. "I can tell you from experience that Lucy would rather live with her daddy in a cardboard box than grow up in a mansion without him." She gripped his arm as he turned away, forcing him to look at her. "What about Lucy's heritage? Since she's

Native American, she's covered by the Indian Child Welfare Act, which substantially reduces the number of foster parents who can even qualify to care for her. She may be sent out of the county, even out of the state.''

He felt as if he'd swallowed a rock.

''And what about you, Johnny? Do you really want your tribal council informed that Johnny Winterhawk has refused custody of his own child? What would happen then?''

''I'd be reviled by my people, I suppose. And rightly so.'' A nonchalant shrug left the answer to hang between them like a foul stench.

Claire moistened her lips. ''You're willing to accept that?''

On the surface, he forced a thoughtful, dispassionate expression honed by years of practice. Inside, he was in turmoil for more reasons that he was willing to acknowledge even to himself. If prodded, he'd have to admit that he felt no intrinsic connection with his heritage, couldn't even remember much of the Ute history handed down through tribal storytellers at the powwows his grandparents had taken him to when he'd been a child. His own parents, like Johnny, had been too engrossed in climbing the ladders of success to pay much attention to genealogy. ''I have no control over what people think of me.''

''These aren't just any people, Johnny. They are your people, your blood.''

A warning tension stiffened his spine. ''They are strangers with whom I share a similar pedigree,'' he snapped. ''Where were 'my people' when my mother ran off with another man? Where were they when my father died five years later? The tribal council didn't raise me, wasn't there when I needed them. Why should I give a damn what they think about me now?''

The sorrow in Claire's eyes took his breath away. ''Maybe you shouldn't care, Johnny, but you do.'' She laid a palm against his cheek, soft and comforting. He was paralyzed by her touch, enthralled by the gentle glow of her eyes, the clarity of her words. ''You pretend that things don't matter to you, that people don't matter, but it's only a ruse, a way of concealing how deeply they truly do matter. You're a man who cares so much that every fiber of your being is shaken by the strength of your emotions. That's why you hide from yourself, Johnny. That's why you try too hard, and in doing so, doom yourself to failure.''

The touch of her hand on his cheek warmed him to the core. ''That sounds like something you learned in Psych 101.''

''No, just routine observation.'' Her smile dazzled him. ''You overfed it, you know.''

''Excuse me?''

''The fish. You overfed it.''

''How on earth can you possibly know that?''

''More routine observation,'' she replied with a shrug. ''The water in the bowl was murky. There was a thick layer of rotting food on the gravel.'' She leaned closer, until her lips were tantalizingly close to his. ''You tried too hard, Johnny Winterhawk. That may not be a good trait in a fish owner, but it's a wonderful trait for a daddy.''

Her scent floated over him, through him, into him. He was dizzied by her nearness, enchanted by her touch. He wanted to kiss her more than he wanted his next breath.

So he did.

Dipping his head, he brushed her mouth with his, and felt a jolt so startling that he instantly snapped back, stunned by the potency of the brief touch.

Claire's eyes widened. She snatched her hand away from his cheek to touch her lips as if assuring herself they were still there. "Wow."

A slow heat crawled up his throat. "I'm sorry. I shouldn't have done that."

She nodded somberly. "No, you shouldn't have. This is what you should have done." Before he could react, she slipped her hand around the back of his neck, pulled his head forward and took his mouth in a kiss so deep and sweet that he felt as if his heart had lurched into his skull to spin wildly around his brain.

Her lips were moist, hot, exquisitely delicious. The experience was wondrous, erotic beyond anything he could have imagined. Colors flashed through his mind, explosions of light, swirling images of slick skin, heated breath, entwined fingers and slow, sensual moans of pleasure. A familiar throb worked its way from lips to groin, an instant arousal so intense it shook him to the core. His arms encircled her of their own volition, crushing her soft body against him until he could feel the hardened tips of her nipples pressing against his chest.

He was wild inside, a raging heat of need, of passion, of desire beyond anything he'd experienced. Only when he heard the familiar high-pitched fuss from what seemed a great distance did his mind plummet back from the heights of sensual pleasure into the droll reality that they were seated on a bench in a public park in plain view of anyone who happened to be strolling past.

In plain view of his child.

Pulling away with a gasp, Johnny released his precious prize long enough to grasp the back of the bench so he wouldn't topple forward. He struggled to breathe, wondering if Claire had also been as affected by the kiss as he had been. To his dismay, she simply smiled up at him, then turned around to tend the fussy baby.

"There, there," she murmured, lifting Lucy from the stroller and cradling the infant in her arms. "Are you ready for your lunch, sweetie? I have a nice bottle all ready for you."

While Johnny took inventory of his mental faculties, all of which seemed to have been thoroughly muddled from the inside out, Claire casually retrieved a bottle of formula and began feeding the baby. It was as if she hadn't noticed that the world was a peculiar shade of violet, and was spinning on a strange axis.

She shifted Lucy in her arms, spoke without so much as a sideways glance. "So we're agreed."

Johnny opened his mouth to respond, but uttered only an eerie croak. He swallowed, cleared his throat and tried again. "Agreed on what?"

"Agreed that you won't allow Lucy to be raised by strangers."

Puffing his cheeks, he blew out a breath. It took a moment for the air to clear his dizzied mind. "All I can do is petition the court for custody, Claire. As I've already told you, there's little chance any judge will grant it."

"You're her father. They have to grant it."

He sighed, dried his palms on his thighs. "No, they don't. I'm not the kind of guardian most courts would look favorably upon, a divorced man who works eighteen hours a day and didn't even know he'd fathered an illegitimate child until said child showed up on his doorstep." He swallowed hard, struck by how harsh the assessment sounded out loud. "The way things look now, there's little chance I'd be awarded custody of Lucy."

Claire shrugged, shifted the bottle in her hand and spoke without looking up. "Then we'll just have to make a few changes."

"Changes?"

"No court in the land would deny that a pediatrician is qualified to care for a child."

"I'm not a pediatrician."

"I am."

"Your credentials won't carry much weight with the court."

"Of course they will," she said with a sly smile. "As soon as we're married."

Chapter Five

"Have you completely lost your mind?" Megan's fork clattered against her dinner plate.

Since her friend's voice had risen to the decibel level only slightly less than that of a jet plane on takeoff, Claire cringed at the speculative glances from nearby diners and feigned interest in the giant slab of Millie's famous meat loaf on her plate.

Her own voice sounded limp, defensive. "I don't know what happened at lunch today. Johnny and I were discussing Lucy's future and his concern that he wouldn't have either the opportunity or the ability to raise her properly, when out of the blue this peculiar, breathless voice suddenly piped up with a marriage proposal." She couldn't bring herself to meet Megan's stunned gaze. "Imagine my surprise when I realized the voice was mine."

Leaning forward, Megan propped her forearms on

the edge of the laminate booth table. "And Johnny actually agreed to this?"

Claire felt a slow flush creep up her throat. "Does it strike you as so ludicrous that a man like Johnny Winterhawk might actually be interested in a stubby-legged, slightly myopic redhead whose profession involves the well-being of children?"

"You're one in a million, Claire. Any man on earth would be lucky to have you. That's not the point."

"What, pray tell, *is* the point?"

Megan pushed her meal aside with a hiss similar to that of an angry snake. "You can't just marry a man because he wants a pediatrician in the house."

"Why not?"

"Because it's not right, that's why."

Claire shrugged, cut off a bite-size hunk of saucy entrée and stabbed it with more force than necessary. "People get married for all kinds of reasons. Who's to say which reasons are right and which are wrong?"

Reaching across the table, Megan grabbed Claire's wrist as she tried to shovel the bite into her mouth. The juicy tidbit slipped off the fork and plopped onto her plate with a delicate splat.

"He's just using you," Megan said, not unkindly. "You're going to get hurt."

As much as Claire wanted to argue the point, she couldn't. Laying down her fork, Claire stalled for time by dabbing her mouth with her napkin, vividly recalling the stunned expression on Johnny's face when she'd suggested marriage. He'd actually gone pale.

For a moment, Claire had feared he'd either run away screaming or laugh in her face. He'd done neither. Instead, he'd focused those piercing black eyes with an intensity that had stolen her breath. "That could work," he'd said. "It could actually work."

Intellectually, she'd realized that he was referring to enhancing his chances of winning a custody petition, but her heart was convinced that he was referring to the marriage itself. Of course it would work. It was destined to work. She'd known that from the moment she'd laid eyes on him.

Claire believed that with all her heart. Of course there was no way to convince Megan or anyone else of that without sounding like a gullible, starry-eyed adolescent. "Marriage doesn't come with a lifetime warranty for anyone, not even you."

The moment she saw the flash of fear in her friend's eyes, she regretted her words. Megan withdrew her hand, laid it quietly in her lap and regarded Claire thoughtfully. "At least Mac and I love each other."

"I know." Claire's heart twisted at the pointed reminder that Johnny Winterhawk did not love her. At least, not yet.

"Love is the glue that binds us," Megan said. "It's the bonding of two souls, doubling the strength of each. It allows us not only to survive the difficult times, but to thrive on them. And it gives us such peace, such joy." A smile trembled on her lips, and moist emotion brightened her eyes. "I can't imagine my life if Mac wasn't a part of it, Claire. I love him so very much. He is everything to me, and the best part is that I know in here—" she laid a palm on her chest "—that I am everything to him, as well. That's what I want for you, that strength, that joy. You deserve that, Claire. You deserve to be loved and cherished. You deserve a real marriage."

Something shivered deep inside Claire, an exquisite throb she couldn't quite identify. Megan's words shook her to her bones. Again that tiny whisper radiated out from the pit of her soul, a chilling inner voice warning that she was secretly justifying the panic of a thirty-two-year-old virgin whose chance of having the family she craved grew dimmer with every passing day.

But another voice, one that resonated from a deeper part of her being, murmured that Johnny Winterhawk was the man she was born to love.

Either way, she was going to marry him, and it would be a real marriage in every sense of the word. Claire would make sure of that.

"Marriage?" Spence nearly choked on his radish, tomato and mashed-mango sandwich. "Are you crazy?"

Johnny steepled his fingers, swallowed a surge of sheer panic and forced a calm, rational tone. "Given the circumstance, marriage makes a great deal of sense."

"Marriage doesn't make sense under any circumstance." Spence set the sandwich aside, leaned back in their usual luncheon booth at Maggie's diner. "You're a braver man than I am to actually allow a woman into your home, into your life, into—" Spence's eyes widened as his lips quirked into a just-between-us-studs grin "—your bed?"

Johnny managed to keep from spewing the iced tea he was sipping. It was lunchtime, twenty-four hours after Claire had issued her startling proposition. He still hadn't come to terms with the full implication that any marriage, even a union generated as a matter of legality and convenience, would mean to his comfortably isolated existence.

"Don't be crude," he muttered, setting the glass aside. "This is purely a business arrangement."

"Yeah, right." Spence's knowing smirk galled Johnny to the bone.

He mustered an appropriately indignant response, to which his friend and law partner seemed oblivious. "If there's one thing my daughter needs in her life right now, it's a maternal role model who adores her. If there's one thing I need in my life, it's an expert on child care. Claire qualifies on both counts."

"And she's not bad to look at, either." Spence forked a chunk of potato salad into his mouth, then raised a hand to capture the server's attention and pointed to his empty iced-tea glass. After it had been refilled, he focused across the table. "Hey, if you don't mind frilly stuff hanging off your shower rods, middle-of-the-night shrieks because the toilet seat was left up or having your razors dulled by defuzzing feminine legs, more power to you. Just don't expect me to be the one to pee on your foot and tell you it's raining."

"Meaning what exactly?"

"Meaning that you're digging yourself a dry well, my man. You may think there's water a hundred feet down, but all you're going to end up with is a shovel full of mud."

Johnny blinked at him. "Is that a legalism used strictly by ranch-law attorneys, or is there some profound message buried in there?"

"Have you ever known me to be profound?"

"Not really."

"Well, there you go." Spence took a healthy swallow of tea, set his glass down and angled a thoughtful glance across the table. "So what's the exit strategy?"

A chill slipped down Johnny's spine. "We haven't worked out all the details."

Spence's eyebrows bunched into a frown. "You mean you haven't agreed how you're going to get out of this marriage once the custody issues have been settled?"

"Not exactly."

"Oh, brother." Heaving a sigh, Spence pushed his plate aside and flung the napkin on the table. "There's no sense in trying to keep you from being reeled in hook, line and sinker when you're already flopping on the pier."

"This was my decision as much as it was Claire's," he replied with what he considered to be appropriate indignation. "It's what is best for Lucy."

"Were you trying to say something?" Spence asked innocently. "I could swear I saw your gills move."

No woman had a right to look that good at the end of a ten-hour work shift, Johnny thought as Claire bounced into the restaurant with a smile that could dazzle diamonds.

He automatically rose to pull out a chair for her. She settled into it, breathless and glowing, shrugged off a warm, cinnamon-colored wool coat that brought out the auburn highlights in her own silky hair and turned in the seat to arrange the garment over the back of the chair. "I'm sorry to be late. We had two fevers and a diaper rash rush into the clinic at the last minute. It's been one of those days.'' She shifted forward, her eyes sparkling. "Have you ordered yet?"

"No. I, ah, was waiting for you."

"How chivalrous!" Her melodic laughter evoked a peculiar fluttering sensation in his chest. "You must be starving, poor man." She glanced around, caught the maître d's attention with a smile that had the fellow hovering like a mesmerized moth in two seconds flat. "We're ready to order now," she said in a voice like melting honey.

The maître d' clicked his heels, snapped his fingers. A tuxedo-clad server appeared like magic to recite the specials. When he'd finished, Claire fixed Johnny with a gaze hot enough to melt bones. "Mr. Winterhawk will make this evening's selection," she whispered.

That startled him. He'd never been called upon to make anyone else's dinner choice before. "But I don't know what you like."

"As long as it doesn't have tentacles or leap off my plate screaming, I'm willing tc give just about anything a try." A slow, sensuous smile brought a mischievous glint to her eye, and erotic huskiness to her voice. "Surprise me, Johnny. I love surprises."

Every drop of moisture evaporated from his mouth. He peeled his lips off his teeth, cleared his throat and tried to behave as if the napkin in his lap hadn't suddenly been propelled upward by an unexpected physical response. "We'll have the, er, grilled swordfish…" He paused, waited for her delicate nod of approval before completing the order, then selected a particularly nice pinot blanc to complement the meal.

"Did you have any problem finding Megan's place?" she asked when the waiter had left.

"No, none." He squirmed, rearranged the napkin to conceal evidence of his physical distress. "It was kind of her to watch Lucy this evening so we could, ah, finalize things."

"Megan is a peach." Claire plucked a bread stick from a nearby basket, broke it with a snap. "Did you see Tyler while you were there?"

He recalled a fat-cheeked infant cooing in a playpen. "Yes."

"He's adorable, isn't he?"

Although Johnny was no expert on attractive infants, he thought Lucy was prettier. "The child seemed quite healthy."

Claire laughed, bit the end off her bread stick and washed it down with a sip of water. "Tyler and Lucy might make a cute couple some day, don't you think?"

For some reason, he was aghast at the suggestion. He didn't stop to consider why. "No, I most certainly do not."

Claire issued a chuckle as she regarded him with amusement. "So, you don't think Tyler Duncan is good enough for your daughter? Or is it simply the thought of your precious baby girl becoming a woman someday that has brought that ashen hue to your face?"

Alerted by a draft on his tongue, Johnny closed his mouth with a snap, found himself smiling at her astute observation. "I'm having enough difficulty adjusting to fatherhood in the first place, let alone considering how I will eventually interview prospective sons-in-law."

She tilted her head prettily, causing her sleek hair

to brush the curve of her left shoulder. "Actually, I think you've adjusted to fatherhood quite well."

"Do you?" For some reason, it pleased him that she thought so.

"Absolutely." Her smile remained, although her eyes seemed more thoughtful than amused. "You're a good man, Johnny Winterhawk, and you'll be a magnificent father. Lucy is a very lucky little girl." Averting her gaze, she added, "I'm lucky, as well, to have been given this opportunity to share her with you."

Johnny's own smile froze into a stiff grimace. Absently touching the lapel of his suit coat, he felt the folded document neatly tucked into the inside breast pocket, and wondered how lucky she'd feel after reading it.

For the next hour, Johnny found himself utterly enamored by the breathtaking woman across the table from him. Claire Davis was a person of extraordinary humor and grace, and she had a way of gazing so deeply into his eyes that she seemed to be reading every nuance of his soul. Everything amused her, from the maître d's peculiar waddle, which she speculated could be alleviated by a simple switch from briefs to boxers, to the twist of orange rind adorning her plate, which she promptly rearranged into the shape of a pointy-nosed fish in deference, she explained, to the one that gave its all for their lovely dinner.

For some odd reason, Johnny found that fascinating. In fact, he found everything about her fascinating, including the melodic laughter that made his blood quiver like warm Jell-O, and the adorable dimple that magically appeared each time she pursed her lips, a habit in which she indulged during moments of thoughtful reflection.

By the time the dessert cart was wheeled to their table, Johnny was utterly beguiled. And he knew it.

"Wow," Claire murmured, eyeing the delicacies with palpable delight. "I can feel my arteries clog already."

The server blinked, shored up his wavering smile. "Chef's fudge torte is a house specialty, and our brandy-sauced caramel custard quite popular. Or perhaps madame would prefer the tart cherry soufflé?"

Issuing a regretful sigh, she laid her napkin beside her plate. "Despite the exquisite selection, I'm afraid I couldn't eat another bite. Please give my compliments to the chef. The meal was magnificent."

Beaming, the server hovered like a solicitous bumblebee to refill Claire's coffee cup and top off her water glass before remembering that she wasn't alone at the table. He gave Johnny what could only be called a look of pure envy. "And would the gentleman care for dessert?"

"No, thank you." He empathized with the smitten waiter. There was something incredibly alluring about Claire Davis, something elusive and subtly erotic that turned heads and made male hearts beat faster. A man who wasn't careful could become besotted by such a woman.

"So, it's settled." With a bright smile, Claire leaned forward, propping her wrists on the linen-draped table. "We'll meet at the courthouse tomorrow at three, do the deed, pick Lucy up from day care and celebrate by rushing back to your place to make sure the movers don't drop my dresser or trip over the portable crib.''

An icy chill stiffened his shoulders at the reminder. He cleared his throat, absently patted the document hidden beneath his lapel. ''I've, ah, taken the liberty of moving my furnishings and personal belongings into the guest room. I thought you'd prefer the master suite.'' When the thoughtful dimple appeared at the corner of her mouth, Johnny averted his gaze. ''There's a private bath,'' he said stupidly.

She remained silent for a moment. From the corner of his eye, he noticed she was staring into her coffee cup. ''It seems inappropriate for me to evict you from your own bedroom.''

''I'm rarely there, anyway.'' When she hiked a brow, he felt his skin heat. ''That is, I don't require much sleep.''

The truth of the matter was that Johnny was a hopeless insomniac who spent long nights working, or prowling the darkened recesses of his home to the comforting combination noise of the television and radio. Or at least he had before Lucy came into his life. Now the TV and radio remained off, lest the noise muffle the sounds of the baby's breathing or conceal a fuss of displeasure.

Claire's delicate amber brows crinkled into a frown. ''Judging from the circles under your eyes, you require more sleep than you're getting. I could prescribe a mild sedative for you.''

''I don't take drugs.''

''What do you do when you get a headache?''

He shrugged. ''I wait for it to go away.''

''How admirably macho of you.'' She laughed, perhaps at his startled expression. ''Antibiotics, vaccines and other modern drugs have given us all safer, healthier lives. Pharmaceuticals are not the enemy, Johnny, although like anything else, they can be abused.'' She regarded him thoughtfully. ''I hope your distrust of modern medicine doesn't extend to childhood vaccinations and regular pediatric examination.''

It had never occurred to him to deny his child the very best medical care available, and he was bothered that Claire would believe otherwise. ''Lucy will have the best care of everything, and that includes medical care. Why else would I marry a doctor?''

The sparkle in her eyes faded. Her smile seemed a bit stiff, he thought.

''Why else indeed?'' She inhaled deeply, twisted the corner of her napkin. ''You're right, of course. It was a silly thought. I should have known better.''

Although he didn't know precisely what she meant, he was fairly certain she wasn't talking about his view of the medical profession. He shifted in his seat, felt the telltale document poke against his armpit and was reminded that they had one final item of business to discuss. Feeling strangely fatalistic, he withdrew the folded legal papers, clearing his throat to capture her attention.

''What's this?'' she asked as he handed the document over. ''A prenuptial agreement?''

''Just a formality, the clarification of a few details.''

She skimmed the first page, then the second and finally the third, all without changing her bland expression. ''This outlines the termination of the marriage within sixty days after the final award of custody.''

Johnny was well aware of the contents. "I thought you'd be more comfortable if the dissolution terms were agreed upon in advance."

"How considerate of you," she murmured. "One hopes the judge in the custody suit is just as forward thinking as you." She glanced up, appearing more unconcerned that he suspected she was. "This will become a public document as soon as it's filed. But of course, as an attorney you're well aware of that."

"Of course I'm aware of that." His heart skipped a beat. Despite his assurance to the contrary, it honestly hadn't occurred to him that the document might find its way into the custody hearing. Feeling like a complete idiot, he covered his lapse with the first thing that popped into his mind. "Which is why the agreement won't be filed until after the custody arrangements have been finalized."

She issued a somber nod. "Then there's clearly no rush in signing them, is there?" As if on cue, a subtle buzz emanated from her midsection. She deftly unhooked the pager from the waistband of her skirt. "It's the clinic," she announced, grabbing her coat from the back of her chair and tucking the legal document in the pocket. "Some perplexed new parent has probably misread the suppository directions again and has a baby with a foamy mouth."

Bewildered, Johnny automatically rose as she stood, and held her coat for her. "But the agreement—"

"We'll talk about it later." She turned on her tiptoes, startled him by brushing his lips with a sweet kiss that jolted him to his toes. "It's the night before our wedding," she whispered against his cheek. "While in public, we should behave as if we can't wait to get our hands on each other. Don't you agree?''

"Uh…"

"Oh, I almost forgot. We're running out of diapers. Can you pick some up on the way home?"

Before Johnny could do any more than nod stupidly, she flashed another dazzling smile, wound her way through the crowded restaurant and disappeared.

Checking his watch for the third time in as many minutes, Johnny hurried out of the supermarket with a huge package of disposable diapers tucked under his arm. Cold night air slapped his face, invigorating him. He'd promised Meg Duncan that he'd pick up Lucy by 9:00 p.m. It was now 8:45, and he'd have to hustle to get there in time.

Crossing the busy parking lot, he was so lost in thought that he momentarily forgot where his vehicle was located. He paused under one of the lot's light poles to orient himself.

"Johnny?" The voice was vaguely familiar. He turned as a woman with thick eyeglasses and sleek, shoulder-length braids stepped out of the shadows. "I thought it was you. Gracious, it's been how long…over a year?" She laughed at his bemused expression. "I'm Greta, Samantha's friend."

"Oh, right. You worked with Sam at that fast-food place out on the highway."

"I still work there, only I've been out of town for a couple of weeks visiting my folks down in Scottsdale." She tilted her head, her expression sober. "I just heard what happened to Sam and Rodney. Wow, talk about bad karma. An awful thing, just awful."

A lump positioned itself in his throat. Not trusting himself to speak, he simply nodded.

"Sam was a good person, although I never liked Rodney much. He was always ordering her around, talked to her like she was a servant or something." Greta studied Johnny intently enough to make him flinch. "I always hoped she'd end up with you, actually."

He managed a nonchalant shrug. "Things happen."

"Yeah, things do." She slipped her index finger under the thick lenses to dab away the moisture. "Sam wrote me a couple of times from Albuquerque. I was always going to answer—" Her voice caught. She coughed away the weakness, heaved a sigh of regret. "I know Sam wasn't close to her folks, but they still must have taken it hard."

"Samantha's parents died last year."

"Both of them?" Greta was clearly shaken by the news. "Geez, that's really the pits. I wonder who's taking care of her baby."

"I am." He managed a smile, shifted to expose the package under his arm. "Lucy is with me now."

"With you?" That clearly startled her. "Why on earth would you be taking care of Sam's daughter?"

Something in the woman's puzzled expression struck a warning chord. "Because she's my daughter, too."

Greta wobbled back a step, chewed her lower lip. She opened her mouth, closed it, then readjusted her spectacles with maddening deliberation. When she'd finished, she took a deep breath, laid a compassionate hand on his arm. "It may not be my place to tell you this, but I think you have a right to know."

Icy fingers of fear clamped hold of his spine. "To know what?"

"Didn't you ever wonder why Sam left you?"

"I presumed because she was in love with Mr. Frye."

"Poor Sam was so crazy and mixed-up, I doubt she even knew the meaning of the word." Greta paused to chew her lip again. "The truth is that Samantha left because she discovered that she was pregnant."

Air rushed out of his lungs as if he'd been gut punched. "She knew she was pregnant, and she left anyway?"

"Sam left *because* she was pregnant, not in spite of it." Greta sighed, shook her head. "Don't you understand, Johnny? You aren't Lucy's father. Rodney is."

And with those words, Johnny's world collapsed.

Chapter Six

"It makes perfect sense, Mom." Tilting her head sideways, Claire clamped the cordless phone between her cheek and shoulder, freeing her hands to quickly sort the day's mail.

It was nearly ten at night, two hours after she'd rushed from the restaurant to check a feverish toddler at the clinic. Her head ached, her spine felt as if it had been stomped by wild horses and she'd have rather chewed worms than have this conversation with her mother.

Since the civil-marriage ceremony was scheduled for tomorrow afternoon, Claire couldn't put it off any longer. "If we don't convince a judge that Lucy will be raised in a stable, nurturing environment, she may be removed from her father's care."

A disappointed sigh filtered over the line. "Of course that would be very sad, but to marry a man you barely know purely for legalities and logistics? It seems rather impulsive, dear, even for you.'' Regina Davis had a maddening manner of conveying disapproval with such calm rationale that any response would by comparison seem defensive and slightly hysterical.

Agreement, Claire had learned, was the only remedy. ''It does seem impulsive, doesn't it?'' A final glance confirmed that the day's mail consisted only of a few bills and an official-looking envelope announcing she was the guaranteed winner of a multi-million-dollar sweepstakes. She tossed the envelopes aside, and managed an airy laugh. ''Oh, well, you know how I am.''

''That's why I'm worried. You're much too altruistic for your own good. Remember in high school, when you loaned your baby-sitting money to some girl who couldn't afford a cheerleading outfit?''

''Mindy wasn't 'some girl'—she was my dearest friend.''

''That's hardly the point, dear. You gave her money you'd been saving all year for a drama-club outing. If your father hadn't accidentally discovered you'd canceled the reservations, you wouldn't have been able to go.''

''It wouldn't have been a disaster if I hadn't.''

''That trip to Broadway was all you'd talked about for months. The fact that you were willing to make such a sacrifice for the sake of a friend shows how…generous you are.''

''I believe *gullible* was the word you used at the time.''

''Yes, well, that's how mothers are when they feel their children are being taken advantage of.'' Regina's soft chuckle faded into a morose sigh. "Which segues into our current discussion, dear."

"No one is taking advantage of me, Mom. This was my idea in the first place."

"I have no doubt of that," she said kindly. "Perhaps it's selfish of me, but since the first day I held you in my arms I've dreamed of your wedding, of seeing you walk down the aisle in the same bridal gown I wore on my wedding day and my mother wore on hers."

The reminder was surprisingly painful for Claire, dredging up memories of old photographs she'd once studied with such reverence, images of both Nana and Regina, smiling and radiant, wearing the same creamy lace-and-silk gown that had been carefully packed away for Claire's wedding.

As a girl, Claire had imagined herself in that gown, had even chosen the accessories she would wear, clipping photographs from glossy magazines of the perfect pearl earrings, the perfect ivory pumps, the perfect satin-and-lace garter. Every detail of that day had been etched in her mind, from the attendants' gossamer ensembles right down to the reception mint cups and table decorations.

Somehow, she'd never quite imagined herself standing in a chamber lined with law books while wearing a practical wool blazer and sturdy rubbersoled shoes.

Regina sniffed, cleared her throat. "I understand that this is just a legal formality, not a real marriage. Still, it's come as a bit of a shock."

The lump in Claire's throat seemed the size of Manhattan. She managed to speak around it. "I understand."

"I can't help but wonder if you've thought this through, darling. I realize you want to help. That's part of your nature. Still, it's difficult to believe you'd jeopardize your own future for the sake of a stranger's child."

"Why not, Mom? You did." The moment the words rolled off her tongue, Claire wished she could yank them back and swallow them whole.

"That's not the same thing at all." The hurt in her mother's voice nearly broke her heart. "Your father and I loved you from the moment we laid eyes on you. I've never given a moment's thought that you weren't the child of my womb. You're the child of my heart. Nothing can ever change that."

"I know, Mom. I love you, too." She swallowed a surge of emotion, stepped from the apartment's small living area, crowded with packing cartons, into a kitchen that was stripped clean, with contents already tucked into several smaller boxes scattered across the linoleum. "The truth is, that's how I feel about Lucy. She's so special, so precious. She's going to grow up without knowing her real mom. I can't bear the thought that she could be taken away from her father, as well."

A vague but perceptible tremor touched Regina's voice. "I knew that you'd always been curious about your birth parents, Claire. I never realized how deeply you felt about having lost them."

Claire would pull out her toenails before she'd purposely wound her beloved adoptive parents, yet every word she uttered seemed to have that unintended affect. "I love you and Daddy more than life itself, Mom, but there's this...this part of me that's missing, a hole in my past that can never, ever be filled. It may not be reasonable. It's not even something I can explain. All I know is that I think about Lucy growing up with that same emotional void, and my heart just breaks for her.''

Frustrated, Claire slumped against the sink. Her mouth was as dry as a desert, and every glass in the apartment had been packed. "I can't imagine what my life would have been like without you and Daddy. I don't want to change anything, Mom. I...I just want to know where I came from, and the realization that I never will—'' Tears leaked onto her lower lashes. She couldn't go on.

"My sweet, sweet girl,'' Regina whispered, her voice soft with love. "Of course it hurts me to know that you have needs that I can't fulfill. I'm a mother. Mothers like to believe they are omnipotent when it comes to making their children happy. Nor can I understand exactly what you're going through because I haven't shared the experience.'' Bemusement distanced her tone, not much, but enough to be unnerving. "I can certainly understand why you'd feel drawn to a child who will share that experience. You will be able to help her, Claire, in a way that I couldn't help you.''

Claire's heart felt as if it had been squeezed. She adored her mother. "I hate disappointing you, Mom, but this is something I need to do.''

"You could never disappoint me,'' Regina said kindly. "Besides, you've always had a soft spot for babies.''

"Yes," she murmured. No way was she going to mention to her doting mom that she had a soft spot for Johnny Winterhawk, as well.

"Your father and I will support any decision you

make, dear, but have you given any thought as to how this will affect your own future?''

"I've thought of little else," Claire murmured. That much was certainly true, although not in the context she'd led her mother to believe. The significance of what would occur tomorrow loomed like a cold spot in a haunted room.

A pained sigh slipped into the receiver. "Don't you think that a woman of, ah—'' a discreet cough "—your age should be spending your time looking for a man with whom you can start a real family? I don't want to be a noodge, dear, but I would so like to be a grandmother while I'm young enough to push a stroller instead of a walker.''

Claire's parched mouth seemed suddenly mummified. Desperate, she turned on the faucet, twisted sideways to lap the running water like a thirsty cat. She'd known the conversation would eventually end up here. It always did. Her mother yearned to be a grandma. Perfectly fine, since Claire yearned to be a mom, except the crux of the matter was that old biological clock, and how long a broken-down gal in her thirties could hope to keep those aging ovum from going to waste before they were used. It made Claire crazy.

Worse, it played on her deepest fears. Was marrying Johnny Winterhawk the right thing to do for Lucy's sake? Or was it merely an excuse to worm her way into the life of a man who until last week had not even known she existed?

"Claire?" Her mother's voice buzzed from the phone Claire held at arm's length, and was barely audible over the rush of running water. "Claire, are you listening? What is that peculiar sound?"

Her thirst temporarily sated, she turned off the faucet, tucked a drippy strand of hair behind her ear and forced a cheery tone. "Nothing, Mother. At any rate, since I'll be moving tomorrow—" she wiped her wet face with the back of her hand "—I just wanted to give you the phone number."

There was a frosty pause. "That would be the phone at this Mr. Winterhawk's residence?"

"Yes."

"I see." Papers shuffled, as if her mother was searching for something on which to jot the number down. "Claire, what if you get attached to this child? It will break your heart to have to leave her."

Claire's fingers throbbed as she squeezed the telephone hard enough to dent steel. The legal agreement Johnny had shown her flashed in front of her eyes. It was now safely tucked into her knapsack, although she'd had to talk herself out of ripping the hated document into a thousand microscopic shreds. She'd reconsidered only because she hadn't wanted to lie about the document's whereabouts or explain the emotional outburst leading to its unfortunate demise should she be asked.

Still, its very existence rankled. She should have expected it—Johnny was an attorney, after all—but actually seeing such a document replete with legal euphemisms describing the dissolution of a marriage before it had even begun was sobering to say the least.

Regina's voice broke into her thoughts. "Claire, are you listening to me?"

"Yes, Mom, I'm listening."

"Eventually, you'll have to give this child up. How will you deal with that emotionally?"

"I'll cross that bridge when I come to it."

But in her mind, in her heart, Claire had already decided it was a bridge that would never be crossed. She would not, could not give Lucy up. Not now.

Not ever.

A sliver of moonlight seeped through the window, softened by the shadowed sway of a nearby aspen. Johnny stood over the crib, gazing down at the sleeping infant as he'd done for the past five hours. It was three in the morning. There would be no sleep for Johnny tonight, not a catnap, not a wink.

You aren't Lucy's father.

Greta's words haunted him. Terrified him, although he couldn't rationally explain why. If it were true, Johnny's problems were over. He had no legal or moral obligation. There was no need to seek custody of a child who wasn't his own, no reason to go through with a marriage designed only to assure the award of said custodial request.

If it were true, he didn't have to continue scheduling his entire life around the needs of one tiny human being.

If it were true, he should be down on his knees giving thanks to the Creator for releasing him from a duty he'd initially accepted with a grudging heart.

Reaching into the crib, Johnny caressed the sleeping baby's cheek, again marveling at the silky softness of her skin. He studied the infant's features, the feathery black hair, the gentle turn of her pudgy nose, a crevice at the chin, a dimple at the corner of her diminutive baby mouth.

Even at this tender age, Lucy favored her mother. She had Samantha's almond-shaped eyes and wispy, slanted brows. There was no evidence of Anglo features. If it were true that Rodney Frye was her father, there should have been.

Johnny brushed a fingertip along the baby's hand as the perfectly formed miniature fingers flexed into a loose fist. The baby shuddered, sighed, moved her tiny lips in a silent sucking motion. Paternity would be simple enough to establish. If it were true that Lucy wasn't his child, a blood test would certainly prove that.

If it were true.

Turning away from the sleeping infant, Johnny glanced around the once sterile home that was now cluttered with diaper bags, stuffed toys, tiny T-shirts and footed pajamas dotted with jovial cartoon characters. He wandered to the once spotless kitchen, regarded the counters cluttered with bottles, measuring apparatuses and cans of formula, the powdered remnants of which stained the tile grout. He hadn't tidied up after Lucy's last feeding, and set about doing so now. He didn't want Claire to see the mess when she arrived tomorrow afternoon.

Of course, if Lucy were not Johnny's child, there would be no reason for Claire to move into his home because there would be no reason for the marriage to take place. For some reason he chose not to explore too closely, that thought was unsettling to him. Secretly, he'd been looking forward to Claire's arrival, to hearing her soft laughter float through hallways that had been silent too long, to sharing conversation and a smile over morning coffee and watching the light in her eyes as she cradled Lucy in her arms.

If what Greta had told him were true, there wouldn't be a marriage. There wouldn't be shared conversation, or the lilt of soft laughter. There wouldn't be any more midnight feedings or the aggravation of tripping over a misplaced toy while stumbling down dark hallways.

If it were true, Lucy would be an orphan, relegated to a gauntlet of state and tribal law. Lucy had no living maternal relatives. Even if there were family members on her father's side willing to undergo the complex and expensive legal process required by the Indian Child Welfare Act, there was no guarantee they'd be awarded custody.

If it were true that Lucy was not Johnny's child, her entire childhood could be one of confusion and uncertainty, a clash of cultures, a bureaucratic power struggle for the heart and heritage of one very small girl.

A small squeak from beneath his shoe captured his attention. Reaching down, he retrieved a duck-shaped stuffed animal that made a peculiar sound when its belly was pressed. Lucy liked the toy. She always turned toward the noise with wide, curious eyes. Dark eyes. Dark hair. Dark skin.

Just like her mother. Just like him.

Johnny couldn't believe Lucy was another man's child, not when the soft weight of her in his arms stirred a secret place in his soul, touched his heart. He had seen the face of his ancestors in the eyes of this special child. If it were true that Lucy was not his daughter, then his eyes and his heart had deceived him.

If it were true.

But it wasn't true, couldn't be true. Lucy was his daughter, his child, his blood.

All he had to do now was prove it.

"You look like you spent the night wrestling alligators," Spence said.

Exhausted, Johnny rubbed the back of a neck so stiff it creaked when he turned his head. "I wasn't aware that alligators were a big problem in Colorado."

"I was speaking metaphorically. Everybody knows gators don't venture north of Phoenix." Spence paused at the base of the courthouse steps. "It's not too late to change your mind, buddy."

Johnny responded with a cool stare.

"Every condemned man is entitled to a final appeal," Spence replied, tucking a small camera in his jacket pocket. "But don't expect a last-minute reprieve from the governor."

Jamming his hands in his pockets, Johnny rocked back on his heels, wondering why his feet refused to move on command. He gazed up at the carved courthouse doors, felt a film of cold sweat gather on his upper lip. Claire was inside, waiting for him. He could feel her presence. It comforted him, yet a war raged inside him, a battle between conscience and pride, logic and instinct, heart and soul.

He told himself that he wasn't using Claire's love for Lucy to manipulate her into a situation that would benefit him at Claire's expense. Marriage had been her idea, after all. Surely she understood the ramifications of her suggestion. Claire Davis was without doubt the most intelligent, levelheaded person Johnny had ever known. She'd offered a perfect solution to what had seemed an insurmountable problem. He wondered if she'd feel the same once he told her what Greta had said.

Then again, there wasn't really any reason to pass

on untrue conclusions based on speculation by a woman who'd never even seen Lucy. If he mentioned the meeting to Claire, she might decide to delay the wedding, which would just muddy the legal waters and postpone the custody procedure for several weeks until the blood tests proved what Johnny already knew.

On the other hand, it was Claire's decision to make. She certainly had a right to know.

Didn't she?

"I'm sure he'll be here any minute," Claire told the doubtful clerk. "You know how lawyers are, one delay after another." She forced a cheery chuckle. It came out high-pitched and slightly maniacal.

The startled clerk sucked in her cheeks until her face looked like a deflated paper bag, took a step back from the counter as if preparing to sprint. "As you can see, the docket is quite full this afternoon."

Claire followed the woman's gaze to the crush of couples milling around the bleak waiting area. Some cooed like hormonal bunnies; some held hands, casting nervous smiles at each other; others avoided eye contact completely, shifting from one foot to the other as if waiting in a grocery line.

"He'll be here," she murmured.

The clerk's expression of practiced sympathy implied that she'd heard the same weak insistence from more than one jilted bride-to-be. "Of course," the woman murmured, then glanced at a handwritten list taped on the frosted-glass barrier. "Miller and Vasquez?"

A smiling, middle-aged couple stepped forward.

"Last room at the end of the hall," the clerk

droned. "Please have your marriage license and personal identification available."

All in all, the process was about as romantic as a trip to the Department of Motor Vehicles. Swallowing a sudden surge of doubt, Claire moved away from the counter to hover in a quiet corner where she could keep an eye on the hallway. Maybe it wouldn't be the worst thing in the world if Johnny didn't show up. Maybe her mother had been right. Maybe Claire hadn't thought this thing through—

Her breath caught in her throat as the courthouse door swung open and the most gorgeous man God ever set on this earth walked inside. With his chin held high enough to be arrogant, he scanned the milling group with a gaze so intense that even before it fell on her, she trembled at its power. When he saw her, his expression softened.

Doubt dissipated like so much steam. This was definitely the man Claire would spend the rest of her life with. He just didn't know it yet.

Heads turned as he crossed the room. Johnny Winterhawk was a man that even betrothed women noticed, much to the chagrin of their future husbands. His presence even garnered attention from the bored counter clerk, who gawked like a starstruck schoolgirl.

He didn't speak until he was close enough for Claire to be dizzied by his scent. "Am I late?"

"A little." So relieved she could have wept, Claire shifted out of her coat and absently brushed the wrinkles from the flowing sleeves of her ivory satin dress with the Victorian lace neckline that was the closest thing in her closet to Nana's wedding dress. There was something about the supple slide of satin on the

skin that soothed her, made her feel almost bridelike.
It was a small thing, Claire supposed, but a woman
was entitled to indulge herself on her wedding day.

Johnny's strained voice broke into her thoughts. As
he spoke, he glanced around the crowded courthouse
foyer. "Claire, there's something we should discuss
before—" His gaze returned to Claire. He took a
sharp breath, expelled it all at once. His lips moved,
but no sound came out. His eyes glowed with soft
reverence. "You look beautiful."

A roar in her ears drowned out the courthouse buzz.
All she could hear was the beating of her own heart,
and all she could see was the face of the man who
haunted her dreams and who thought her beautiful.
"Thank you."

A moment ticked by, then another. Perhaps a minute. Perhaps an hour. Time didn't matter. The world
didn't matter. Nothing existed except the man who
gazed upon her with eyes glowing like soft starlight
in a midnight sky.

An unfamiliar voice shattered the moment. "I said,
I hate to break this up."

Johnny blinked as if awakened from a trance.
Frowning, he glanced around to focus on the source
of the annoying interruption.

With some effort, Claire followed his gaze to the
handsome fellow with pleasant eyes and a killer grin
who stepped forward. "We haven't been officially introduced. Spence McBride, at your service."

"You're Rose McBride's son." Accepting his
proffered hand, Claire recalled having noticed him at
the clinic on occasion, although they'd never been
officially introduced. "It's so nice to see you again."

"Ditto," he said cheerily. "And I second my esteemed friend's observation. You look lovely. I can't wait to kiss the bride.''

Claire was certain she must be glowing like a neon tomato. She skimmed a questioning glance at Johnny, who was still gazing at her with a peculiar, hungry light in his eyes.

It was Spence who answered Claire's unspoken question. ''I'm the best man,'' he explained. ''Although Johnny here is a close second, so you haven't made a bad deal. I'm also your official ring bearer, wedding photographer and certified matrimonial witness, should testimony to the authenticity of the nuptials be required.''

''I see.'' She flinched at the reminder as Spence echoed Johnny's point of view that this entire process was merely a charade for the benefit of future custody hearings.

And why should he believe it to be otherwise? It wasn't Johnny who was fantasizing and romanticizing every glance, every touch, every whispered word.

It wasn't Johnny who secretly believed that a temporary marriage of convenience would evolve into a lifetime of love.

It wasn't Johnny whose pulse raced at the thought of sultry nights under the same roof, whose heart pounded with sensual images of soft moans and slick skin, of moist lips and kisses so sweet that her knees nearly buckled at the memory.

That was Claire's fantasy, not Johnny's. At least, it wasn't his fantasy yet. But it would be. She'd make sure of it.

''Winterhawk and Davis.''

Claire blinked.

''That's us.'' Johnny took a shuddering breath,

gripped her elbow and propelled her down the hallway so quickly Claire had to run to keep up. An angled glance confirmed that he was three shades paler
than he'd been moments ago.

Guilt gnawed her. "Wait."

She planted her feet, stopping so suddenly he stumbled back a step, and Spence ran into both of them.
Both men gawked at her.

Claire's hands were cold as ice. She wanted to tell
him that he didn't have to go through with this, that
there might be other ways for him to assure custody
of his daughter without marrying a woman he didn't
love.

She wanted to, but when she opened her mouth, a
question fell out. "What was it you wanted to discuss?"

"Discuss?" For a moment, he stared blankly, as if
he'd forgotten himself. Then his jaw clenched, his lips
tightened and his complexion went gray. "We need
to talk about something that happened last night,
while I was picking up diapers...." He shifted his
weight from one foot to another, twisted his mouth
as if trying to spit out an unpleasant taste.

Alarmed, Claire first thought that Johnny would re-
fuse to go through with the ceremony until she'd
signed the hated prenuptial agreement. Thank heavens
she hadn't ripped the danged thing up. "Whatever it
is, I'm sure we can take care of it later."

"No, this is important." Johnny sucked a deep
breath. "Last night, I was at the store."

Claire waited a beat before prodding him. "You
were at the store to buy diapers."

"Yes, diapers."

"And...?"

"When I returned to the parking lot, I..." Beads of perspiration gleamed along his upper lip. "I..."

Now she was getting worried. She'd never seen Johnny look quite so distraught, never observed such a blatant crack in his stoic demeanor. "You what, Johnny?"

A shuddering sigh. He closed his eyes, and when he opened them again, he looked as if he'd been cut off at the knees. His chin quivered once, then seemed to collapse in on itself as he clenched his jaw. "I realized that I'd purchased the wrong brand."

Claire blinked. "The wrong brand of diapers?"

"Yes." He moistened his lips. "They don't fit Lucy properly. I thought you should know." With that, he pressed his palm to her waist and ushered her toward the judge's chambers.

Fifteen minutes later, they emerged as husband and wife. For better or worse, the deed was done.

Let the honeymoon begin.

Chapter Seven

Claire eased the nipple from the sleeping baby's mouth and set the bottle on the kitchen table just as Johnny entered the room carrying a box of small appliances.

"This is the last of it," he announced, placing the carton beside several others containing Claire's china, flatware and kitchen utensils. He lifted a ceramic crock out of the box, clearly mystified. "What is this?"

"An electric vegetable steamer."

"You need a separate appliance just to cook carrots?" His perplexed expression amused her.

"If you find that astounding, wait until you see my professional food processor, my pasta maker and my ten-speed electric mixer complete with color-coordinated dough hook."

"I didn't know you were such an avid cook."

"We've only been married six hours. There's a lot you don't know about me." She angled a grin. "And vice versa, I'm sure."

To her delight, he smiled back at her. "In that case, you'll probably be surprised to realize that I am also the proud owner of professional-quality cooking equipment."

"You are?"

"Indeed." He reached into a drawer, pulled out a large knife and a wooden spoon. "One all-purpose food processor, one handy-dandy mixing device."

She laughed. "And the pasta maker?"

"A pot of boiling water and a bag of noodles. Works like a charm."

"You may feel differently after you've tasted my homemade spinach linguine."

A faint frown wrinkled his forehead. Replacing the utensils, he glanced over his shoulder. "I don't expect you to cook for me, Claire."

"Good, because you'd starve. Between my Lamaze classes and my flaky clinic hours, I'm lucky to indulge my love of cooking twice a week. The rest of the time, you're on your own."

She shifted the sleeping infant in her arms, chanced a glance in his direction. Her heart lurched. God, he was handsome, particularly with his brow furrowed and his lips thoughtfully pursed.

For a brief moment, she glimpsed an image of how he would look in twenty years, with distinguished gray at the temples and character creases at the corners of still intense eyes. He would age well, Claire decided, and was surprised at how clearly she could envision that in her mind's eye.

When he glanced up and caught her staring at him,

he flushed and turned away so quickly that he tripped over a carton, spun around and knocked over a potted palm Claire had placed beside the sliding glass door to take advantage of morning light.

"Sorry," he muttered, heaving the palm upright. He brushed his palms together, as if the touch of foliage had singed his skin, then hovered in one spot as if fearing to take another step while his nervous gaze searched for more botanical booby traps.

Embarrassed by the clutter her arrival had wrought, she glanced at the profusion of plants and boxes tossed about his once meticulous home. Most of her furniture had been placed in storage, although cartons containing her personal belongings were scattered throughout the house, and a riot of live plants spilled from every shelf, table and windowsill.

She moistened her lips, absently used a free hand to smooth the floppy sweater she'd changed into after the ceremony. It had seemed more appropriate for the unpacking process than the ivory Victorian garment she'd ended up wearing for the wedding, but it made her feel frumpy and drab. "I'm sorry about the mess."

"It's not a problem." Despite the assurance, he gazed around as if disquieted by the transformation. "I didn't realize you owned an indoor jungle."

"Don't you like plants?"

"I like them well enough, but they don't like me. Living things don't do well in my care." He eyed an African violet heavy with pink blooms. "That's pretty."

"Is it in your way sitting on the counter? I can move it—"

"No, it's fine."

"I don't want to intrude on your space."

The comment seemed to startle him. "Your presence isn't an intrusion, Claire. It's a blessing."

So touched was she by his words and the sincerity with which they were issued that her eyes instantly filled with grateful tears.

When one leaked onto her cheek, Johnny sprang around a carton, reached her in two giant steps, assisting her by pulling back the kitchen chair as she stood. "What is it, Claire? What's wrong?"

Barely able to speak, Claire lifted the baby to her shoulder. Her voice, when she found it, was little more than a broken whisper. "That was just such a nice thing you said."

"Nice things make you cry?"

He was so clearly concerned, so endearingly bewildered that she couldn't help but smile. "It's my wedding day. I'm entitled to a moment of irrational emotionalism."

A peculiar glow settled in his eyes, a spark of wonder, perhaps, or even subtle apprehension. "That reminds me..." He touched his thumb to her cheek, wiping away the moisture in a gesture so intimate and gentle that it took her breath away. "I still haven't had a chance to kiss my bride."

Her legs wobbled like a pair of Johnny's infamous boiled noodles. "I wondered when you'd get around to that."

"How about now?" A provocative, husky whisper.

"Now is good." A pitifully breathless squeak.

If Claire hadn't been holding Lucy, she probably would have leaped at him before he could change his mind, just as she'd done at the park on the day she'd so boldly proposed marriage to him.

When it came to Johnny Winterhawk, Claire simply couldn't trust herself to behave with the calm logic that had always been her trademark. She barely recognized the palpitating, impulsive person she'd become, giggling like a schoolgirl one minute, leaking irrational tears the next. There was something about Johnny that made her feel both clumsy and beautiful, wildly erratic and sinfully erotic, a bewildering collage of emotion that she didn't understand and couldn't control.

If her turmoil was visible, Johnny gave no indication he noticed. He gazed at her with the same smoldering warmth Claire recognized from the other men in her life, men who had kissed her, had wanted her, had proceeded to demonstrate the seduction process from step to step without deviation, as if each had memorized the same human-sexuality text. Despite natural curiosity and the urging of her own well-developed hormones, Claire had routinely closed the book before the final chapter.

She knew how the story ended. She was, after all, a doctor. The biological realities of human reproduction were hardly a mystery to her. But the emotional turmoil, the current of sensation swirling deep inside—these were new to her. This was uncharted territory.

Johnny slid his thumb beneath her chin, urging her to tilt her face back gently, taking care not to disturb the sleeping infant she held at her shoulder. "Have I mentioned how lovely you are?"

"Feel free to mention it again." A quiver of anticipation vibrated down her spine.

His mouth moved closer, closer still. "I was the envy of every man at the courthouse." The moist heat of his breath touched her skin with minty warmth, a fresh scent of chewing gum mingling with the subtle hint of smooth liquor from the nightcap he'd sipped earlier that evening.

"I was the envy of every woman." Claire waited, trembling, breathless, her lips parted in welcome.

"They were humbled by your beauty."

Instead of taking her mouth in a single crushing swoop, Johnny merely shifted slightly, then traced the outline of her lips with his fingertip. One hand massaged the nape of her neck. The other probed every contour of her face, caressing the curve of her jaw, brushing a wisp of hair from her brow with infinite care. Every unhurried touch, every exquisite stroke warmed her skin, nourished her soul. Her own breath quickened. Every nerve in her body was alive, pulsing with need.

Slowly, oh so very slowly, he fitted his mouth against hers, moving his lips in a sensual rhythm that evoked tiny explosions of pleasure in parts of her body that had lain dormant for far too long. A provocative hunger twisted deep inside, a desire so intense that her legs wavered and her heart raced and her blood hissed through her veins like heated steam.

Claire had been kissed before, more times than she could count. But she'd never been kissed like this, never felt the ground move beneath her feet, never felt as if the stars had shifted in the sky and the earth had wobbled off its axis.

Johnny stepped back, looking startled. He said nothing. He didn't have to. The experience had been too powerful, too jolting not to have been felt by both of them.

They gawked at each other for an awkward moment. "I guess it's bedtime," Johnny said.

Claire nearly fell over. "Yes," she murmured as sensual images circled her mind. "Bedtime."

When Johnny opened his arms, Claire stepped forward, and would have melted into his embrace had he not spoken again. "I'll put her down."

"Her?" It took a moment for Claire to realize that he was talking about the dozing infant nestled against her shoulder. "Oh. Lucy's bedtime." She shifted, allowing Johnny to gather the baby in his arms without waking her, a display of parental expertise he'd not have been able to manage a week earlier. "Actually, it's probably bedtime for the grown-ups, as well." The bold statement slipped out unbidden, bringing a prickle of heat to her cheeks. "It's been a long day."

Johnny cleared his throat. "Yes."

"Well, then." She licked her lips, managed a bright smile as she sidled toward the hallway. "I'll, ah, just go get ready."

He nodded.

"For bed."

He nodded again.

"Yep." She clasped her hands behind her, rocked back and forth on the balls of her feet. "Ready for bed."

A tiny glint of amusement twinkled in his eye. "Sounds like a plan."

Fearing that if she opened her mouth again, even more lunacy would emerge, Claire backed out of the room and sagged against the hallway wall to catch her breath. She heard Johnny's footsteps mute on carpet, and knew that he'd taken Lucy into the living room, where for some odd reason he insisted on keeping her crib. A masculine whisper caught her ear. Intrigued, she slipped down the hall to the foyer that opened into the living area.

"There you go, small one. May your dreams be as sweet as your smile."

There was a tinkling sound, as if his shoulder had brushed the crib mobile. Claire wished she could see him. She loved watching him with his baby, loved the awkward gentleness he displayed, the tender warmth in his eyes. The first time Lucy had grasped his finger, he'd lit up like a child at Christmas and bragged about his daughter's athletic prowess for days. It touched Claire. *He* touched Claire.

Another whisper had her straining to hear. "Claire's here now," he murmured. "You're going to be all right." He paused a beat. "We're both going to be all right."

Covering her mouth, Claire muffled the sound of her breath catching in her throat and slipped silently back down the hallway to the master bedroom. Once inside, she closed the door behind her and sagged against the jamb, shaken to the core.

He cared about her—he actually cared. And he wanted her here every bit as much as she wanted to be here. Thrilled, relieved, so grateful she could weep, Claire darted a frantic gaze to the supple silk-and-satin negligee draped hopefully across the bed. A honeymoon gown if she'd ever seen one, which was exactly why she'd purchased it a few days ago in an impulsive fit of romantic optimism. She'd told herself that a woman was entitled to wear something deliciously slinky on her wedding night, even if the groom never saw it. Of course, she couldn't help but hope that he would not only see the beautiful gown, but also assist her in removing it.

What would happen after that, Claire could only imagine, based on whispers from her female friends who'd experienced such pleasures and her own clinical knowledge of sexual function. The former quite frankly seemed a great deal more interesting than the latter.

The image evoked a delicious shiver.

Discussion of postnuptial intimacy had been avoided during the rush to legitimize their relationship, although there was little doubt that Johnny intended to respect her privacy. He had, after all, moved his furniture, clothing and personal belongings into the guest room. Claire had been partly relieved, partly disappointed. She did, however, understand. Theirs was a unique relationship. Courtship usually preceded the wedding rather than the other way around.

Still, they'd never agreed that a convenient marriage had to be platonic, and there was no doubt in Claire's mind as to the meaning of the signals Johnny had been sending. That melting kiss, that smoldering gaze. Oh, yes. He was ready.

Men were always ready, or so it seemed to Claire, who'd yet to meet any male over the age of puberty whose urge to merge hadn't been the driving force of his dating life. It was always Claire who'd been reluctant, who'd refused because the timing was wrong, or the person was wrong, or she simply hadn't been ready for the emotional commitment of such intimacy.

Well, she was ready now. The right time, the right man, a ring on her finger and lust in her heart. This was the moment she'd waited for all her life. She was determined to make the most of it.

Twenty minutes later, Claire emerged from a luxurious bubble bath, fluffed her damp hair and slipped into the most sensual garment she'd ever owned in her life. The silk slid over her hips with a supple swish, caressing her skin so sweetly that a sigh slipped from her lips. Surely the angels themselves wore satin and silk in heaven. There could be no more glorious way to spend eternity. Except, of course, to spend it nested in Johnny Winterhawk's arms.

Which was just where she planned to be in about ten minutes. The anticipation made her tingle all over and gave her skin a rosy glow that was, she decided, rather attractive. She scrutinized her reflection in the mirror, touched up her makeup, then turned sideways to eye the drape of the fabric over her body. Silken cords hugged her shoulders; the bodice dipped low between her breasts, revealing nothing but suggesting a great deal. The sleek fabric hugged her like a satin skin, skimmed her ankles with a sophisticated flare.

Her gaze settled on a small abdominal pouch. She frowned, sucked in her stomach. That was better. All she had to do was hold her breath for the rest of the night. No problem.

A nervous giggle slipped out. She slapped her hands over her mouth, mentally scolding herself. Giggling was not sexy. Men did not appreciate women who laughed during, er, the performance. Claire forgot where she'd heard that, but it certainly made sense. No matter what happened, she must not display even a hint of amusement.

A final glance in the mirror, a spritz of enticing

fragrance, a deep cleansing breath, and she slipped out of the bedroom, hoping the peculiar vibration that greeted her was not the sound of her knees knocking together.

It took a moment to realize that the intermittent rumbling was emanating from the darkened living room. She turned on a lamp, and her heart sank. Johnny was seated on the sofa, one hand on the baby's crib rail and his head slumped against the back cushion. He was sound asleep. And he was snoring.

Claire sighed, but never considered waking him. He'd looked exceptionally tired today. In fact, he'd looked tired since Lucy had arrived, with good reason. He'd refused to place her crib in his own bedroom, fearing he wouldn't hear her when he was in the far side of the house, and he'd insisted that moving the crib from room to room might disturb her. Claire suspected that he'd spent every night since his daughter's arrival slumped on the sofa.

It was such a sweet sight, actually, a protective father and his slumbering child. Smiling, she slipped off his shoes, lifted his legs onto the sofa. After covering her new husband with a blanket, Claire returned to her bedroom and spent her wedding night alone.

With Lucy safely cradled in a carrier on the kitchen table and a women's magazine lying open on the counter, Claire set down the spatula long enough to flip the page to the article she was seeking.

"'Enticing your man,'" she murmured aloud. "'Everything you ever wanted to know about the art of seduction.'" She puffed her cheeks, angled a glance at the bright-eyed infant. "You see what I'm reduced to? Advice for the lovelorn from perfect strangers.''

Lucy gurgled happily.

''That's easy for you to say. You haven't spent your first week of married life doing everything short of a nude belly dance on the dinner table to garner masculine attention.''

The baby grinned, waved a tiny fist, which Claire took as a gesture of encouragement. ''Yes, well, I must admit I'm not particularly accomplished at this sort of thing at the moment. But don't worry, sweetie. By the time you're old enough for some serious mother-daughter talks on the subject, I guarantee I'll have some delightful tidbits of advice to share with you.''

An ominous sizzle from the frying pan captured her attention. She flattened the bacon strips, lowered the flame and spent a cautious moment listening to shower sounds to assure herself that Johnny was still safely occupied with his morning ritual.

She could barely imagine such a large man folded into the cramped room at the end of the hall using a diminutive, curtain-lined tub that provided only a handheld showerhead attached to the faucet with an annoying loop of hose. In comparison, the spacious master bath provided a massive glass-enclosed shower stall and luxurious Jacuzzi large enough for two. It seemed a shame to waste all that magnificent space on one small female.

Claire smiled. If she couldn't entice Johnny into her bed, perhaps she could entice him into her bathroom. ''What do you think, Lucy? Is the way to a man's heart through a hot shower?'' When the baby yawned, Claire shrugged. "Okay, okay, we'll see what the experts say."

She took a moment to turn the bacon strips, then continued reading aloud.

"Like the wild creatures from which they evolved, men rely on senses, not emotions. Forget candlelight dinners and mood music. Men prefer visual stimuli, are unwilling to consume what they cannot see, and are unable to concentrate on amorous pursuits while their stomachs are empty. Mom was right, ladies. Food really is the first stop on the way to their hearts."

Claire tapped the page with her fingertip. "Hmm… Well, at least we're on the right track. If it's one thing your daddy does appreciate, it's a nicely prepared meal. I don't know about the rest of this, though. It seems rather complex for something that's supposed to come naturally."

Forcing her mind into the same study mode that she'd used so successfully through the grind of medical school, Claire told herself that learning seduction techniques was no different from any other course of study. One simply gathered information, processed it efficiently, then put the knowledge to use.

Visual stimuli, for instance—impulses transmitted via optic nerves from the retina to the occipital lobe, where they were transformed into vision. That was something Claire could understand. Science, biology, anatomical facts.

Intellectually, she was also aware that the sight of the unclothed female form had a powerful physical effect on the male of the species. This reaction seemed to occur even if the female in question was available only on celluloid, or as a two-dimensional photograph in a glossy magazine.

That struck Claire as peculiar. After all, she'd seen her share of nude males. Although she could appreciate the beauty of a well-formed and muscular physique, she'd yet to be physically aroused by the mere sight of one.

Issuing a pained sigh, Claire propped an elbow on the counter, rested her forehead on her fist and used her free hand to turn the page.

"Remember those senses, ladies. Sight, smell, sound, touch, taste. No man born can resist a naked, perfumed woman who whispers naughty suggestions while gently stroking—

"Oh, my!" Jolting upright, Claire closed the magazine, pushed it aside as if it were a coiled snake.

"Well." She cleared her throat, foolishly averted her gaze from the cooing infant. "You're much too young to hear about… that."

Folding her arms, she propped a hip against the counter, feeling utterly foolish and completely lost. She wasn't an idiot, nor was she a naive schoolgirl. She knew exactly what men wanted, even if she couldn't quite appreciate why such things were so important.

She huffed, annoyed at the implication that men required no more than a glance at erotica, a whiff of sultry scent or a single seductive whisper to morph into carnal beasts hell-bent on sexual conquest. "It was a silly article, Lucy. Forget everything you heard.

Men have emotions, just like we do. They feel compassion and empathy. They fall in love.''

Exhaling all at once, she rubbed her forehead. Men did indeed fall in love. Over her own life, some had professed to having fallen in love with Claire, although she hadn't returned those feelings. None of them had been the right man.

None had been Johnny Winterhawk.

As if on cue, a tremendous thud rattled the walls, followed by a bloodcurdling bellow. Claire leaped forward, sprinted down the hall. A string of furious epithets filtered from behind the bathroom door, along with more ominous thumps.

"Johnny?" She beat the door with her fist. "Are you all right?"

When the only response was a chilling crash and a yelp of pain, she yanked the door open.

"Johnny—" She gasped, jerked to a stop, stunned by the sight of a wet, naked man writhing on the bathroom floor and fighting to extricate himself from a sheath of torn shower curtain.

Cursing furiously, Johnny flung off the confining fabric, jumped to his feet and kicked the tangle of tattered plastic before realizing he was no longer alone. When he saw Claire, he froze into a bronze and burnished statue of masculine perfection.

It took a moment for Claire to realize that she'd forgotten to breathe. She inhaled deeply, almost desperately, then emptied her lungs all at once.

"Visual stimuli," she murmured. "It works."

Chapter Eight

Naked and dripping, Johnny snatched a corner of the torn curtain from which he'd just disentangled himself, judiciously positioned it to achieve some modicum of modesty.

"Don't be embarrassed," Claire murmured, her unapologetic gaze riveted below his navel. "I'm a doctor."

"Don't doctors believe in knocking?"

"I did knock. Apparently, you were screaming too loudly to notice." Her gaze meandered upward with unnerving deliberation, pausing at his chest. She issued a peculiar gurgle.

Johnny presumed her apparent difficulty in peeling her lips off her teeth was a futile effort to disguise amusement.

Clearing her throat, she nodded at the tattered wad of plastic. "Nice kill, soldier. Shall we give it a hu-

manitarian burial, or would you prefer to mount it on
the wall to memorialize a warrior's great victory?''

A humiliating heat crawled up his neck. He was
certain she had a vivid mental picture of how the
entire embarrassing incident had occurred, of how
he'd been squished inside the cramped tub struggling
to rinse his hair with the awkward hand spray, then
lost his balance and crashed through the shower curtain with all the grace of a toe-dancing bison. He felt
stupid, clumsy.

Exposed.

It wasn't nudity that made him feel vulnerable.
He'd been raised in a culture that believed the unclothed body was as natural as a leafless tree in winter. Nor was he particularly overwrought at having
been caught in a decidedly childish fit of pique. What
truly unnerved him was a sudden sensation of intimacy, and all the frightening emotions that went with
that.

''You try taking a shower in a teacup,'' he growled.

''I know, I'm sorry. You shouldn't be relegated to
a child-size bathroom in your own home.'' Her smile
was empathetic, oddly wistful. ''You're bleeding.''

Vaguely aware of a stinging sensation above his
left eyebrow, he touched the area, stared stupidly at
the red stain on his fingertips. He must have struck
his head on the sink when he fell.

''Let me take a look.'' She extended her hand, her
smile fading when he automatically pulled back. ''I
won't hurt you.''

A lump of panic wedged in his throat. Claire could
indeed hurt him, would do so if he allowed it. Not
physically, however. The minor injury was of no concern to him. Emotional pain, the devastation of loss

that savaged the spirit and eviscerated the soul—that was what terrified him.

Johnny Winterhawk had deeply cared for three women in his life...his mother, his wife and Samantha Cloud. All had betrayed him; all had abandoned him. Females, he'd decided, were not to be trusted with a man's heart.

The problem was that a certain delightful redhead had already touched his heart, and was tightening her grip with every passing day. That unnerved him, since he'd taken great pains not to allow anyone close enough to hurt him again. And he'd been successful, until Claire Davis had entered his life.

Sweet, gentle, beautiful Claire, with her sparkling eyes and lyrical laugh that could charm the cougar from its mountain and the moon from the sky. Smoldering, sensual Claire, who stood before him like a sultry goddess draped in moss-green satin and ivory silk, her Titian hair glowing hot, spilling to her shoulders like russet flame.

She had bewitched him, enamored him, pervaded his thoughts, invaded his dreams. Sleep, once the enemy of darkness, had become a breathless world of wonder where lush lips parted for him alone, and exotic hair tousled with passion fanned the pillows of his mind.

"Sit down."

He blinked, realized Claire had retrieved antiseptic and bandages from the medicine cabinet. "You don't have to—"

"Would you rather go to the emergency room?" She shrugged, angled a mischievous glance. "They're a bit suture happy, but otherwise quite competent."

"I don't need stitches."

"I quite agree. A couple of butterfly fasteners should do nicely, ~~but I'm not going to fight~~ my way through six yards of flower-print plastic to get at you. Here." She handed him a bath towel, turned around as if to give him privacy.

Feeling incredibly idiotic, he fumbled with the tangled curtain only to glance up and meet her curious reflection staring at him from the mirror. Despite her awkward pretense of adjusting the silken lapel of her blouse, she met his gaze in the mirror with an embarrassed smile, mouthed the word "Oops," then made a production of covering her eyes with her hands. Within the space of a heartbeat, she peeked between her fingers with a mischievous, taunting grin.

Acting on instinct, Johnny did what most red-blooded males did when challenged by a beautiful, seductive female. He accepted.

Staring directly at her reflection, he casually tossed the shower curtain into the tub and waited until the grin beneath her open fingers faded into a slack-jawed gape before he casually wrapped the towel around his waist and sat down.

"So tell me, Doctor, will I live?"

She slumped against the sink, wiped her brow with a trembling forearm. "You will. I may not." Puffing her cheeks, she blew out a breath. "Anatomy class was never like this."

Despite his intention to remain aloof, Johnny found himself chuckling. "Shall I take that as a compliment?"

"If it pleases you to be compared to a cadaver," she muttered, pouring antiseptic on a cotton ball. "Now hold still."

The next sound he heard was the pathetic hiss of his own deflating ego.

Claire was fairly certain she was going to either rip his towel off and devour him whole, or faint on the spot. Her body temperature had risen five degrees in as many minutes, and competent, professionally trained fingers nimble enough to suture a wriggling toddler were now shaking so hard she ended up disinfecting his eyebrow. Frustrated, she tossed the cotton ball aside and cleaned the wound with a washcloth.

The scent of him drove her wild. Fresh bath gel, woodsy and tart, mingled with the erotic aroma of distinctly aroused male. That vibrating bulge beneath the concealing terry cloth drew her gaze like a sexual magnet. She couldn't keep her eyes off him.

She couldn't keep her hands off him, either. Her fingertips grazed his shoulder each time she reached for a first-aid item from the sink. She constantly stroked his cheek, pretending to adjust the tilt of his head or take advantage of the light from the small, frosted-glass window. She even managed to slide her palms down his incredibly well-contoured, smoothly hairless chest with the lame excuse of straightening his torso so she could work more easily.

If Johnny realized he was being shamelessly groped, he gave no indication. At least, not from the waist up. His striking profile remained stoic, impassive, his dark gaze fixed on a spot in thin air. An occasional muscle twitch beneath her curious fingers was the only indication that he was even aware of her.

Claire, on the other hand, had never been more

intimately or acutely aware of anyone in her life. She bent close to him, spending so much time arranging the butterfly adhesive strips along his injured forehead that he must have wondered if she were weaving them into his skin. She simply couldn't help herself. He just smelled so good, so incredibly delicious that she repeatedly filled her lungs with his scent, absorbing the essence of him deep inside of herself.

Ah, those physical senses. The sight of his bronzed muscles; the soft rhythmic sound of his breath; the smell of his maleness; the feel of his slick, damp skin. She judiciously suppressed the urge to nibble his earlobe, thus adding taste to the other four items on the completed checklist.

For the first time, she was utterly immersed in the masculine perspective of sheer physicality. And it was magnificent.

"Claire?"

"Yes?" The word floated out on a sigh.

"I can't feel my bottom, and blood flow to my legs stopped twenty minutes ago. Are you nearly through?"

"Hmm? Oh, yes. All done."

"Good." He stood stiffly, rolled his head from side to side and massaged the small of his back. Turning, he reached toward her, leaned so close that his lips nearly grazed her cheek.

Dizzied by his nearness, Claire was about to fling herself into his arms when she realized he was only retrieving his elegant watch from the edge of the sink behind her.

"Damn," he muttered, when he saw the time. "I'm late."

She licked her lips, figured she was probably late,

as well, and idly wondered why she wasn't bothered by that, since she was usually punctual to the point of neurotic. "You can work late tonight if you need to. I'll pick Lucy up at day care—"

"No!" Glancing away, Johnny slipped the gleaming gold watch band over his folded hand, fastened the clasp without looking at it. "We agreed that I'd pick her up on Tuesdays and Thursdays so you have time to grab supper before your Lamaze classes."

"It's no problem. Tonight's class has been canceled. The clinic is using the classroom for a nursing seminar." Noting that he seemed oddly distressed by such benign information, she added, "My shift will be over by five this afternoon. The center is practically next door to the clinic. It's much more convenient for me to pick her up."

He set his jaw, continued to avert his gaze. "Thanks, but I'll take care of it. I've already made arrangements."

She flattened against the sink as he brushed past her. "What arrangements?" When he didn't reply, she followed him into the hallway just as he closed the guest-room door. She heard noises from inside, the squeak of a closet hinge, the scrape of drawers being opened and closed.

A thought struck her. "You know," she called out. "Since we're both going to be off early, maybe we could try that new Italian restaurant in Durango. I've heard the chicken *picata* is to die for."

The door opened, startling her. Johnny stood there wearing a pair of gray wool slacks and a white shirt, still open at the collar. A blue knit tie was loosely draped around his neck. A matching gray wool suit coat was folded over his arm. "Another time."

She followed him into the kitchen, where he poured a quick cup of coffee, downed half of it in a single gulp. "It's not that often our schedules allow us both to be off at a reasonable hour. It seems a shame to waste that."

He grunted, dropped the coat over the back of a chair and fiddled with a cufflink. "I have errands to run."

It didn't occur to her to question that. "Then wouldn't it be easier if I took care of Lucy while you attended to them?" She thought his shoulders slumped for a moment, but by the time she'd blinked, his spine was straight as a bowstring.

"Lucy hasn't been officially entered in the tribal membership rolls," he said finally.

"You're going to the tribal administrative offices? That's wonderful!" That he'd neither confirmed nor denied her presumption vaguely occurred to Claire, but she dismissed the notion. Every time she'd previously mentioned anything about Southern Ute government or tradition, Johnny had clammed up and changed the subject. She understood that he felt estranged from his people, although he'd never been willing to discuss the reasons. "May I go, too? I saw a flyer in the clinic lobby about the annual Bear Dance this weekend, and was hoping to learn more about it before we went."

His double take would have been comical if his angry gaze hadn't scorched the air between them. "I will not attend."

"Why not? It's tradition—"

"I have...other plans." He snatched up his coat, headed to the dining room to scoop the documents he'd been working on last night into a valise.

"It runs all weekend."

"I'll be busy all weekend."

"Busy doing what?" Claire spied the fat appointment book, with its worn leather cover and the bristling forest of loose notes tucked between scrawled calendar pages.

When not in his valise, the book was frequently left lying on the dining table, amid a clutter of documents. His entire life was penciled inside. She made a dive only to have it snatched out of reach.

She sighed. "These are your people, Johnny. They're Lucy's people, too. I don't know much about Southern Ute culture, but I do know that the annual Bear Dance is one of their happiest, most cherished social rituals. What could possibly be more important than that?"

"Trimming my sideburns, spraying the lawn for crabgrass." Johnny dropped the appointment book into his valise, snapped the case shut. "I'll think of something." With that, he grabbed his coat, hoisted the valise, strode out of the house.

It was nearly dusk when Johnny pulled into the driveway. Light spilled through the windows of the house, a cheery welcome that warmed him. He'd always hated coming home to a cold, dark house, had even considered buying one of those electronic timing devices that would turn on the lights automatically before he arrived home. Eventually, he'd discarded the notion as too pathetic for serious consideration. A man who had chosen to spend his life alone must adjust to turning on his own lights. It had never occurred to him that he'd ever share his home, or his life, with anyone ever again, even on a temporary basis.

And no matter how pleasant Claire's sojourn into Johnny's private world may be, he knew perfectly well that it was temporary. He couldn't afford to forget that even for a moment.

An irked fuss from the back seat caught his attention. He glanced in the rearview mirror, suppressed a twinge of guilt at the infant's distress. After all, he had caused it. Casting a swift glance at the house to make certain Claire hadn't emerged, Johnny exited the vehicle and opened the passenger's door to retrieve his cranky child. "I know, small one. It had to be done. You were very brave."

Soothed by the sound of his voice, Lucy turned her head, struggling to focus while he unbuckled the carseat harness. The cuff of his right sleeve was still unfastened. He pushed the fabric up to remove a Band-Aid from the crook of his arm, then slipped off one of Lucy's booties and removed a similar adhesive strip from the heel of her tiny foot. A small but visible bruise was already forming around the prick. His heart sank. Any pediatrician would instantly recognize the minor blemish and know exactly what had caused it.

Casting yet another guilty glance over his shoulder to ensure he wasn't being observed from inside the home, he replaced Lucy's booties and lifted her from the car seat.

She cooed happily at his touch, her head bobbling backward as she focused huge dark eyes on him. His heart melted like ice in sunshine. "I would have taken the pain for you if I could have," he whispered, and meant it from the depth of his soul. He would have taken a bullet for this precious child. He would have died for her.

A sharpness stabbed his chest at the thought that he might lose her. He willed it away. Lucy would not be taken from him. She was his daughter, his child. Soon he would have proof.

He brushed his lips across the baby's soft hair. "It was necessary."

Lucy smiled, her eyes huge and trusting. Because he couldn't help himself, he smiled back, despite the heavy toll the day had taken on them both. He was still haunted by the baby's cry of pain when the blood had been drawn. She'd stiffened in his arms. Her small lip had quivered, her chin puckering. She had trusted him, and he'd betrayed her.

He'd betrayed Claire, as well. What he'd told her was true enough. Lucy hadn't been officially entered on the tribal rolls, because it wasn't necessary to do so. Lucy was Ute by blood. She was automatically a member of the tribe.

Realistically, Johnny had no choice but to deceive Claire. If anyone discovered that he'd secretly arranged for DNA tests to prove his paternity, it could affect his custody case. Of course, it would only affect the case if he were not Lucy's father, a concept Johnny firmly rejected. But the test would provide the proof he'd need if Greta's claims to the contrary were ever brought to the court's attention.

He couldn't explain even to himself why he was so unnerved by the prospect of Claire discovering that his paternity had been questioned. Once he'd considered himself a man of truth and honor. Now he'd been reduced to subterfuge, deceit, hairsplitting lies of omission that he'd repeatedly justified in his mind, but for which his heart made no excuse.

Shame left a tawdry taste on the tongue. There was no doubt in his mind that Lucy was his child. Deep down, he feared Claire might doubt it. And if she did doubt it, she might leave. And if she did leave, his heart would revert to an empty house. Cold. Dark. Lonely.

"There you are!" Dropping the watering can beside a thirsty ficus, Claire swooped into the foyer, took Lucy from Johnny's arms and covered her chubby face with kisses. "Did you have a good day with your daddy? I've missed you so much!"

The infant squirmed, struggling against being held so tightly. Reluctantly, Claire loosened her fierce hug, nestled the infant comfortably against her shoulder and turned her attention to the man who dropped the diaper bag on a nearby chair while carefully averting his gaze. "So, is she officially listed on the tribal rolls?"

Johnny cleared his throat, rolled one shoulder in a halfhearted shrug. "Yes."

"Terrific!" Turning her face, she kissed the baby's ear. "Hear that, sweetie-bug? You are official. No matter where you go, how you choose to live your life, you will always know where you came from, always know where you belong." Her voice cracked slightly, embarrassing her. "Well. You must be ready for your supper bottle by now."

"Is that so important?" Johnny asked quietly.

"Of course it's important. She's probably starving."

"I meant the tribal-roll thing, knowing where she comes from."

She regarded him. "You know that it is."

"No, I don't know that." His jaw hardened, twitched. "Pedigrees don't matter except with show animals. Humans are not the sum of their ancestry. We choose our own path in life, our own destiny. Where we come from, our genealogy is merely an accident of birth, a biological directive. Nothing more."

The sadness in his eyes, the heaviness in a voice that would have seemed firm and unforgiving to one who could not perceive a hidden meaning, belied the strength of his statement. "That's not true," Claire said quietly. "It's the essence of who we are, of our strength as individuals and as a part of something larger than ourselves. It's blood, Johnny."

His head snapped around, startling her. His gaze darted to the infant in her arms as if expecting to see something worrisome. Apparently relieved, he exhaled all at once. "Whatever."

Although bothered by Johnny's strident reaction to any mention of his ancestry, Claire chose not to pursue the matter. Pride in his culture was visible all around her, from the embroidered replica of the Ute tribal flag that hung in a place of honor in his home to the child-size moccasins prominently displayed on a bookcase beside a hide bag sewn with sinew thread and decorated with intricate beadwork.

When Claire had asked about the items, Johnny had replied that they'd been handmade by his grandmother to celebrate his rites of childhood passage. There had been pride in his eyes as he spoke, and the warmth of love.

No, this was not a man without a deep and abiding emotional bond to his people. He was, however, a man who'd clearly been hurt and disillusioned, intent upon protecting himself. From what or whom, Claire wasn't certain, but she was nothing if not determined. Eventually, she'd ferret out the truth.

But not tonight.

Shifting Lucy in her arms, she angled a sideways glance. "I hope you're hungry."

"I could eat." A subtle smile revealed relief at the change in topic. He followed her into the kitchen. "Would you like me to fix something?"

She retrieved a bottle of formula from the refrigerator and placed it in the microwave for a quick warm-up. "Using that handy-dandy, professional-quality, gourmet food-processing unit known as a paring knife?"

"Ah, the food-processing unit won't be required." His smile broadened into a breathtaking grin. "Perhaps the word *something* was a misnomer, since my culinary repertoire is limited to scrambled eggs and toast."

"Buttered toast?"

"That complicates matters."

"Just as well. Even perfect human specimens such as yourself must watch the old cholesterol." The microwave buzzed. She removed the bottle, nodded toward several covered pots on the stove. "Anyway, I've already planned a smashing supper for you. As soon as Lucy has been fed and bathed, I'll—"

"Bathed?" His smile flattened, his eyes widened in what appeared to be absolute panic. "She doesn't need a bath."

"Has she had a bath today?"

"Ah…no."

"Then she needs one."

He swallowed hard. "Very well. I'll do it."

"Excuse me?"

He sucked a deep breath, took the baby out of her arms, snatched the warm bottle from the counter. "You've been kind enough to prepare a meal for us. The least I can do is feed and bathe my own child."

Claire couldn't believe her ears. Johnny was terrified of bathing the baby, and to her knowledge had not done so since his first attempt weeks earlier. "That would be great. I'll just clear a few things from the counter—"

"I'll use the tub."

Now she really was stunned. "The tub?"

"Ah, perhaps the bathroom sink would be a better choice."

"That's a small sink."

"She's a small person." Tucking the baby against his shoulder, he headed for the hallway.

"Johnny?"

He paused, angled a wary glance over his shoulder.

"Don't just dunk her like a doughnut, okay?"

"Okay," he muttered, with the hint of a frown that implied he'd planned to do just that.

Perhaps if Claire hadn't been so preoccupied with her own plans for the evening she'd have been more attuned to the subtle fear in his eyes. Instead, she simply rubbed her hands together in anticipation, and began sautéing mushrooms and onion for the wine sauce. The meal would be scrumptious.

If all went as Claire planned, the dessert would be unforgettable.

Grinning stupidly, she retrieved the boned chicken

breasts from the fridge, sliced them into neat ribbons of meat and was stir-frying them to a golden brown when she heard water running in the bathroom.

A glance at the clock confirmed that about fifteen minutes had passed since he'd left the kitchen, which was approximately how long it took Lucy to drain a bottle. She picked up the pace, humming happily as she stirring bubbling sauce, steamed vegetables and browned dinner rolls to crispy perfection.

She'd just finished fluffing the rice with a fork when she decided to check on the bathing process. Wiping her hands on a tea towel, she hurried down the hall. The bathroom door was not completely closed, and she could see him wrapping the baby in a towel. She peeked inside. "All done?"

He jumped as if shot, then whirled around clutching both towel and infant as if his life depended on it. "Ah, yes—" he fumbled to cover a tiny bare foot with terrycloth "—all done."

"Why is the back of her hair dry?"

He flushed, paused a moment. "The front is wet. Isn't that enough?"

"You just gave her a sponge bath, didn't you?"

"You didn't tell me not to." His defensive posture tickled Claire immensely. "You simply said not to dunk her, and I didn't."

She could barely contain a snort of laughter. "It's the effort that counts. I'll get her dressed for bed, then we'll have dinner."

When she reached out for the baby, he made no move to hand her over. "I can do it." Lucy squirmed in his arms, and a bare leg emerged. Johnny immediately tucked the tiny extremity beneath the towel wrapping, and hustled past Claire toward the newly furnished nursery. "Pajamas I can handle."

"Don't forget the diaper."

He shot a look over his shoulder, then hurried into the small bedroom and closed the door.

Once inside, Johnny laid the baby in the oak crib they'd just purchased days ago, and waited a moment for his heart rate to slow. The nursery was impressive, he had to admit, and the portable crib had been turned into a playpen. It still bothered him to have the baby sleeping so far away, so he made several nightly trips to check on her, and make certain she was still breathing.

Claire's presence was a calming influence, though. If she believed it was preferable that Lucy get used to sleeping in her own room, then Johnny was willing to accept that. Particularly when she pointed out that a well-equipped nursery would be impressive when child-welfare representatives did a home inspection as part of the custody process.

When Johnny's nerves were under control, he set about preparing his daughter for bed and took a moment to study her bruised heel. It was barely visible, not nearly obvious enough for the child-care providers at day care to notice. He had no illusions about Claire, though, and was certain she'd spot the tiny blemish instantly if given the opportunity.

He'd have to spend the next few days making certain she didn't have that opportunity. The thought of providing complete care for his infant daughter didn't frighten him as much as it would have a couple of weeks ago. Only baths frightened him. Holding on to a wriggling, wet baby was like trying to peel grapes underwater.

Tonight Johnny had cradled the baby in his arms and sponged her clean with a washcloth. He should have realized that Claire would figure that out with no more than a casual glance. He'd have to be more careful in the future.

And more devious.

Sighing, he diapered the baby with considerable expertise, slipped on a pair of footed pajama bottoms, snapped them to pajama top and tucked her into her crib. He wound up the musical mobile, turned on a night-light and crept out of the room.

A delicious aroma caught his attention. He sniffed his way into the kitchen. "Whatever you're cooking, it certainly smells wonderful."

Claire glanced up from the table, her eyes sparkling. "Aha. Smell. One down, four to go."

"I beg your pardon?"

"Never mind. Sit." She yanked out a chair at the kitchen table, half hauled him into it, then grabbed a potholder and retrieved a steaming plate from the oven. She placed it in front of him with a flourish. "How does that look?"

"Magnificent," he murmured, his mouth watering. Ribbons of tender chicken and chunks of colorful vegetables were heaped on a mound of white rice, garnished with sprigs of fresh cilantro.

"Smells good, looks good. We're on a roll." She retrieved a second plate, set out a basket of hot rolls and seated herself across the table from him. "Listen."

"Listen to what?"

"That soft sound of bubbling sauce. Can you hear it?"

Johnny tilted his head. "Actually, I do hear something."

"Doesn't it make you even hungrier?"

"It does indeed." He grabbed a fork, speared a golden strip of meat. It melted in his mouth. He chewed slowly, savoring every delicious bite.

"Taste good?"

"Umm."

"What about the texture?"

"Perfect, absolutely perfect. A sensory banquet." He savored another bite, washed it down with a sip of chardonnay.

For the next twenty minutes, he ravenously consumed what was without doubt the most delicious meal he'd tasted in his life.

"Would you like more?" Claire asked when he finally pushed his plate away.

"No, thank you. I'm absolutely stuffed." He suppressed an urge to loosen his slacks, noticed for the first time that her own meal had barely been touched.

She moistened her lips, her eyes demurely averted from his questioning gaze. "I hope you left room for dessert."

If the meal was this magnificent, his mind boggled at the possibilities for a sweet finale. Regretfully, he couldn't have eaten another bite, and said so.

"Perhaps," she murmured, "you'll feel differently by the time it's ready to serve."

Thirty minutes later, Johnny relaxed on the living-room sofa sipping the last of his after-dinner coffee while he edited a contract draft for a client he would meet first thing in the morning.

Claire had refused his offer to clean the kitchen,

had practically pushed him out of the room insisting that she had everything under control. He'd heard her bustling around, noted the occasional clunk of pots, the clatter of flatware being loaded into the dish-washer, running water as the utensils and dinnerware were being rinsed. The comforting domestic sounds had ceased about fifteen minutes ago. Johnny kept glancing up from his work, hoping Claire would join him.

A few minutes later, she did.

He hadn't heard her enter; he'd just felt an im-mutable shiver along his spine and glanced up and saw her there, pooled in soft lamplight like a flame-haired goddess draped in flowing ivory silk. A gulp of air caught in his throat, nearly choking him.

Her voice was husky, soft as a lover's touch. "Sight," she whispered, extending her arms and per-forming a fluid pirouette.

Johnny rose as if lifted by unseen arms. She seemed to float toward him, her bare feet silently skimming the thick carpet like wings on a breeze. When she was close enough that her body heat radi-ated against his chest, a sensual fragrance wafted around him, a scent so delicate and fragile that his nostrils instinctively flared, drawing it deep inside him.

"Smell," she murmured, lifting herself on tiptoes to purr against his ear. "Sound."

A draft on his tongue alerted him that he was trying to speak. The only sound he made was a thin hiss as she lifted his hand to press his palm over one firm, lush breast.

"Touch," she said softly.

Every nerve in his body exploded. He was completely captivated, enraptured by her beauty, so aroused by her sensual seduction that he was unable to move, unable to breathe, unable to utter a single coherent word.

Claire spoke for him. "Dessert is served," she whispered, her lush lips mere inches from his mouth. "You have only to taste."

No power on earth could have stopped him.

Chapter Nine

Before Johnny's mind could react, his arms were around her. He drew her to him desperately, almost roughly, until her breasts flattened against his chest and the hardened points of her nipples tightened against his own skin.

Her lips parted with a gasp, and her eyes widened with surprise, with smoldering passion and perhaps a subtle glint of apprehension so mild that his mind vaguely registered it before being overwhelmed by the passion of his own aroused body. Sexual instinct was in control, a lust beyond measure that drove him not merely to kiss her lush mouth, but also to devour it. All the leashed passion, the desire, the sensual torment he'd been repressing burst forth to flood his senses, overwhelm the resistance he'd so staunchly maintained.

Johnny had wanted Claire since the first moment

he'd laid eyes on her. Now he would have her. Nothing would stop him. Nothing.

With his mind spinning and his body afire, the pliant body in his arms tightened. He felt a stab of panic as she tried to pull away. Instinct begged him to hold her even tighter; another, more potent instinct instantly loosened his grasp. He nearly wept with disappointment as he stepped back, dizzy, gasping for breath and mystified by a peculiar buzzing in his ears.

Although Johnny was perplexed by the intermittent sound, Claire was focused upon it. She steadied herself for a moment, grasping his shoulders as if she feared she'd collapse if she released him too suddenly. Then she took a shuddering breath and turned away.

When Johnny's head began to clear, he vaguely realized that the buzzing sound was coming from Claire's beeper, which was lying on the bookcase beside the canvas satchel that doubled as both purse and briefcase.

Palming the small electronic pager, she read the message and went pale. "I have to go."

"Right now?" Still befuddled by a persistent mental fog, he spun around as she rushed past. "Why? Where?" It took a moment to realize that he was talking to himself. The room was empty, silent except for muted sounds emanating from the master bedroom.

By the time he'd regained enough physical mobility to stumble toward the hallway, Claire rushed out wearing a pair of jeans and a floppy sweatshirt. The beeper was clutched in her hand. He spun around as she brushed past, followed her back to the living room.

He finally managed a single coherent sentence. "Where are you going?"

"A woman is in premature labor. The infant will need immediate care." She fastened the pager to her waistband, plucked her bag from the bookcase and sprinted to the front door. "I'll be home late," she muttered.

The door whipped upon, shuddered shut, and she was gone.

Johnny didn't know how long he stood there, overwhelmed by the sudden silence. His body cooled; his mind cleared. He finally went to the wet bar, poured himself two fingers of whiskey and downed it standing up.

The evening's events replayed through his mind. He remembered it all, every scent, every sound, every sensation coursing through his veins. His brain had shut down; his body had taken over.

It had almost happened, he thought, everything he'd been determined to avoid, that physical union that inevitably bonded spirit and soul into an emotional connection that led only to loss and grief.

Johnny Winterhawk was a man for whom sexual liaison was not sport. It was a spiritual joining of a man and a woman, a gift of the Creator to be accepted with joy and humility. It was also a lifetime commitment of the heart. He had tasted the sweet fruit of lovemaking with few women in his lifetime; each of them now owned a secret part of him.

Claire would own it all.

His feelings for her frightened him. He couldn't allow himself to expose his heart again, to suffer again the agony of inevitable loss.

There was also a chivalry in his determination to

maintain a platonic relationship. Claire was a unique woman, a woman of tenderness and compassion who deserved more than a flight of fancy and a physical release. She deserved a lifetime of love bestowed by a man whose repeated failures had not already deemed him unworthy.

From Johnny's perspective, all marriage was temporary, even those naively portrayed as lifetime commitment. At least this union was an honest one, with scope and purpose set forth at the outset. Johnny had no right to change the rules at this point; he had no right to taste the sweetness of her body, test the tenderness of her heart. He had no right to take advantage, to sate his raging hunger at her expense.

Even as Johnny swore to himself that what had happened tonight must not happen again, a whisper in his mind promised that it would, that it must. When it did, life as he'd known it would cease to exist.

Surrounded by darkness, he awoke to feel her presence before he recognized her silhouette beside the crib. She was immobile, unmoving, her profile stiff as a statue except for the slight tilt of her head as she gazed down at the sleeping infant.

From the corner of his eye, he noted a subtle gray pall touch the window, and guessed the time to be about an hour before dawn. A sudden stab of pain twisted through his spine. He'd fallen asleep in the nursery rocking chair a few feet from Lucy's crib.

He was perfectly comfortable allowing Lucy to sleep alone in the nursery as long as Claire was home. When she was gone, all his fears and insecurities took over, propelling him to stand guard over his slumbering child, monitoring every breath she took. He was upset with himself for having dozed off, having slept so soundly that he hadn't even heard Claire come in.

The rocking chair creaked as he shifted. Claire made no indication that she'd noticed, not even turning her head as he crossed the room and stood beside her.

Even through shadowed darkness, he perceived sorrow in the subtle slump of her shoulders, the rigidity of her fingers grasping the crib rail. He pressed a palm over her hand. Claire neither moved nor spoke, didn't appear to notice that he was even there.

Finally, he heard the soft rush of breath, words so distant he barely heard them. "She was so tiny," she whispered. "So very, very tiny."

Johnny's heart felt swollen, raw. He knew the infant she had rushed to care for had not survived. "You're a doctor, not a god. You did what you could."

"It wasn't enough."

She said nothing more; she simply continued to gaze into the crib until night shadows softened into silver. Then she turned into the circle of his embrace, and he held her as she cried.

"You're late." Johnny mopped his face with a towel and glanced up as Spence sauntered into the locker room of the Eastridge Health Club, where most of Buttonwood's movers and shakers met to work up a healthy sweat between business deals. "You'll have to work out by yourself today. I've got a meeting in twenty minutes."

"No problem. I'll get someone else to spot while I work the weights." Spence dropped a duffel on the gym bench, hung his jacket on the door hook of an open locker. "By the way, Hank is having a poker game tonight. Care to join us?"

There was something perversely amusing about the sheriff's love of poker. Die-hard card players took solace in knowing that the games would not be raided since the guy in charge of enforcing the town's anti-gambling laws was the host. "No, thanks. I'm lousy at poker."

"I know." Spence grinned, loosened his tie into a sloppy loop and lifted it over his head. "That's why you're so popular around the old card table. Everybody comes away richer when you ante up."

"Everyone but me." Johnny stood, propped a foot on the bench to tie his shoelace. "Much as I'd like to make my monthly contribution to your retirement fund, I promised to take Claire and Lucy to a movie tonight."

Spence hiked a brow, glanced around the small room to assure himself they were indeed alone. "Taking this marriage stuff pretty seriously, aren't you?"

"Public appearances as a family unit may prove helpful later on." Johnny tied the second shoe, tucked in his shirt and fastened his slacks without meeting his friend's speculative gaze. "Besides, Claire has already given up enough of her life and her freedom on my behalf. Escorting her to a movie or buying dinner at a nice restaurant once in a while can't begin to repay that kindness."

"You mean the business arrangement."

"Yes."

"Nothing personal going on between the two of you."

Johnny reached for his suit coat, chose his words carefully. "We're friends."

"Good friends."

"Yes, good friends." Johnny slammed the locker, whirled in frustration. "Are you practicing cross-examination techniques for your next court appearance? Because if you are, I've got to say you should refund your client's money and give serious consideration to taking up another profession."

"Thanks for the tip." A widening grin revealed that Spence was neither offended nor intimidated. "I'll give it some thought."

"You do that."

"I was just curious, because I checked with Myra the other day, and she said you'd never filed the executed prenuptial agreement."

"Explain again why that's your business."

"In the eyes of the law, your marriage gives Claire a future financial claim on your share of our partnership. By signing the agreement, she'd have given up that right."

"Would you expect your future wife to give up financial stability to which she was legally entitled?"

"No." Spence finished unbuttoning his shirt and shrugged the garment off. "Not unless the marriage was a temporary business agreement created to fake out the court system in a custody matter."

"Point taken." Adjusting his necktie, Johnny avoided his friend's gaze. Spence was right, of course, which had been the reason for the agreement in the first place. Well, it had been one of the reasons. "I'll talk to Claire about it."

"When?"

"When I get around to it." He skewered Spence with a look. "There's no rush, is there?"

"Not anymore. It's kind of like putting in the fire hydrant after the building has burned to the ground. Since you're already officially wed, Claire can basically laugh in your face and start spending half of your retirement if she wants."

"Claire isn't after money."

"I know," Spence agreed cheerfully.

"Then why are you hassling me about it?"

"Hassling friends is a hobby. It's fun, and I'm good at it." Having exchanged his business attire for a sweatshirt and workout shorts, Spence sat on the bench to replace his black leather oxfords with sneakers from his duffel. "That, and my own innate curiosity as to whether you'd finally figured out the real reason you married Claire Davis."

Something in his friend's voice sent a warning chill down Johnny's spine. "You know the reason."

"Yep, I do now." Reaching back into the duffel, Spence retrieved an envelope emblazoned with the logo of a local film developer. "Your wedding pictures."

Johnny took the envelope, held it for a moment before tucking it into his jacket pocket. "Thanks."

"You really ought to look at them."

"Why should I? Was my fly open?"

"No, but your heart was." With that peculiar profundity, Spence tossed his duffel in the locker and sauntered away, whistling.

Every nerve in Johnny's body twitched. The envelope seemed to fuse itself to his chest, growing heavier with every passing moment. He smoothed his hair, straightened his tie, tried to ignore the mounting

pressure. He told himself that the photographs were
of no personal or sentimental value, were merely another link in a chain of circumstance meticulously
created for the custody hearings. They were documentation, nothing more, nothing less.

Yet the knowledge that Claire's image was inside
the envelope pressed over his heart made Johnny's
pulse race ridiculously. It annoyed him, frustrated
him. But in the end, it compelled him to retrieve the
envelope, and examine its contents.

The first picture made him suck in his breath.
Claire was just as he remembered, an angel in ivory
satin with floral wisps tucked into her gorgeous auburn hair. In photograph after photograph, she gazed
up at him alternately laughing or with touching reverence or with a sparkle of what could easily have
been interpreted as real emotion by one who didn't
know that the scene itself had been carefully crafted
for effect. Claire looked so ravishing, so breathtak-
ingly bridelike that the photographs would easily convince a judge. They almost convinced him.

He should have been pleased by the results; instead, he was shocked and chagrined, not by Claire's
image, but by his own. The man in the photographs
resembled the person he saw in the mirror every
morning. Except the man in the photographs gazed at
his bride with a glowing wonder that went well beyond merely playing a part.

Johnny had always considered himself a circum-
spect man, one who concealed his essence from a
world that used such weakness as a weapon. What he
saw in the photographs changed all that. In his own
image, he recognized honest emotion, real happiness

and true joy beyond any image reflected in the mirror, beyond any image reflected in his own mind.

The pictures revealed a man stripped of emotional armor, a man whose emotions were bared to the world and displayed in the glow of his eyes. He saw a man in love.

It scared the life out of him, so he simply refused to accept what he saw as real.

"I think the movie was too intense for Lucy." Feeling free, exhilarated and happier than she'd been in years, Claire shifted the baby in her arms, used her free hand to dig the final kernels of popcorn from the container Johnny held. "I mean, when the witch boomed onto the screen cackling, I almost had a heart attack myself."

"It was a cartoon," Johnny said.

"It was an animated feature film. There's a difference."

"Whatever it was, she slept through most of it. She's too young for movies, anyway."

"She's not too young to learn about the world around her, or to spend time with people who love her. Babies are sensory sponges. Part of their learning process is adapting to unfamiliar surroundings and new experiences."

From the corner of her eye, she saw Johnny shrug, toss a handful of popcorn into his mouth, then throw the empty container in a nearby receptacle. He brushed his palms together, glancing at the group of moviegoers heading toward the parking lot.

Earlier Claire had picked up Lucy from day care, then driven to Johnny's office, which was only a couple of blocks from the theater.

Now they meandered down the sidewalk toward the professional building where Johnny's law firm was located, passing intermittent pools of amber light from the quaint street lamps and glittering retail establishments lining Buttonwood's main street.

Claire studied him thoughtfully. He'd been quiet tonight, more reserved than usual. Once she'd turned suddenly in her seat to find him staring at her. He'd looked away without comment, but not before the light from the movie screen had illuminated a peculiar sadness in his eyes.

A disquieting thought struck her. "Has there been a problem with the custody petition?"

The question seemed to startle him. "No, the papers have been filed. It's just a matter of trudging through all the interested bureaucracies, then finding space on the court docket to schedule a hearing."

"Are you sure?"

"Yes." He shifted the diaper bag back over his shoulder, slipped his hands in his pockets, fell into step beside her as she sauntered down the darkened sidewalk. "Why do you ask?"

"I don't know." She sighed, shifted the infant from her arms to her shoulder. "Actually, I do know. You've spent so much more time caring for Lucy the past couple of days, insisting on bathing her, changing her and dressing her, I guess I was wondering if you've decided that my presence in her life is—" she coughed away a dry spot in her throat "—unnecessary."

When he didn't immediately respond, she angled a glance and saw his jaw tighten. "You could never be unnecessary, Claire. Lucy needs you more than she needs me."

"You are her father," Claire said simply. "She will always need you."

They walked in silence for a few moments before Johnny spoke again. "The man who raised you, your adopted father..." He hesitated, cleared his throat. "Did you love him?"

"With all my heart."

"But you don't love him as much as you love your biological father, a man you've never even met."

Startled, Claire looked up and realized that Johnny was serious. "I don't actually love my biological father in the sense you mean," she said carefully. "As you've pointed out, I don't even know him. Perhaps it's more accurate to say that it's the not knowing that haunts me, the emptiness of realizing that I don't really know who I am or where I come from."

"And that is truly important to you?"

"Of course. Isn't it important to you?"

"Not really."

She frowned. "I can't believe that."

"Why not? It's true." He spoke calmly, without a hint of emotion, and yet there was an underlying tension to his body language that belied his soft voice. "The act of reproducing does not in itself make parents out of people who have no desire to raise and nurture children."

Claire couldn't dispute that, but was touched not only by the statement, but also by the inadvertent revelation it made about Johnny's own background. "Do you believe your own parents were such people?"

"My mother clearly felt fettered by the responsibility of having a child." A subtle streak of pain flashed through his eyes, then was gone.

"Is that what she told you, Johnny?"

"She told me nothing. She simply left."

"And you haven't spoken to her since?"

He shrugged, obviously uncomfortable with the subject. "We've spoken on occasion."

"When you can't avoid it."

"Yes, when I can't avoid it."

That saddened Claire, because despite his attempt to feign otherwise, she could see that the estrangement with his mother was hurtful to him. "Do you feel the same way about your father?"

"No. My father worked too hard, died too young. But he was a good man, a good father, who raised me the best he could. I respected him."

"And you loved him."

"Yes, I loved him."

"Just as Lucy loves you." The assurance didn't seem to mollify him, although he accepted it without debate. That alone was unusual, since Claire would have expected him to point out that his daughter was too young to experience the emotion of love as such. Rational concepts were as natural to Johnny as his inborn stoicism. She wondered what had moved him to bring up the subject of biological parenthood in the first place.

"I used to come here when I was a kid," Johnny said.

Snapped from the solitude of her thoughts, Claire glanced up, delighted to realize they were in front of an ice-cream parlor. Outside, sparkling lights rimmed the window like dancing stars. Inside, families gathered around tiny round tables, filling the air with happy laughter. "So, now that you're all grown up, can you still be tempted by a hot-fudge sundae?"

He smiled. "When I was nine, I sold my bike for

the price of a two-scoop mocha fudge, double whipped cream, caramel sauce on the side.''

''You traded a bike for ice cream?''

''What can I say? It's a weakness.''

''The great Johnny Winterhawk has a weakness?'' She fanned herself with her hand. ''Call the media, this is major.''

His smile broadened into a genuine grin. ''Don't you dare. My reputation would be ruined.''

''I might be willing to keep your secret. I might even be willing to forego my fetish for serving only healthy, low-fat foods long enough to stock the freezer with the most decadent premium ice cream and stack a few jars of caramel sauce in the pantry.'' She batted her eyes. ''For a price.''

He eyed her warily. ''What kind of price?''

''Nothing you can't afford.'' Smiling, Claire opened the ice-cream-parlor door and led the skeptical man inside. Even the wiliest fish in the lake could be hooked if you used the right bait.

Sometimes it was just too easy.

Chapter Ten

"Listen to the music!" Breathless with excitement, Claire exited the vehicle, and opened the rear door to retrieve Lucy from the car seat. "The parking lot is jammed. There are so many people. I had no idea!"

Johnny barely heard her. Instead, he curled his fingers around the steering wheel like talons on prey while drumbeats pounded his brain, and the voices of his people raised in song struck a secret chord in his heart. Scenes from his childhood raced through his mind. Happy scenes, cherished memories. To relive them was to relive the pain of having lost that reality, having lost all the people who had made those memories so joyful.

The driver's door opened, startling him. Claire shifted the infant in her arms, her eyes sparkling with delighted mischief. "Come on, slowpoke. We had a deal. Last night you wolfed down a scrumptious hot-fudge-and-caramel creation prepared by my own little hands, and in return I expect you to dance with me until your feet blister.''

Wondering how he'd allowed himself to be manipulated into such a promise, Johnny exited the car, shot a grumpy glance at the radiant woman balancing his beautiful child in the crook of her arm. ''We're husband and wife,'' he said quietly, ''and therefore related in the eyes of the tribe.'' Her smile softened, glowed. ''Relatives may not dance with each other.''

The glow faded. ''Why not?''

''It's a rule.'' He retrieved the diaper bag and stroller from the back seat. ''Bear Dance is a social event, the welcoming of spring where old friends reacquaint themselves, and new friends are made through the dancing. It's a good place for young people to gather and size up prospective mates.''

''Prospective mates? You make it sound rather unromantic.''

He shrugged, opened the stroller and hooked the strap of the diaper bag over the handle. ''In the spring, a young warrior or maiden's fancy turns to matters of the heart. It's the way of things, no less or more romantic than Anglo versions of the same events.''

When a blanket had been spread over the reclining stroller bed, Claire placed the infant inside, pausing to fuss with the baby's elastic headband, which had been decorated with a beaded bow and tiny feather. After obsessing half the morning to select the perfect attire for Lucy's public debut, Claire had finally chosen a brightly colored dress with lace-trimmed collar and puffy ruffled sleeves.

Fortunately, the tiny telltale bruise on the baby's

heel had faded after the first day, allowing Johnny to gratefully relinquish his temporary position as sole care provider. Poor Claire had been utterly perplexed by his behavior, which must have seemed almost schizophrenic to her. One day he was terrified of dressing and bathing his fragile baby daughter, the next he was insisting on doing just that, only to perform yet another parental pirouette as soon as the injection site had healed enough to return Lucy to the one person on earth who could give the long-suffering infant a decent bath.

Through it all, Claire had been a saint, encouraging his peculiar spurt of fatherly devotion without question, and accepting his relinquishment of same in a similar manner. She never quizzed him, never attempted intrusion into his private thoughts or demanded explanations that would force him to expand the web of lies he'd already so shamefully woven. She simply accepted what was with grace, dignity and that dazzling smile that curled his toes and warmed him to the marrow.

Johnny liked that about Claire. He liked everything about her, including her bouts of adorable ditziness when she obsessed about something silly, as she'd done this morning while dressing Lucy.

Johnny had to admit the results of her obsession were certainly worthy of the effort. Lucy looked absolutely adorable. Heads would turn to admire such a child, and to admire the woman at his side. A beautiful daughter, a beautiful wife. A puff of pride swelled inside him, although he knew it was misplaced. Physical appearance was unimportant.

His grandfather's voice whispered through his

mind. *The Creator sees only purity of spirit, hears only songs from the heart.*

He was here, Johnny realized. Grandfather was here, smiling over his shoulder, walking beside him, beckoning to the circle of dancers in the corral. In his heart, he felt as if he'd come home, home to a place where happiness had once dwelled, a happiness that belonged only in the past, relegated to memory as were historic victories of a once great people whose numbers continued to dwindle.

That was yesterday, and yesterday was gone. To celebrate all that was gone seemed ghoulish. Johnny didn't want to celebrate the past, didn't want to remember the disillusionment or the loss.

"Are you sure this is supposed to be a happy ritual?" Claire's voice yanked him back to the present.

"Why do you ask?"

"Because the way you've been sulking and skulking all morning, one would think this is the grumpy-as-a-bear dance." She adjusted the stroller sunshade, tossed him a bright grin. "Well, you can just be as cranky as you please, Mr. Winterhawk. Lucy and I are going to have a magnificent time whether you like it or not."

Guilt pricked him. He didn't want to spoil Claire's day; he'd rather draw his own blood than cause her a moment's grief. "I'm sorry. I do want you to have a good time."

"Then smile, buster."

He attempted to comply.

She rolled her eyes. "Nice try." With that, she steered the stroller toward the cacophony of music and laughter.

Johnny stood beside the car, as if his polished loaf-

ers were glued to the earth. Ghosts from the past
spoke on the breeze, whispered in the voices raised
in song from the corral where his people gathered to
dance, to feast, to celebrate the change of season. Yet
he wanted only to escape, to burrow into the sanctuary of his modern life, a life he'd created on his own
without tribal blessing. Without tribal help.

But a deeper wish was for Claire to be happy. If it
pleased her to be here, he was determined to allow
her that joy. He caught up with her before she entered
the laughing crowd that surrounded the dance corral,
a circle of trees hewn each year for this purpose.

Laying his hands over hers, he took possession of
the stroller, a protective gesture that she acknowledged with an appreciative smile. They entered the
festival as a family, melding into the throng as if they
truly belonged.

Despite his qualms at being there, Johnny couldn't
suppress that sense of belonging. In fact, he savored
it, while the mood and the music seeped into his soul.

The aroma of fried bread and chili made his mouth
water; the sweet smell of sun-warmed earth filled his
lungs. The drums grew louder, like the percussive
rhythm of a thousand heartbeats above which the
sound of singing floated on air, a joyous greeting of
springtime.

In the dancing place, males dressed in bright shirts,
wide-brimmed hats and beaded belts were lined up
facing east. Females wearing long, colorful dresses
and shawls lined up facing west. Both lines swayed
with the beat of the music. Dust rose from beneath
their feet, laughter bubbled from their lips and everywhere the sound of music soared with the wind.

Beside him, Claire studied the line of dancers with

a worried eye. "Please tell me that the unique costumes of the dancers are just a coincidence."

That pesky prick of guilt poked at him once again. "The Bear Dance chief has issued rules for the dress of Indian dancers. It does not affect visitors and tourists, as you can see." He emphasized that with a subtle gesture to encompass the variety of clothing worn by the multicultural throng enjoying the festivities.

"But I wanted to dance!" Clearly disappointed, she absently touched the scoop-necked, apple-green tank top that flattered her creamy complexion and flame-colored hair. "You should have told me."

"All are invited to dance. The dress requirements are only for tribe members."

"So why are you wearing a white golf shirt and khaki pants? You're full-bloodied Ute."

"You aren't." The moment the words slipped from his lips, he regretted them. "I didn't mean that the way it sounded."

"Yes, you did." Claire managed a thin smile, chewed her lower lip for a moment. "You're right, of course. Maybe I'd fit in better if I dyed my hair brown—"

"That's nonsense!" He was horrified that she'd even consider such blasphemy. "Don't even think about it."

"But I've always envied people with dark, lustrous hair."

"Others would envy hair like yours." Deliberately lifting a few silky locks cascading to her shoulder, he watched the shimmering strands slip through his fingers. "Spun copper," he murmured, "shining with flaming brilliance, brighter than a thousand suns."

Claire widened her eyes, took a sharp breath that jolted Johnny back to reality. He yanked his hand back, annoyed with himself for the inadvertent display of emotion. When he spoke again, his voice was rougher than he'd intended. "Artificially altering your appearance will not change who you are."

The flare of hope in her eyes faded. "I don't know who I am, Johnny. You have a history, a heritage. You know where you come from, where you belong. You have everything I've always wanted, yet it doesn't seem to mean anything to you. I can't understand that."

Seeing her pain, realizing how disconnected she felt from her own bloodline affected Johnny like a punch in the stomach. From deep inside, he felt a resurgence of something he'd thought lost, a need in his soul to reconnect with his heritage, with those who had gone before him and those who had given him life.

"It means something to me," he said finally, and was stunned to realize that he meant it. "It means everything to me." The strength of emotion shocked him, shocked him so much that he fought it. Still, seeds sown a lifetime ago had germinated. If nourished, they would grow.

"I'm glad." Claire touched his hand, a casual gesture ripe with quiet intimacy.

He cleared his throat, felt oddly light-headed. "So no more talk about coloring your hair."

"I just don't want to embarrass you, Johnny."

"You could never embarrass me, Claire." He was hurt that she believed otherwise, stunned to recognize that beneath the veneer of polished, professional confidence was a vulnerable heart desperate to fit in and belong. "I'm the one who is embarrassed. Pride is unseemly, a narcissistic emotion appealing to ego, not accomplishment. Yet it swells within me when you're at my side, even though I understand what those who eye me with envy can't know—that you aren't here because of my prowess as a man, but because of your compassion as a woman."

A sheen of moisture brightened her gaze. "I do believe that's the sweetest thing anyone has ever said to me." She touched his cheek, a gentle caress that warmed him to the bone. Her lips parted as if she were preparing to speak. "I'm here because I want to be, Johnny, because I—"

A voice from the crowd, interrupted. "Claire! Yoohoo, over here!" A large woman wearing a ridiculous floppy sunhat and garish feathered earrings that looped down to her collarbone waved frantically from in front of a beverage stand.

Johnny was annoyed by the intrusion, although Claire's delight at seeing the woman seemed genuine. She waved back. "It's Nell Hastings," she said, as if that explained everything. "I really should go speak with her." She angled a fretful glance over her shoulder. "Do you mind?"

"Of course not," Johnny lied, curling his fingers around the handle of the stroller. "Visit with your friends, enjoy yourself. Lucy and I will wait here."

"I won't be long." Hoisting on tiptoes, she surprised him by kissing his cheek, then melted into the crowd.

Feeling strangely alone, Johnny squatted beside the stroller to straighten the baby's blanket, smooth her pretty dress and assure himself that she was contented. Lucy focused her dark eyes on him, grinned in recognition. Johnny grinned back, stroked her delicate cheek, chuckling aloud when the infant turned to suck on his knuckle. "Looks like someone is ready for lunch."

The baby bunched her brows into a fierce frown when he extricated his hand long enough to retrieve a bottle from the diaper bag. "Here you go, small one." With a delighted gurgle, Lucy suckled hungrily.

Johnny smiled, sat back on his heels and gazed around the crowd while his daughter fed. A woman smiled at him. He recognized her as the receptionist at an insurance company down the hall from his office. Still crouched beside the stroller, Johnny acknowledged her greeting, grateful she paused only long enough to admire the baby before moving on.

As he watched the crowd, he recognized other people, as well, those he saw on a regular basis, those he hadn't seen in years. Some spoke, while others passed by without noticing him. It was surrealistic, actually, a sense of déjà vu that was both futile and disturbing.

When his ankles began to throb from the awkward position, he shifted to relieve the pressure. As he did, the crowd parted as if by magic, revealing an old man with long, silver-streaked hair seated on a tree stump just beyond the dancing circle. The man wore the traditional Bear Dance costume, a brightly colored shirt, jeans and a beaded belt, along with a wide-brimmed black hat clearly battered by time and boots scuffed by years of hard use. His hands were wrinkled, gnarled with age, yet he deftly wielded a glinting pocket knife to whittle bark from a fat twig, perhaps crafting a whistle for the wide-eyed youngster sitting cross-legged in the dust.

Although Johnny couldn't see the older man's face, the rapt attention of the boy confirmed that the man was speaking. It was the Bear Dance, after all, a time for stories, for the passing of history from one generation to another. Once Johnny had been like that fascinated child, hanging on his grandfather's every word, words that still reverberated in his mind.

Two brothers were hunting in the mountains. One became tired, and stopped to rest. The other continued hunting. The brother who was resting saw a bear standing upright, clawing a tree. The bear was making noises and seemed to be dancing with the tree. The young man learned the song of the Bear Dance, then returned to teach it to his people. Every spring the people sing the song and perform the dance to welcome the warmth of spring, and to show respect for the spirit of the bear.

The story was as real to Johnny now as it had been the first time it was spoken. He watched the old man and the young boy, not through the eyes of an observing stranger, but through the heart of a man reliving his own past, a memory from another time, another world.

Then the crowd surged forward, blocking his view. A peculiar panic knifed through him. A quick glance revealed that Lucy had fallen asleep. After easing the nipple from her slack mouth, Johnny stood, shading his eyes, straining to see. In less than a heartbeat, the crowd thinned. The stump was empty, and there was not so much as a disturbance of dust on the ground where the youngster had been sitting. A chill slipped down his spine.

"Welcome, Johnny Winterhawk. You have grown much since we last saw you."

Startled, Johnny spun around. Familiar eyes, dark and piercing, gazed back at him from a face creased with wisdom, tanned with age. No one knew exactly how old Ezra Buck was, although he'd been a revered elder and powerful influence in the tribe for more decades than most could remember. Johnny's grandfather had called him friend.

"It's good to see you, Ezra." Johnny accepted the proffered hand, was not surprised by the strength of the older man's grip. "Yes, it has been a long time."

"Too long." Ezra's eyes were dark and somber, but his face creased in a smile as he gazed at the sleeping infant. "She is a beautiful child. Looks much like her mother."

"Yes." He shifted, realizing that one of Ezra's many duties was maintaining vital statistics in the offices of the tribal chairman. It didn't surprise him that Ezra was aware of Lucy even though no official notification had been made, despite his deceptive implication to Claire that he had done so. He would, of course, but not until the legalities had been attended to and his daughter's birth certificate was revised to reflect his name instead of the stigma of illegitimacy.

Still, Lucy's existence was hardly a secret, and the tribe was like an extended family, with information passed informally among members.

"I am pleased that you have finally returned to us," Ezra said. "Too long have you turned your back on your people."

An icy lump settled in Johnny's chest. From his perspective, it was his people who'd turn their backs on him. Out of respect for his elder, he clamped his jaw until his teeth ached, but he said nothing.

Ezra regarded him with astute eyes. "You have nothing to tell me after all this time?"

"Nothing you would care to hear."

"It's not for you to decide what I wish to hear."

"This is not the time or place to open wounds of the past."

"It is the perfect time." The old man nodded, gazed around the crowd, tapped his booted foot to the rhythm of the music. "It is the perfect place."

Anger boiled up inside, a seething rage of loss and fury. Fists clenched at his side, he balled his fingers so tightly that his knuckles ached. He dared not release it, dared not expose the years of pain, of heartache.

Beside him, Ezra Buck tucked his thumbs in the loops threaded around his beaded belt and spoke so softly he could barely be heard above the singing and the drumbeats and the din of the crowd. "Your people need you, Johnny Winterhawk. You have not been there for them."

"And they have been there for me?" Johnny spun around, all caution lost to the fury in his blood. "Where were 'my people' when my mother abandoned her family? When my father died?" It poured out like bitter bile, grief of a lifetime exploding all at once. "Where were 'my people' when my wife dishonored me, when I was alone, grieving, filled with rage? Where were they, Ezra? Do you know? Do you care? Does anyone care?"

The old man shrugged. "The wisdom to seek lends the courage to find, my son." He laid a firm hand on Johnny's shoulder, let the warmth radiate from one body to the next. "Ask your grandfather to guide you."

By the time Johnny blinked twice, Ezra was gone.

Claire was aghast. "He gave *how* much money to the clinic?"

"Nobody knows for sure," Nell said importantly. "But rumor is that it's enough to make Dennis Reid sit up and take notice. I hear that there's talk of a merger."

That was news to Claire. She'd never been particularly fond of Dr. Reid, finding him to be a bit too arrogant and secretive for her taste. Still, he was the clinic's chief of staff, so she'd always kept her views to herself. "I wonder how that will affect the staff?"

Nell shrugged. "I don't know, but the clinic could sure use the money, and I for one am not going to look a gift benefactor in the mouth, especially when the guy is a bona fide hunk, drop-dead gorgeous and a millionaire to boot. Also—" Nell lowered her voice and glanced around to make sure they weren't being overheard "—I hear he's looking for a wife."

"A wife? In Buttonwood?" Claire burst out laughing, much to Nell's distress. She wiped her eyes, tried to stifle her mirth. "I'm sorry, Nell, but you have to admit there are more lucrative places for a drop-dead gorgeous millionaire to wife hunt than little old Buttonwood."

Huffing only a bit, Nell nodded hard enough to vibrate her gaudy feather earrings. "It does make one think there's more to the story than we've heard so far. Fact is, one of the maternity nurses says that she heard from someone on the surgical staff, who heard directly from Rose McBride's office that—Claire? Are you listening?"

"Hmm?" Actually, Claire had only been half listening. She'd been keeping watch on Johnny from the corner of her eye and had noticed a distinct change in body language when he'd been joined by an older man wearing the distinctive costume of the bear dancers. "Who's that man, Nell?"

"Which man?"

"The one talking to Johnny."

Shading her eyes, Nell squinted through the crowd. "Oh, that's Ezra Buck, an elder in the tribal-records office."

Johnny's errand with Lucy crossed her mind. "Is that where the membership enrollments are kept?"

"I suppose."

A thought struck her. "Do you suppose the administration office keeps track of all tribal members, even the ones who, say, remarry and move out of state?"

A crease of annoyance was visible between Nell's brows. "I honestly don't know. I do know, however, that there's been an interesting rumor about who fathered Rachel Arquette's baby. Now, everyone knows that Dr. Reid has been courting Rachel since word got out she was pregnant, but I happen to know..."

The woman's voice droned into a thin buzz. Claire nodded, pretended to listen, but couldn't keep her gaze off Johnny and Ezra Buck. Johnny was clearly tense, even angry. A moment later, Ezra Buck disappeared into the crowd.

Claire stiffened, laid an apologetic hand on Nell's arm. "I'm sorry, I have to go."

"But you haven't heard the good part—"

"We'll talk tomorrow, okay?" Without waiting for a reply, Claire pushed into the crowd, weaving her way through the throng, searching for the elusive man who could very well hold the key to her husband's past, as well as his future.

Frustrated, Claire hurried past the dance corral, circled around the singers into an area behind the food stands. Just as she was about to give up, she turned around, found herself gazing into a pair of dark, wise eyes.

"What can I do for you, child?"

It didn't occur to Claire to ask how he'd known she was looking for him. "I'm trying to get in touch with someone who moved away from here a long time ago. Can you help?"

Ezra smiled.

"It was a wonderful day." Sighing, Claire twirled around the living room on her toes, arms circled in front of her as if holding an invisible beach ball. "The music, the dancing—" she skipped around the dining-room table to snag Johnny's arm, preventing him from reaching into the valise he'd just opened "—the singing, the magnificent food. Tell me you had fun, Johnny."

He laughed, really laughed. The happy sound gave her goose bumps. "Yes, I had fun."

"So you're glad we went?"

Still smiling, he brushed a knuckle along her jaw. "Yes, I'm glad we went."

Breathless, she rose up on tiptoes, leaned in close. "There are lots of fun things we can do together."

"Really?" His eyes darkened, smoldered with a heat Claire fervently hoped was desire. "What did you have in mind?"

"We have some leftover whipped cream and caramel sauce."

"I thought the ice cream was gone."

"It is." She managed a seductive, throaty purr. "There are more appealing uses for sweet toppings, don't you think?"

It took a moment for his eyes to reflect a gleam of comprehension. He wavered a moment, as if his knees had gone weak. "I, ah..." Clearing his throat, he tugging at his knit collar. "You are a temptress, aren't you?"

"I try."

"We, ah, we never actually discussed these matters."

"Let's discuss them now."

"Is it hot in here?"

"I hope so."

He blew out a breath and took a step back, only to find himself caught between the table edge and a daring woman determined to prevent a case of chronic virginity from becoming terminal. Inexperience was her problem. That could be cured, but not without a little cooperation. She tried for a sultry cover-model pout, and batted her eyelashes.

"Work with me here," she whispered. "It's not nearly as much fun alone."

Johnny nearly choked. "I...I..." His gaze was riveted on her cleavage. With a shuddering gasp, he reached blindly into his briefcase, pulled out an indiscriminate fistful of documents. "I have work to do."

Sighing, Claire stepped away, blaming herself for not knowing how on earth to make him want her. Every time she saw the glaze of passion in his eyes, she'd leap in for the kill only to have her prey skitter away at the last moment. A work plea was one of his favorite escape mechanisms.

Glaring at the hated briefcase, she mentally planned a satisfying bonfire with its contents when she spotted a familiar document bound with blue legal paper and folded to fit in a man's pocket. Her heart thudded once, then went silent for a beat before returning to normal rhythm. Instinct told her the document in his briefcase was the prenuptial agreement she'd refused to sign the night before they were married.

The reminder that this had begun as a business deal flustered her. "Okay, fine." Raking her fingers through her hair, she stumbled back a step, feeling oddly disoriented. "I was only kidding anyway."

"Claire, it's just that—"

"You know me, just one practical joke after another." Her laughter was high-pitched, sounded strained even to her own ears. "Actually, I've got work to do, as well. Files to update, medical journals to peruse. Tons of stuff."

As she spoke, she edged toward the hallway, flashing a fake smile a moment before she spun and bolted to the safety of her bedroom. Closing the door, she sagged forward, scrubbed her face with the heels of her hands and called herself six kinds of fool.

"What is wrong with me?" she wailed, flinging herself on the bed. "I use mouthwash and deodorant. I keep my hair clean and my fingernails tidy." Grabbing the worn and beloved stuffed bunny that had decorated her bed since she'd been a child, she wailed her frustration. "I just don't get it, Flopsy. Boys chased me all through high school, men chased me all through medical school, I've had three marriage proposals and more indecent proposals than I can count, but I still can't manage to entice the only man on the entire planet that I actually want.'' She squeezed the bunny's throat, shook it hard enough to vibrate its floppy polyester ears. *"What is wrong with me?"*

One of the bunny's glass eyes fell off, and plopped into her lap. She groaned. "Oh, great. Sexual incompetence *and* bunny abuse. What a prize.''

Laying the one-eyed creature aside, she carefully saved the displaced eye for future repairs, then retrieved a women's magazine from her nightstand drawer and peevishly flipped through the pages. She was missing something here, some nuance of sensuality that had eluded her grasp. There must be a secret to seduction, some subtle but significant behavior required for satisfactory masculine arousal.

Stimulating all five senses had been a positive step. Johnny had looked like a man on the verge of sexual meltdown. His eyes had darkened, his slacks had bulged, he'd nearly had smoke coming out of his ears. Claire had been close, so close she'd nearly fainted with the joy of victory.

Too bad her beeper had gone off before he had.

Frustrated, she roughly turned one page, then another and another until she spotted an article that intrigued her. "'The Aphrodisiac Of Danger,'" she read aloud.

"The exhilaration of the unexpected, the excitement of surprise, the urgency of risk, all are powerful enticements for the masculine mystique. For some men, the allure of adrenaline is more potent than Viagra.''

Flopping the magazine closed, Claire bolted upright. "Of course!" She jumped off the bed, stunned that she hadn't thought of it sooner. "You want danger, Johnny Winterhawk, something unexpected to spice up those old adrenaline glands?"

Rubbing her hands together, she retrieved a Polaroid camera from the closet shelf. "Oh, yeah," she murmured, caressing the knobby plastic case as if it were a lover. "Hold on to your moccasins, Johnny. You're in for the surprise of your life."

Chapter Eleven

The alarm went off as usual. Johnny ignored it for a while, just continued to stand beside the window staring into the darkness. He'd been awake most of the night, his gut knotted with tension, his loins throbbing with need.

Damn.

It wasn't enough that Claire was the most perfect woman on earth; she had to be the most desirable one, too.

Damn.

Using his shoulder to push away from the wall, he sauntered over to turn off the clock radio. Loud music usually soothed him, enticed his weary mind away from that which haunted it. Now it simply jangled his last nerve.

He didn't know how long he could hold out. His thoughts swirled with erotic images, shared passion, moments he could only dream about because to experience the reality would change him forever. He remembered the soft glow of love that seemed to be evident in their wedding pictures. It hadn't been real, of course. It was merely a trick of the light. Still, Claire was a woman he could fall in love with, *would* fall in love with if he allowed it.

But he simply could not allow it, couldn't permit his heart to expose its tattered core to another betrayal, another shattering loss.

Frustrated, he slipped on his hated robe, a concession to modesty that was necessary since accepting Claire's invitation to use the master bathroom for his daily shower. He went quietly to her room. She'd left the door open, as was her custom. He supposed she did so to more easily hear the baby's cry, although Lucy rarely fussed in the middle of the night. When she did, Claire attended to her so quickly that Johnny usually heard footsteps in the hallway before he'd even roused himself from bed.

Now he moved through her room with practiced silence, pausing a few feet from her bed to watch her sleep. She was lovely in slumber, tousled and vulnerable, her brilliant hair splayed across the pillow. She was a woman made to be desired, one who desired in return. Only a fool would have been oblivious to her blatant sexual overtures during their time together.

Johnny wasn't a fool. He understood her needs, realized that a woman of such obvious zest and passion required the physical satisfaction of a man. That didn't make her unique.

In Johnny's experience, every woman he'd cared about had experienced such needs, and required the services of more than one man to satisfy them. Monogamy was an old-fashioned notion, he supposed. Too bad his heart was stuck with it. When he loved a woman, he loved her body and soul, with a passion so intense he was blinded by it.

It was his greatest weakness. He understood that about himself. He also understood that his weakness was not Claire's fault.

Stifling a sigh, Johnny turned into the bathroom, quietly closed the door. He undressed methodically, stepped into the steaming shower, performed the perfunctory ritual while his mind churned and his stomach tightened.

Their marriage was a blessing to him and Lucy; it was of no benefit to Claire. At least, none that he could see. On the contrary, it apparently restricted her in ways he'd never previously considered, and he was embarrassed that they'd never thought to discuss the sexual implications of the arrangement.

In truth it hadn't occurred to him that there would be such an aspect to discuss. After all, marriage had never affected his first wife's outside activities. Her sexual liaisons, he'd later learned, had been legend, and hadn't even slowed during the brief tenure of their wedded bliss.

Although he'd never given himself permission to consciously consider Claire's personal life, he'd presumed that she would continue to pursue it. Discreetly, of course. To do so blatantly would have jeopardized the custody matter on which the basis of their current relationship was formed.

Never in Johnny's wildest dreams could he have imagined that her sweet, sensual suggestions would send him into a spiral of erotic arousal beyond his control. Self-restraint was nearly exhausted; he was on the brink of collapse. A whisper, a touch, a single provocative smile might be enough to shatter that final barrier to conquer his still bleeding heart.

He simply couldn't let that happen.

A sudden chill raised bumps on his skin. Stunned to realize he'd been in the shower long enough to drain the hot-water tank, Johnny exited, dried himself, barely remembered to slip back into his robe before he opened the bathroom door.

The bed was empty. Claire was already up. Johnny hurried into the guest room to finish dressing.

Fifteen minutes later, he headed to the kitchen, helped himself to a cup of fresh coffee, which he downed in a few healthy gulps, then took a shortcut to the dining room through a sliding pocket door that was usually closed.

At the sound of the door opening, Claire gasped, spun away from the dining table on which his valise had been left open among a few scattered documents.

Her face went pink. "Good morning." As she spoke, her hand snaked behind her back. "You look nice today."

He automatically glanced down at his attire, a gray business suit with a pin-striped dress shirt and a burgundy print tie. "Thank you." He leaned left, trying to see what she was fiddling with. "Sorry about the mess on the table. I should have cleaned up my work before I went to bed last night."

"Gracious, it's your table. It's your house." Her laugh was high-pitched and a bit peculiar. "You can leave your work anywhere you want." As she followed his narrowed gaze, her cheeks turned from pale pink to the color of a ripe tomato. "I was just, ah, putting things back into your briefcase so they wouldn't get lost.''

To prove the point, she whirled around, jammed his appointment book into the open case, followed by a frenetic flurry of legal documents snatched from the table and stuffed into the valise without the slightest care.

Johnny leaped forward, tugged a crumpled contract from her grasp. ''Thanks. I'll take it from here.''

''Oh.'' She moistened her lips, avoided his gaze. Oddly enough, she giggled. ''Okay, then.''

''Isn't this your day off?''

''Yes.''

''Lucy isn't awake yet. You could have slept in.''

''Doctors don't require sleep. We're cured of that pesky waste of time during our internship.''

A too bright gleam in her eye gave him pause. Frowning, he touched the back of his hand to her forehead. Her skin was cool to the touch. ''Are you feeling all right?''

''Never better.'' Her eyes widened like speckled blue saucers. ''How about you?''

''Fine, thanks.'' If he hadn't been running late, he might have asked why she seemed nervous enough to jump out of her skin. ''I have a breakfast meeting,'' he mumbled, grabbing the valise and heading toward the door. ''I'll see you later.''

''Yes.'' Clasping her hands behind her back, Claire rocked back on her heels, grinning like a cat with feathers in its teeth. ''You certainly will.''

Gathered at one end of the conference table, three men hunched over a documents stained by handwritten alterations. Johnny finished jotting a marginal note, glanced at Spence, who was engaged in quiet conversation with Douglas Moorehead, senior partner of the speculative land-venture firm that was also their newest client.

"How long will you need to codify these changes in the water-rights clause?" Johnny asked.

Spence shifted one of the loose documents for a better view. "A couple of days at most. It's just a matter of validating the abstract of title on each parcel, checking deed conveyances and verifying precedents and case law."

The question had been posed for the client's benefit, since Johnny already knew the answer. Still, there was a certain decorum to maintain. "I'll review the easements, assess the applicable zoning, assure sufficient egress has been maintained in conjunction with contiguous properties. The fiduciary agreements should be finalized by the end of the week."

Moorehead nodded his approval. "I'll present your findings when the board meets next month." Straightening, he adjusted his glasses. "I presume you'll make yourself available to answer questions?"

"Absolutely." Johnny reached for his appointment book. "Date and time?"

"The evening of the fifteenth."

"Evenings aren't usually good for me," Johnny muttered. Claire was frequently away conducting Lamaze classes or on emergency calls, which left him to care for Lucy. "Let me check my schedule...."

As Johnny flipped through the pages of his appointment book, a photograph slipped out to plop on the conference table. Johnny glanced down at it, did a double take and froze in disbelief at the image of his beautiful flame-haired wife wearing nothing but a provocatively arranged bedsheet and a sultry smile.

Across the conference table, Spence hissed like a flattened tire.

Moorehead merely readjusted his glasses and bent over for a closer look. "Yes," he murmured. "I can certainly see why you'd prefer to have your evenings free."

Johnny snatched up the photo and shoved it in his pocket. He opened his mouth to explain, but all that emerged was a choked gurgle. Not that it mattered. An erotic photograph of his wife had just been blatantly displayed to a prospective client. What possible explanation could there be?

"You're a lucky man, Winterhawk. If I had something that lovely waiting for me, I'd resent working late, too." Heaving a wistful sigh, Moorehead removed his glasses, tucked them in his coat pocket. "I'll reschedule the meeting."

The curling iron tangled in her hair, turning a soft swirl into a chaotic knot. Claire uttered a cry of dismay. One hank of hair spewed out like electrified tinsel; the rest hung from her head like limp red rags. Frantic, she tossed the curling iron aside, stuck her head under the faucet, then reached for the blow dryer.

When she'd finished, her hair looked pretty much as it always did, sleek, smooth and boring. It would have to do.

So nervous her hands shook, she somehow managed to apply her makeup, adding extra liner to brighten her eyes, and a third coat of mascara for glamor. She finished up with glossy lip color called

Kiss Me Crimson, which seemed ironically appropriate under the circumstance.

Inhaling deeply, she smoothed her coat collar, gave her reflection a final glance and snatched her handbag from the bed. "Wish me luck, Flopsy." The ragged one-eyed bunny peered morosely from between a pair of ruffle-scounced pillows. Claire sighed. "Yes, I know. I'm going to need it."

She peeled her lips off her teeth, and headed out the door.

Sunlight streamed through the office blinds, the diagonal strips of brilliance broken only by the shadow of the man sitting at the desk. Johnny felt the late-afternoon warmth behind him, vaguely aware of the creeping light streaks on each side of his silhouette. It was for him an internal timer, a constant reminder of the sun's position in the sky, and a silent celebration of the warm season to come.

Winter was over. The erratic personality of spring had evened into mellow comfort, would soon step aside for the bold sizzle of summer. Heat. Burning heat. Smoldering heat. Heat to rival the fire burning in his belly, the passion of unrequited desire.

After the morning's meeting, he'd returned to his office determined quench the sensual burn in his body by focusing his mind on work. Work was his catharsis; work was his friend. Work was all he could count on to hold up its end of the bargain. Work, unlike personal relationships, had never betrayed him, never shocked him, never left him feeling unworthy, less of a man. He'd always taken solace from it, been able to close out the failures from other facets of his life. Always, until now.

Now he couldn't focus on anything but the photograph in his hand. He'd studied it for hours, every exposed curve, every concealed contour, the lush, pouty mouth and the taunting, twinkling eyes. A sweep of auburn tresses following with the jaunty tilt of her head, gathering softly on one shoulder, while the other side fell forward to caress the creamy curve of her throat.

Neatly printed on the white rim of the picture were the words, "Do you like surprises?" That was all the explanation offered. It was all he'd needed.

This woman, this exquisitely beautiful woman was his wife. And he wanted her more than he wanted his next breath.

He didn't glance up when the office door opened. "I told you to hold my calls, Myra. I don't wish to be disturbed."

"Myra has left for the day," came the sultry reply. "And some disturbances are more pleasant than others."

Swiveling his chair so quickly that it nearly toppled over, Johnny sucked in a breath, gripped the edge of his desk. "What are you doing here?"

Claire shut the door behind her, unfastened the top button of a supple cashmere coat that flowed gently to her shapely calves. "I came for an answer to my question." Her gaze settled on the photograph in his hand. "Did you like my surprise?"

His mouth went dry. He dared not stand, lest she note from his physical distress how affected he'd been by her surprise. "It was...unexpected."

"And dangerous?" Smiling, she unfastened the next button, lowered her voice to a whisper. "Do you like danger, Johnny?"

"Danger?"

"Mmm-hmm." Another button popped free. "A rush of excitement, a tiny thrill of being just a little bit naughty?"

"Naughty?" He coughed, laid the photograph on his desk with the image side down. Knowing she would be embarrassed to learn that the picture had been accidentally viewed by others, he kept that information to himself. Only when his lungs began to throb did he force himself to breathe again. "I, ah, know you meant it as a joke, Claire, but the truth is—"

"It was no joke, Johnny. And neither is this."

To his utter astonishment, she shrugged the coat off her shoulders, and stood before him in all her splendor. Except for a sensual satin gift bow affixed to her navel, she was totally nude.

It was the most erotic thing Johnny had ever seen in his life. Which is just what he would have told her if his larynx hadn't gone into spasm. He felt the draft on his tongue, knew he was staring like a slack-jawed adolescent, but couldn't have closed his mouth if his life depended on it.

She moistened her lips, blinked. Her fingers curled nervously at her side. "Well?"

With some effort, he forced a sound from his paralyzed throat. It wasn't a word, exactly. More like the deflating croak of a squashed frog. Even that much was progress, considering that when she'd dropped her coat, Johnny had damned near swallowed his tongue.

She flexed her fingers, curved her mouth into a quivering smile. "I was hoping for a more positive reaction."

He sucked in a breath, exhaled slowly. "If my reaction gets any more positive, I'll need a new pair of slacks to wear home."

"That can be arranged," she purred, stepping out of the cashmere puddle at her feet. "Meanwhile, I have it on good authority that Spence has a meeting in Ignacio, and won't be back for hours."

She glided across the floor, pirouetting once as she reached the corner of his desk. "Of course, his meeting might not last as long as expected. The cleaning crew might show up early. There could be a delivery, or a client who drops in without an appointment."

Moving around the desk, she pressed her hips against the edge of the polished wood, so close to him that her scent surrounded him like loving arms. "There's always the danger of being caught, of being surprised."

A subtle shiver slipped down her flesh. Johnny followed it with his gaze as it moved from her bare shoulders to her bow-bedecked belly, and down curvaceous thighs, accented at their apex by an erotic nest of silky auburn hair.

Her voice was low, throaty, so sensual he felt the vibration all the way to his toes. "So tell me, Johnny, do you like surprises?"

"Yes," he whispered, raising his gaze to her voluptuous breasts with pale nipples tight as tiny pink fists. "I like surprises."

"I like them, too." Leaning back, she provocatively parted her lips, sensually lowered her eyelids. "Surprise me, Johnny."

What happened next was more than a mere surprise. It was astounding, at least to Johnny, who felt

as if he'd lost all control of body and mind, and was
compelled by a force beyond the earthly plane.

Aroused beyond rational thought, Johnny reacted
on pure instinct. He rose from his chair, swept Claire
into his arms and kissed her until she was limp and
gasping. He was dizzy with passion, burning with desire, unable to think beyond a singular purpose of
sating the fire in his manhood, quenching the sensual
thirst that had tormented him since he'd first laid eyes
on this incredible woman who was now his wife.

With a single sweep of his arm, the desk was
cleared. Files flew across the room, pencils bounced
to the floor, the in basket crashed, spewing a desperate
tangle of documents across the lush carpeting.

Weeks of wanting, of suppressed desire spilled out
in a tumble of crazed passion and desperate need. He
spun her in his arms, tasting her lips, her throat, taking
one breast into his mouth, then the other. He heard
her gasps, her startled murmurs, felt her flesh tremble
at his touch and knew that she wanted him as much
as he wanted her.

"You are so beautiful," he whispered against her
moist skin. "I've wanted you for so long, Claire, so
very, very long."

"I've…wanted you, too, Johnny."

The tiny pause, a quaver of hesitation in her voice
gave credence to her passion, and to her impatience.
Johnny couldn't wait another moment to consummate
what they both so desperately craved.

In less than a heartbeat, Claire was lying on his
desk, while he fumbled with his zipper. "Johnny,
I—" The words caught in her throat when his manhood sprang free. Her eyes widened.

He felt her thighs tense as he parted them, heard

her sharp intake of breath as he wrapped her legs around his waist. She squirmed, her hips writhing so sensually that he feared he wouldn't be able to contain himself another moment. "I know." He panted the words out one at a time. "I'm hurrying."

"Johnny—"

"Almost there, honey." Lifting her buttocks, he pressed himself against the moist threshold. He shuddered, whispered her name and, with a single stroke, sheathed himself in her welcoming warmth.

Claire cried out at the same moment Johnny's mind cleared enough to comprehend the meaning of the tiny tug during his entrance, the stiffening of her body when the barrier had opened to him.

Stunned, he went completely still, staring down at Claire in utter bewilderment. Her eyes were closed, a flash of tooth gleamed white as she bit her lower lip. Her breath came in short, frantic gulps.

At that moment, he knew.

He instantly withdrew, shocked and horrified. "Why didn't you tell me?"

A touch of color was returning to skin that had paled to the shade of eggshells. Breathing hard, she moistened her lips. "I didn't think it mattered." She reached up, touched his shoulders to urge him forward. "It's all right now, the worst is over. Or so I've been told."

"The worst is—?" Stepping back, Johnny yanked up his pants, so bewildered and shocked he didn't know what to do. "I can't believe it," he muttered more to himself than to her. "A virgin, you're a virgin."

Awkwardly levering up on one elbow, she offered

a thin smile. "Not anymore. At least, not techni-
cally."

A groan of sheer misery slipped out without permission. "What have I done?"

Her smile quivered, fell away. "You've made love
to your wife."

"Made love?" Shaking his head, he raked his fingers through his hair, then scrubbed his eyelids with
the heels of his hands.

In his mind, he replayed the memory and cringed.
She'd been innocent, inexperienced. That he hadn't
known was no excuse. He'd taken her too roughly,
as if her body had been expressly created for his pleasure. She'd deserved wooing and gentleness, sweet
words and soft caresses until her body quivered with
a passion that matched his own.

Instead, he'd behaved like a rutting elk. "That
wasn't lovemaking, Claire, it was unbridled lust. I'm
so sorry."

"Sorry? *Sorry?*" She bounded up, pushed him
aside, her face flaming with embarrassment. "Do forgive me for forcing you into something that you so
clearly regret."

He groaned. "Honey, wait—"

Skittering away as he reached for her, she scooped
up her coat off the floor. "You'll be pleased to know
that I'll not be bothering you with any more carnal
demands. If that's all there is to sex, it's far more
trouble than it's worth."

With that stunning pronouncement, she donned her
coat and left.

Nell Hastings entered just as Claire finished slipping into the sweater and spare pair of slacks she kept

in her locker. "I thought you were off today," she said.

"I need to catch up on some paperwork." Claire hung her coat in the locker, finger combed her mussed hair. "I'll be available for emergencies. Otherwise, pretend I'm not here."

"Okay." Nell hesitated. "You all right, hon? You look kind of pale."

"I'm fine, just fine." She spun around, headed to the doctors' lounge, hoping to find it empty. Thankfully, it was. Collapsing on a vinyl settee that had seen better days, Claire fought a surge of nausea and tried to eliminate the horror of the past hour from her mind.

What had she been thinking? Was she now so pathetically desperate that she had to force herself on a man who quite clearly did not want her?

The answer was resoundingly affirmative. That's exactly what she'd just done, not only at the expense of her own dignity, but also Johnny's. He'd probably never forgive her. Certainly, she'd never forgive herself.

Fighting tears, she spotted a worn issue of the same magazine she kept in her nightstand, the one that had extolled the virtues of adding a little danger to spice up one's love life. She flung it against the wall, furious at herself for being so gullible, so stupid. How could she have humiliated herself that way?

Even worse, she'd humiliated Johnny. She'd never be able to look him in the eye again. For which he'd no doubt be eternally grateful.

Her face heated at the memory of Johnny's horrified expression, of the shock in his eyes. And of the disgust.

Claire couldn't remember leaving the office. All she knew was that she had to get away, had to retreat to the one place on earth where she was confident and in control. Work was her sanctuary. It had always been so.

Apparently, it always would be.

By the time Claire gathered the courage to return home, a midnight moon had risen high over the horizon. Johnny would be asleep by now. At least, she fervently prayed that he was.

Slipping quietly inside, she was relieved to find the house dark except for a single lamp in the foyer, the one used as a night-light to illuminate the hall in case Lucy awoke.

She tiptoed down the hall, into the nursery, where the baby slept peacefully in her crib. Claire smoothed the blanket, stroked her knuckles over the baby's soft hair. As she returned to the hall, soft music startled her. A spray of light emanated from the open door of the master bedroom, which had been dark only a moment earlier.

Hesitantly, she moved toward the doorway, pausing to catch her breath before peeking inside. The heady scent of fresh roses wafted to greet her. She saw the source, an immense vase of fragrant blooms on one nightstand; on the other, two fluted goblets flanked a silver ice bucket chilling a bottle of champagne.

At the foot of the bed stood her handsome husband, wearing only a sheepish smile and a bright red ribbon adorning an intimate portion of his anatomy.

''Do you still like surprises?'' he asked, reaching for the chilled champagne bottle.

She swallowed hard. "That depends."

"Depends on what?"

Her gaze was riveted on his bow-bedecked manhood. "On how you plan to pop that cork."

Chapter Twelve

"You are so lovely," he whispered, crossing the room, so lithe and graceful in his nudity that she was mesmerized by his perfection. Muscles rippled in the soft amber lamplight, emphasizing the fluidity of his stride, the masculinity of movement. Bronzed beauty, a supple strength that was chillingly primitive, yet clearly composed and controlled.

When he drew close enough for her to feel the heat of his body, her breath slid out on a sigh. "You're not bad yourself."

"I'm simply a man."

"There is nothing simple about you, Johnny Winterhawk. You are a mystery enveloped by an enigma. You are also the kindest, sweetest, most gentle person I've ever known."

Claire wanted him desperately, wanted to melt into his strong embrace and accept what he offered without a thought as to what tomorrow might bring. But she couldn't.

"Despite having embarrassed myself completely this afternoon, I am not as pathetic as I have allowed myself to appear. This—" she encompassed the romantic setting he had created for her "—this is so exquisite, so magnificently generous, but…but…" Moistening her lips, she lowered her gaze. "I want you to want me, but not this way."

Genuine bafflement clouded his eyes. "I don't understand."

"It was never my intention to coerce you into a relationship that didn't feel right to you." The words slipped out with a flinch. Intention or not, that had been the obvious result.

"Do you believe me so easily manipulated?"

"Of course not, but—"

"Good. I'd be deeply wounded if you thought me such a fool. I'm here because I wish to be, because you're a whisper in my heart, a fever in my blood. You haunt me, Claire, haunt my thoughts, my dreams." He smiled, stroked her cheek with his knuckles, a caress so tender it brought tears to her eyes. "It's rare to find a beauty that extends to the soul. Yours does so. That makes you remarkable, unique among women. You have brought great joy to my life. If I am privileged to bring even a small happiness into yours, it would be my greatest honor."

She touched her throat, felt the frantic pulse jitter beneath her fingertips. The soul of a poet. Deep down, she'd known that about him, had frequently been moved by his prose, by a particularly poignant observation, a descriptive phrase lifted from the heart rather than the mind.

Never in all of her life had she been so profoundly touched, not just by the sweetness of his words, but by the tender acts of kindness visible all around her. Vibrant crimson rose petals had been scattered over the bed; flickering candles had been thoughtfully positioned to enhance the romantic ambience; soft music floated on floral-scented air. The room was a swirl of sweet seduction, a jeweled reflection of candlelight and cut crystal, a sensual feast spread with exquisite care simply to please her.

To please her.

Her voice, when she found it, pulsed with emotion. "I don't know what to say."

"Say nothing." He tipped his head forward, brushed the side of her neck with his lips. "Simply feel, be, experience."

She shivered as his mouth explored her throat, her jawline, the sensitive flesh at the base of her earlobe. Vaguely aware, she felt the soft moan slip from somewhere inside as his palms caressed her arms through the sweater's sleeves before moving downward to the hem. When his fingers slid beneath the knit fabric, the delicious warmth of skin on skin drew a gasp of delight.

"Raise your arms," he whispered against her cheek. Cool air brushed her belly as he lifted the sweater over her head. She shivered, more from anticipation than a chill, but he was immediately concerned. "You're cold."

Protest died on her lips as his gentle hands stroked her back, warming her to the bone. Her eyelids grew heavy; her muscles turned to butter. "Mmm."

"You like that?"

"Oh, yes."

Emboldened, he massaged his way downward from her shoulder blades to hook his thumbs in the waistband of her slacks. Slowly, expertly, he lowered the garment, and himself, until the fabric pooled at her feet, and his cheek nested against her soft belly. "Beautiful," he murmured, touching his lips to her navel.

Only when the moist trail of kisses reached her inner thigh did she realize that her panties had been removed with the same deft swoop. Trembling, she steadied herself on his shoulders, stepped out of the discarded clothing, and allowed him to remove her shoes.

Then he stood before her, his dark eyes glowing with approval. "You are exquisite."

She dared not test her voice. Her knees were so weak she feared they would buckle, and her skin was alive with sensation as his hands stroked, probed and caressed areas of her body that before this moment she'd never considered to be erogenous zones.

Until now.

Johnny slid his thumb along the crook of her arm, a fluttering caress that excited and aroused in a most remarkable manner. He traced her collarbone first with the pad of his thumb, then moistened the same path with the tip of his tongue. She uttered a tiny cry of pleasure, and gripped his biceps to keep from falling over. When his fingertips glided down along her rib cage, then up between her breasts, she closed her eyes and felt as if she might faint from sheer joy.

Behind her shuttered eyelids, soft lights flickered with electric intensity. Her body was alive, pulsing with sensuality beyond her wildest imagination. Anticipation replaced apprehension, wonder replaced fear. What she'd experienced that afternoon had been sudden, painful, singularly unpleasant. But this…this was a slice of warm heaven, an intimate tenderness that seeped straight to the heated core.

The silky brush of his hair against her shoulder was the only warning she had as he bent to lift her into his arms. Her eyes sprang open. She wrapped her arms around his neck, stiffened slightly as he carried her toward the bed…then past it into the bathroom.

Smiling, he lowered her legs, but kept one arm protectively wrapped around her waist as he turned on the shower. "An enjoyable prelude," he explained when she gazed up in bewilderment. "Please, allow me to pamper you."

At that moment, he could have requested permission to paint her hair green and she would have acquiesced. She took the hand he offered, and followed him into the billowing steam.

For the next twenty minutes, Johnny ministered to Claire's body and soul as if she were a goddess. He washed her hair, his strong fingers leisurely massaging the thick lather until her scalp tingled deliciously and every muscle in her neck was limp as a soft noodle.

He soaped up a washcloth with devilish sensuality, then used it to nuzzle every inch of her skin, from the delicate flesh of her breasts—the tips of which received special attention until they stood like tiny pink soldiers, stiff and proud—to the buttery warmth between her thighs. Every touch brought a new sensation, heralded by a tiny cry, a moan of passion, a gasp of delight.

When he'd finished, he embraced her beneath the running water, kissing her nape as the hot spray sluiced over her breasts and belly, then turning her around, cradling her wet head between his palms, feathering sweet kisses along her lips while the shower sensually massaged her back and buttocks.

Claire felt strangely bereft when he stepped away long enough to rinse the washcloth. The distance of only a few inches seemed unbearable to her, but within the space of a heartbeat he returned to gently wipe soapy remnants from her face.

When he reached up to turn off the shower, she stopped him. "My turn," she whispered, taking the washcloth from him.

His eyes widened, but he issued no protest. A smile quirked the corner of his mouth as she also made a production of soaping the cloth, teasing him at the same time by running her tongue along her upper lip. "You learn fast."

"Top ten percent of my class." Setting the soap aside, she rotated the cloth over his chest, marveling at the sculpted contours, the muscled strength. She caressed his arms, washing them with exquisite care, even lifting each magnificent hand one finger at a time.

Then she turned her attention to his lower body. Despite the billow of steam surrounding them, Claire's mouth went dry. He was gorgeous. He was deliciously aroused. And he was still sporting a bow, albeit a wet one.

Licking her lips, she set the cloth aside long enough to gently untie the ribbon. "I have always enjoyed unwrapping presents," she murmured, "but never quite so much."

He shuddered as she soaped him with smooth, gentle strokes. When she slipped beneath him to test the weight of his masculinity, he uttered a hoarse cry and gritted his teeth.

She was instantly alarmed. "Have I hurt you?"

"No...no..." He panted between words, paused to gulp a breath. "You've learned your lessons too well."

"Too well?"

Befuddled, she drew away, only to have him gather her in his arms with a chuckle. "A man is different from a woman in more ways than the obvious. A woman is more tactile, passion is slower to build. A man requires only a look. Sometimes a touch is too exquisite to bear."

"I knew that," she muttered, certain her face must be flaming. "Human biology is hardly a mystery to me."

"Books are useful." Agreement was punctuated with an affable smile. "But experience—" she gasped as his fingers gently probed the apex of her thighs "—is invaluable."

He held her up as her knees finally gave way, then guided her from the shower and toweled her dry with great reverence, as if she were exquisitely precious, immeasurably dear. Scooping her into his arms, he carried her to the bed, laid her gently upon it. Removing the chilled champagne from the ice bucket, he slid her a wry look. "I wish I was man enough to open this as you suggested."

She couldn't help it. She giggled. "The conventional manner will do."

"Your understanding is appreciated." He bowed as if honoring royalty, then wrapped a towel around the bottle and expertly popped the cork with his thumbs.

"Well done," she said, noting only a dribble had

escaped into the terry-cloth sheath. "Luck or practice?"

"Strictly luck. The last time I did this—" he paused to pour bubbling liquid into each crystal goblet "—was a friend's birthday party. The resulting geyser ruined his carpet, and it cost me two hundred dollars to repair the cork-shaped hole in his wall."

She accepted one goblet, cradled it between her palms. The mattress dipped as he casually sat beside her, so at ease with his own nakedness that she was surprisingly compliant about her own.

He extending his goblet until the fluted rim touched hers with a melodic chime. "To magical moments."

"Yes," she murmured. "Magical." She pretended to sip, but was too nervous to do more than touch her tongue to the champagne's liquid bite while its tangy fizz tickled her nostrils. Her skin prickled as if touched. She knew without looking that he had done that with his gaze. It was magical indeed, the way he could affect her physically with no more than a glance. The ardor that had built into a bonfire still simmered; she squirmed, frustrated by a need she could identify, but wasn't certain how to quench. "I'm ready now."

A lazy smile. "Ready for what?"

"You know what."

"Do I?"

He was teasing her. She knew that. "I still have my med-school texts. Would you like to borrow one?"

"Ah, a brush-up course?"

"Only if you've forgotten what comes next."

He chuckled again, took another sip of champagne, and stretched out, half reclining on the plush comforter draping her bed. "What do you think comes next?"

"You know...*it*."

"*It?*"

"Yes, *it*." Grinning, she gave his shoulder a playful shove, but inside she was more than a touch desperate.

In the shower, she'd experienced the blossom of sexual desire that had vibrated her to the soles of her feet. She'd expected him to sweep her directly into bed, and make mad, passionate love to her. Instead, they were engaged in a conversation that seemed startlingly casual considering the subject matter. And, of course, the fact that they were both stark naked. "I'd hate to have all that lovely foreplay go to waste because, um, things have cooled off."

The twinkle in his eye taunted her. "Are you cooling off?"

"No, not yet." In fact, Claire was quivering inside to the point that she could barely sit still. Her body cried out for movement, her lips tingled to taste him, her fingertips flexed with an almost desperate need for touch. "I'm, you know, ready."

"No, you're not." He took her glass, set both goblets on the nightstand. "But you will be," he murmured, reaching for her. "You will be."

In the blink of an eye, he'd rolled her gently onto the mattress, fitted his lips over hers and kissed her so deeply, so powerfully, with such profundity and poignancy that her entire body vibrated. She felt the low moan rumble up from her chest, but could hear nothing beyond the rush of blood pounding her veins and the frantic rhythm of her heartbeat.

He tasted her lips, sipped the corners of her mouth

as if testing a fine wine, then continued to alternate between feathery tenderness and plundering ravishment until she was limp, weak and dizzy with desire.

Words whispered in her ear, sweetness without form, sound without context. Her mind translated, her heart soared, her body throbbed as if preparing to turn itself inside out. He shifted subtly, dipped his head and took the tip of her breast into his mouth. The sweet sensation nearly drove her wild. When he teased the other nipple with the pad of his thumb, she rolled her head on the pillow, and a guttural moan of sheer ecstasy floated from somewhere deep inside.

Sparks shot from her breasts to her thighs, joining in an explosion of intimate heat. She was engulfed in sensation: the electricity of his clever fingers doing things she'd never imagined; the lingering taste of him; the whisper of his breath; the pounding of his heart; the rustle of bedclothes mingled with tiny gasps, rumbling groans.

"Now," she croaked, certain she would die without him inside of her. "Please, now."

"Soon." His tongue flicked her nipple; his fingers blazed a burning trail down her belly. He parted her thighs with his knee, exposing her to his touch.

She arched her back, cried out with pleasure as he probed her deeply. Her fingers convulsed, dug into his shoulders. Her hips moved without conscious thought, rotating an instinctive erotic dance against the palm of his hand. "Please…" She could barely breathe. "Oh, please…now…now…"

With a shocked gasp, she went rigid, her body shaking with a sweetness beyond anything she'd ever experienced. Fire, liquid fire. She was engulfed in it, drowning in its erotic heat. Wave after wave washed over her as spasms of white-hot pleasure exerted complete control.

When she fell back panting and spent, Johnny moved over her, smiling. He brushed the damp hair from her brow, kissed each eyelid. ''Now,'' he said quietly.

Then he entered her slowly, tenderly, brought her to the frenzied brink of madness to carry her over the threshold again, and again.

And again.

Moonlight streamed through the undraped window, bathing her dear face in a silvery glow. Johnny shifted, drawing her closer. Claire murmured in her sleep, nuzzled against his chest, her breath warm against his bare skin. Deep inside, his heart swelled with a joy beyond his wildest dreams. This was the woman he had been created for, the woman who completed his soul. He was safe with her. His heart was safe.

There was no doubt in Johnny's mind that Claire was his destiny. He cherished her beyond measure.

A sated sigh slipped from her lips. He stroked the corner of her mouth with his fingertip, smiled as she turned toward his touch. A mussed strand of vibrant hair fell across her cheek. He smoothed it back into the sleek tresses splayed across his pillow, allowed himself the luxury of a lingering touch, a gentle caress. She was so beautiful, so precious. So pure.

Claire was his destiny, a woman who had saved her love only for him, as he should have saved himself for her. All these years, Johnny had been frantically seeking this purity of soul, this aching sweetness of spirit. He'd sought completion, absolution, but had confused physical acceptance as a cleansing of the soul.

Everything he'd experienced before had been a prelude, a pretense of desperation, counterfeit emotion that had seemed genuine only because he'd had nothing to compare it with. Until now. Until Claire.

How could he have known that such perfection existed, and that he would be blessed with it?

Johnny was awed; he was humbled. He was also deeply, irrevocably in love. And for the moment, he forgot that love, like happiness, was always temporary.

"Claire! Come quick, hurry!"

Startled, Claire dashed into the nursery, still buttoning her blouse. She found Johnny leaning over the crib, his eyes alight with wonder.

He glanced up with a dazzling grin, motioned her over. "She turned over! Lucy turned over, all by herself."

"She did?" Joining him at the crib rail, she gazed down at the bright-eyed infant who was lying on her back, whacking her fat tummy and kicking happily. "Did you actually see her do it?"

"Yes! I was playing with her…you know, doing that peekaboo thing behind the crib rail. Then her head bobbled up, her back arched and she just flipped right over!"

Claire laughed, so amused by Johnny's excitement that she didn't have the heart to tell him that such motor-skill development was normal for an infant of Lucy's age. "See if she'll do it again."

"Okay." Beaming, Johnny turned the baby onto her tummy with paternal expertise, then positioned himself where the infant had to bobble her head backward to see him. "Come on, small one, you can do it."

Lucy craned her tiny neck, focusing dark little eyes on her exuberant daddy. She grinned, squeaked, got so excited that she flung out her arms and fell forward with a startled grunt.

Claire chuckled.

Johnny straightened, frowning. "Give her a minute. She's just warming up."

On cue, Lucy regained control long enough to push her upper torso upright, much to her father's delight. He stepped to the end of the crib, which forced the baby to hold her head up even higher to keep him in her sights.

"That's a girl," he murmured, "that's a big girl. Come on now, all the way…"

Claire found herself holding her breath, grimacing, making peculiar hand gestures in midair as if offering kinetic assistance. Over the years, she'd listened with polite interest as the parents of her tiny patients bragged about physical achievements as if their child were the only one on earth to take a step or sprout a tooth. Intellectually, she'd understood the parental pride, although she'd never appreciated why they seemed to view normal biological development as a personal victory. Now, however, she found herself experiencing that heart-pounding anticipation on a visceral level.

"Come on, sweetie," she murmured. "Do it one more time. Show us what a big girl you are."

"Peekaboo!" Johnny said, sounding almost panicked.

"That's a big girl," Claire said, sounding more desperate than encouraging.

Lucy's little head swiveled, focusing first on the man who kept popping up from behind the headboard of her crib, then on the woman who appeared to be shoveling invisible snow with her hands. After what seemed a small eternity, the baby let out a happy squeak, twisted and flipped onto her back so suddenly that her legs jerked and she flung her arms out in shock.

"All right!" Johnny crowed.

"Way to go, Lucy!"

Lifting his baby daughter out of the crib, Johnny cradled the infant in his arms. "You think you're big stuff, don't you?" Lucy replied with a smile and a happy coo. Johnny laughed, looked at Claire with an expression of pure joy that made her heart ache. "She's perfect, isn't she, Claire?"

"Yes," Claire whispered. "And so is her daddy."

Thirty minutes later, Claire melted into Johnny's arms and was thrilled by the passion of his kiss. "Wow," she murmured when he reluctantly released her. "Maybe we should both call in sick today."

He chuckled, smoothed her hair with the back of his hand. "I've never felt better in my life. But I'll admit the idea of staying in bed all day has tremendous appeal, particularly if I had company."

"That could be arranged."

"You're insatiable."

"You make me insatiable." She laid her palm on his cheek, shivered as he turned his face to kiss it. "If I'd known how wonderful making love with you would be—" The words ended in a gasp as he pulled her against him, fitted his mouth over hers in a ravishment that left her panting and breathless.

He, too, seemed shaken. Without releasing her, he took a half step back, lifted her left hand and rolled the golden wedding band on her ring finger. "You deserve diamonds."

"I don't need diamonds."

"You're my wife." The words were spoken firmly, decisively, with a sense of awe that warmed her heart. "You will have diamonds."

Perhaps because of last night's intimacy, Claire read more into those words than the material offering of expensive gems. There was something in his eyes, something in his voice. He cared about her. Claire knew it, could feel it. They were a real family now, in every sense of the word.

Johnny glanced at his watch, puckered his lips in annoyance. "I have a breakfast meeting."

"You'd better go, then," Claire said when she'd regained control of her voice.

He nodded, took his valise from the table, angled a smoldering glance in her direction. "I'll see you tonight."

"Count on it," she whispered.

Reluctantly, he flexed his fingers around the valise handle, flickered a glance at the baby, then heaved a resigned sigh and left.

After Claire heard the front door close, she sagged against the counter, replaying everything over in her mind. Details of how his voice had quavered when he'd told her she was beautiful, and how his touch had been so exquisitely tender as he'd loved her. She knew beyond doubt that he, too, had been moved by

what they'd shared last night. She didn't believe for
a moment that he regretted their lovemaking.

Still, she was bothered by a soft shadow in his gaze
this morning, a nearly imperceptible sadness that only
one who loved him more than life could have noticed.

Claire had noticed.

A secret still haunted him, an emptiness that Claire
believed that she understood, because she shared it.
The past hovered on the periphery of their happiness,
the phantoms of those who had given them life, then
disappeared without becoming a part of those lives.

The search for her own heritage had ended years
ago, when the document trail had disappeared into a
wall of secrecy. Someday that wall might weaken and
collapse, allowing her a tantalizing glimpse into her
own past. Until then, there was nothing more she
could do. Not for herself, anyway, but there was certainly something she could do for Johnny.

Family was all that mattered. Johnny needed family. He needed to belong.

Retrieving the information provided by Ezra Buck,
Claire placed a long-distance telephone call that
would, for better or worse, change the course of more
lives than she could have possibly imagined.

Myra gaped as if he'd lost his mind. "Do you
know how much two dozen white roses are going to
cost you?"

"It doesn't matter. I want them delivered to the
clinic today, before the end of Claire's shift."

Pushing her glasses up the bridge of her nose, Myra
issued a strained clucking sound and thrust a stack of
messages into Johnny's hand. "She must have cooked
some kind of special dinner last night."

"Very special." A warm sensation settled in his chest at the memory. "Myra?" He spoke without looking up from the stack of messages he was perusing. "Hypothetically, would you rather pick out your own diamond ring or receive it as a gift?"

"You've been married for weeks. You're just now getting around to buying her a ring?"

"Are you going to answer my question or not?"

"All right, don't get your briefs in a knot." Myra grinned. "A little lawyer humor. Briefs, as in legal briefs...?"

"Shall I repeat the original question?" Without awaiting an answer from his wisecracking clerk, he clasped his hands behind his back and used his best cross-examination voice. "Hypothetically, would you rather pick out your own diamond ring or receive it as a gift?"

Myna shrugged. "Hypothetically, it wouldn't make any difference," she replied without cracking a smile. "I'd just hock it to supplement my pitiful salary."

Startled, he stopped shuffling messages. "I just gave you a raise."

"I know, but I'm greedy."

He smiled. "That's what we love about you, Myra."

"You mean it's not my girlish good looks?" Eyes twinkling, she patted her curly gray hair. "Too bad I can't afford a boob job and a tummy tuck."

Johnny laughed, handed one of the messages back to her. "Get Douglas Moorehead on the phone for me, will you. And see if Spence has finished the revisions on that water-rights clause."

Nodding, Myra swiveled toward the office door to

greet a courier who'd just entered. "May I help you?"

"Delivery for Johnny Winterhawk."

"I'll sign," Myra said.

The courier scrawled on his clipboard, replied in a bored tone, "I'm instructed to release to the addressee only."

"I'll take it," Johnny said.

"Identification, please."

Startled, Johnny glanced at the letter in the courier's hand, recognized the return address and felt as if he'd been punched in the gut. Somehow he managed to fumble for his wallet, produce the requested ID and keep his fingers from shaking long enough to sign his name.

"Is everything all right?"

Johnny heard Myra's question, would have responded if he'd trusted his voice. Instead, he simply went into his office and closed the door. Dread settled over him like an icy shroud. His lungs felt tight. His stomach knotted into a ball of pain.

The envelope was from the DNA laboratory, and no doubt contained the results of the paternity test. For a moment, he considered shredding the unopened envelope along with its contents. It wasn't logical, of course, but he wasn't dealing with logic at the moment. He was dealing with instinct, and with fear.

He laid the unopened envelope in the center of his desk, then sat in his chair and stared at it. He cursed his reticence, his weakness, telling himself that the proof he needed to ensure custody of his child was within the envelope. There was no doubt that Lucy was his daughter, his child. No doubt. None.

The report would simply confirm that, provide scientific documentation, irrefutable evidence. Intellectually, Johnny understood that. Emotionally, he was terrified, and he didn't know why.

Minutes ticked by. He jumped when the phone rang, told Myra to hold his calls. He paced, stared at the envelope, paced some more. An hour passed, then two, then four. When he finally mustered the courage, he read the report.

The news was devastating.

Chapter Thirteen

"What do you think, sweetie? Is it positively smashing?"

Claire performed a pirouette around the master bedroom to display the sensuous black teddy impetuously purchased during a lunch-hour shopping trip. It was daringly naughty, translucent in all the right places, and constructed to squash her otherwise average breasts upward until they bulged from the sensual midnight lace like lush, ripe melons.

"You don't think the high hip cut makes my thighs look too big, do you?"

Lucy, lying on a crib blanket spread on the king-size bed, stuffed a fist in her mouth and gurgled.

Claire grinned. "Thank you. A fellow female's opinion is important in such matters. If your daddy likes it as much as you do, there might be a brother or sister in your future."

Lucy cooed as if enthralled by the prospect.

"I'm glad you approve," Claire murmured, hurriedly changing into a loose shirt and pair of slacks. "If I have my way, you'll have lots of siblings, dozens of them. Even if being an only child has its advantages."

She paused to give the silky black fabric a final caress before tucking the sexy garment into a drawer to be retrieved later that night. "An only child doesn't have to share the last bowl of ice cream, or fight over who gets the television remote. But it's lonely. You, my precious—" she scooped the baby into her arms to kiss her downy-soft cheek "—you deserve to grow up in a house full of love and laughter, with lots of arguments over who got the biggest slice of pie."

Humming softly, Claire carried Lucy to the portable crib, which had been set in the breakfast nook so Claire could watch her while cooking. As she retrieved a sauté pan and selected fresh vegetables and a package of fat prawns from the refrigerator, she continued to chat with the bright-eyed infant as if conversing with a trusted friend.

"Today your daddy sent me flowers. Did you know that?" Lucy widened her eyes. "Yes, indeed, the most magnificent bouquet of white roses I've ever seen in my life. Everyone at the clinic was pea green with envy." She sighed, glanced through the open door leading into the dining room to admire the gorgeous flowers. "I brought them home so we could all admire them. Don't you think they look lovely on the dining-room table?"

Lucy emitted a tiny squeak.

"Hmm? Oh, that's right. You can't see them from there. I suppose I'll just have to carry you in for a closer look.'' Just as Claire bent to retrieve the baby, the phone rang. ''A slight delay, sweetums,'' she murmured. ''I'll be right back.''

She snatched a wall phone beside the kitchen counter, answering almost breathlessly. When she heard Johnny's voice, her heart gave a wild leap. ''Thank goodness you called! I've left so many messages for you—''

He interrupted brusquely. ''I drove down to Farmington this afternoon.''

''Farmington? Isn't that in New Mexico?''

''I'll be staying here tonight.''

''You're not coming home?'' Her gaze fell on the prawns she'd planned to sauté in rich butter and serve on a bed of saffron rice. ''Well, I'm disappointed, of course. I'd planned a special supper for you, but I suppose the surprise can wait until tomorrow.''

The strain in his voice was palpable. ''Don't plan anything for me. I'm not sure when I'll be in.''

''Is something wrong, Johnny?'' A chill slid down her spine. ''You don't…regret what happened last night, do you?''

In the silence that followed, Claire died a little. She couldn't bear it if he regretted the beauty of their lovemaking, if he didn't cherish it as much as she did. He'd seemed so jubilant this morning, so loving and sweet.

When he finally spoke, his voice quavered with emotion. ''I don't regret it, Claire. I…'' The word dissipated in a choked sigh. ''I have to go. I have a meeting.''

''Johnny, wait!'' Claire paused to catch her breath. ''The roses were beautiful.''

A sound filtered down the line, a muted rustle as

if he'd lowered the receiver, then lifted it again. "I'm glad you liked them."

Before she could find her voice to reply, there was a soft click. Something buzzed in her ear. When she realized it was a dial tone, she hung up, staring at the telephone as if it held a secret she could somehow psychically extract.

Heaving a sigh, Claire returned the prawns and vegetables to the refrigerator. "Well, sweetie, I guess I won't be modeling my pretty new lingerie until tomorrow night."

Claire tried to tell herself that tomorrow wasn't all that far away. But a pesky voice in her mind whispered that it was further away than she could ever imagine.

"Johnny?"

It was 6:00 a.m. when he looked up from the work spread over the dining table. His eyes were reddened from lack of sleep. "Yes?"

"You've worked all night again." It wasn't a question. He gave no reply.

Claire shifted, bewildered by the sudden coolness that had settled between them without warning. The night after his trip to Farmington, he'd called to say he'd be home late. She had waited up until midnight, then fallen asleep. When she'd awakened the following morning, the guest-room bed was mussed, and Johnny was gone. A note on the fridge said he hadn't wanted to wake her, that he would be late again tonight, and not to wait dinner for him.

He'd finally come home at 11:00 p.m., only to settle at the dining-room table to work.

Bewildered by his withdrawal, Claire confronted

him gently. "You've hardly spoken for the past two days. You've worked late, left early, seemed completely preoccupied. What is it, Johnny? What's wrong?"

She reached up to touch a snowy blossom sprouting from the crystal vase. The roses hadn't wilted yet. The relationship, it seemed, had. That terrified her.

Johnny wouldn't meet her eyes. "I've been busy."

Unwilling to accept that, she sat across the table from him, her mind spinning. Claire understood the pressures of business, the unanticipated emergencies that disrupted one's private life without warning. She also understood that Johnny played his own professional dealings close to the vest, rarely discussing his clients or current projects. She didn't want to pressure him, didn't want to nag.

Forcing a smile, she reached out to touch his hand. "Would you like breakfast? I could fix some eggs before I go—"

"No, thank you. I have a meeting in forty-five minutes." He aimed a pointed glance at the document he was reading. "I really should finish this."

"Of course." She placed her hand in her lap, moistened lips so dry they felt cracked and sore. Panic swelled inside, a sense of terror that had blossomed over the past days with increasing fervor. His emotional withdrawal frightened her, particularly since she'd made an impulsive decision, one that would soon bear consequences. "Johnny?"

His pen froze over the paper. He didn't look up. "Claire, I really have to complete these revisions before my meeting—"

"You mother is coming for a visit."

His head snapped up, the bruised-looking crescents

of flesh beneath his tired eyes seeming to sink even deeper into his skull. "What?"

Rushing forward before she lost her courage, Claire blurted, "Ezra Buck gave me her phone number, Johnny, so I called a few days ago—" She flushed, recalling that she had made the phone call in a burst of joy after their one night of wild, wonderful sex. "I called and I invited her."

"You did *what?*"

"She's your mother, Johnny, your blood. She loves you. I thought—" Claire flinched as he flung the pen down, clamped his lips together, pushed away from the table so quickly the chair fell over. She swallowed hard, clasped her hands together to quell their shaking. "I thought it was time for the two of you to let go of the past and become a family again."

Johnny raked his hair, bent his head and stood for a long moment, with only his ragged breath breaking the silence between them. "You had no right," he said finally, his voice thick with anger.

"Perhaps I didn't, Johnny. I'm sorry." She swallowed hard, stood and extended a pleading hand. "But your mother has rights, and so does Lucy."

His head swung around, eyes wide and horrified. "You told her about Lucy?"

"Of course I told her. Lucy is her only grandchild. She was so happy she cried, Johnny, actually cried."

"My God." Wiping his face with his palms, he turned away. "You don't know what you've done, Claire. You have no earthly idea."

The silence was deafening. A few engine noises filtered from outside, the hum of a passing car, the muted buzz of a lawnmower. A clock on the bookcase ticked. The refrigerator thrummed in the kitchen. But in the living room, an icy shroud of silence smothered the soul.

Claire sat rigid, immobile, her knuckles white against the wrinkled lab report clutched in her fingers. Her world had turned to ashes; her heart had turned to dust. "When were you planning to tell me?"

Across the room, Johnny gazed out the window, arms crossed, shoulders squared. "I don't know."

"Let me rephrase. Were you ever planning to tell me that Lucy isn't your child?"

A telltale quiver moved down his spine, visible through the thin cotton dress shirt. "I hadn't decided."

"So you would have gone on living the lie forever?"

A heartbeat passed, then another. Finally, he turned to face her with bleak eyes. "I considered it."

Tears pressed her lids, seemed to freeze there, leaving her eyes tight, dry. Cold. "Why? I mean, you went to a great deal of effort skulking around in secret. It makes one wonder what kind of results you were hoping for."

"I was hoping to prove Lucy was mine."

Claire flung the hated report aside. Somewhere in the recesses of her mind she understood that rationality had been replaced by emotion, but she couldn't control the terror, the fear. The pain. "She *is* yours! Samantha gave her to you, and in just a matter of weeks, a judge would have made it legal. You were looking for a way out, Johnny. At least have the guts to admit it."

A flash of pain was covered quickly. "Believe what you want, Claire."

"I believe what I see, Johnny, and I see a man who never wanted a child, who never wanted a family, who has done everything in his power to...to..." Air slipped out of her lungs all at once. To what? To marry a woman he didn't love, to care for a child that wasn't his? That was the crux of it, the core of her terror. Claire could never doubt how deeply Johnny loved Lucy, knew that he loved her so much that he had married a woman he didn't love simply to give his child a mother. If Lucy weren't his child—

Pain knifed her like a blade. She was going to lose Johnny, and she was going to lose Lucy, too.

"We don't have to tell anyone," she said finally. "No one has to know."

Johnny moved to the sofa, sat beside her. He took her hand, flinched when she pulled it away. "Someone already knows."

"Yes, yes, that Greta person. You told me." Claire knew she was making no sense. She didn't care. Lucy wasn't the child of her womb, but she was the child of her heart. She couldn't lose her. She wouldn't. "We can deal with her. I have money in the bank. We'll pay her."

"Claire—"

"Or we'll say she's lying. She can't prove otherwise. The DNA tests are secret. No one can get them. No one."

Johnny rubbed his forehead. "The court can subpoena them, Claire."

Her stomach lurched. "The court can't subpoena something that doesn't exist." Frantically, she dropped from the sofa to the floor, grabbed the report and would have ripped it into shreds if Johnny had not stopped her.

''The court can order its own test.'' He took the report, laid it on the table, lifted her up and gathered her into his arms. ''Lucy would be put through that all over again.''

Claire collapsed against him, tangling her fingers in his shirt. He was right. She knew he was right, but her mind, her heart simply couldn't accept the inevitable. ''There's no reason for the court to order a test unless paternity is questioned. This Greta person, she didn't say she was going to tell anyone, did she? I mean, there's no reason for her to tell, and there's no reason the judge would ask. We could just wait and see if everything turns out okay...couldn't we?'' She wadded his shirt in her fists, and shook him. ''Tell me, Johnny, tell me you're not going to let them take Lucy away.''

A shudder ran through his torso. His jaw clamped, a muscle twitching below his ear. His lips were tight, whitened at the corners. His eyes were black, emotionless.

Claire drew back, her skin suddenly so cold she shivered. ''You're not going to fight for her, are you? You're just going to give her up.''

He took a moment to answer. ''I don't know yet.''

''You don't *know?*'' Her voice rose, trembled with fear. ''How could you not know?''

''I've needed time to think, to check some things out.'' He swallowed, refused to look at her. ''Rodney Frye's parents are still living. He has two sisters and a brother, all of whom have children of their own.''

With every word, Claire's breathing shallowed and her pulse weakened.

''Lucy has grandparents, aunts, an uncle, cousins. She has family, a real family. They have a right to know her, and she has a right to know them." He swallowed a crack in his voice before adding, "I thought you of all people would understand what that means."

Stunned, sick at heart, Claire moved away from him. She stood, vaguely surprised that her legs were firm enough to support her. "Is that why you went to Farmington?"

He paused before responding. "Frye was raised there. Most of his family is still in the area."

"Did you meet with them?"

"No."

"Why not? I mean, that's why you went there, isn't it? To see if they'd take Lucy off your hands?"

He flinched. "I went there to get information about Frye's family, and that's exactly what I got."

"And what are you going to do with that information?

"I don't know."

For a long moment, Claire couldn't speak. Her heart was breaking. Everything she loved was being ripped away, the child she adored, the man she loved with every fiber of her being. She couldn't face this, couldn't imagine her life without the family that was as much a part of her as her own skin.

A few feet away, Johnny stood stoic, with the implacable expression of a man unmoved that her world had just been shattered.

Johnny was not unmoved. His world had also been shattered, although he concealed his turmoil with feigned dispassion, an apathetic shield behind which he'd always hidden a wounded heart.

Inside, he was dying.

Johnny couldn't look at Claire, couldn't bear to see

the agony in her eyes. He understood she'd only married him because of her love for Lucy. Without Lucy, Claire wouldn't want him. The loss of the child she adored would devastate Claire; it would devastate him, as well. Johnny loved Lucy more than he loved his own life. It didn't matter that she wasn't the child of his body. In his heart, in his soul, she would always be his daughter.

His first instinct had been the same as Claire's, to simply destroy the evidence and pretend he didn't know the truth. In the end, he couldn't deceive Claire, even if living the lie was his only chance of happiness.

Johnny desperately wanted to do the right thing for Lucy, and had made the decision to search for Frye's family because of Claire's own desperate quest to find her bloodline, to understand the heritage of her own ancestors. "I had to know if Lucy had people out there, people who would want her and love her."

"I want her!" Claire spun around, her fists clenched at her side. "I love her, Johnny! I thought you did, too."

With some effort, he kept his expression immobile. "You've spent much of your life wondering about your own ancestry, searching for your heritage, those who were and perhaps are related to you by blood. I didn't want Lucy to grow up feeling that lost, that disconnected from her past. I thought she had a right to know who she is. I presumed that you'd agree."

Claire's expression crumpled before his eyes. Tears slipped down her cheeks in twin rivulets of misery. Her shoulders quivered; her lips tightened and twisted in a silent sob.

It was all he could do to keep from reaching for

her, from gathering her in his arms and promising that they'd take Lucy and run far away from here, live the lie forever if that was what it would take to make her happy. He folded his arms to remove the temptation.

Claire bit her lip, turned away. Her fingers tangled together into a desperate knot. "What about us, Johnny?" Her voice cracked; a sob caught deep in her throat. She stiffened, inhaled deeply and repeated the question as she glanced over her shoulder. "What about us?"

It was the question he feared most. He couldn't force her to stay with him, couldn't expect her to forgive him for allowing the child she adored to be taken away. "The marriage was meant to be temporary."

The life drained out of her eyes. "To you everything is temporary. You've never cared enough about anyone or anything to fight for it."

That hurt. "Claire—"

She pulled back as he reached for her, holding up her arms as a shield. "Go to work, Johnny. Just…go."

Defeated, he did as she asked. As he drove away from the house on that gray and dreary morning, he knew that neither she nor Lucy would be there when he returned.

Chapter Fourteen

It was dark. Cold. Empty.

Parked in the driveway, Johnny felt the loneliness devour him whole. No beckoning light seeped from the windows. No welcoming warmth emanated from the house that for a few brief and joyous weeks had been transformed into a home.

It was a taste of heaven that had dried into ashes on his tongue. He had lost all that was dear to him. Again.

Pain twisted through his gut, knifed into his chest. His breath caught, backed up in his throat. When he'd composed himself, he strode up the walkway, unlocked the front door and entered the cold, dank foyer.

He shivered, turned on one light, then another and another until the house radiated wattage like an overdressed Christmas tree. Evidence of Claire's influence was everywhere, from the lush foliage sprouting in every windowsill and spilling from hanging baskets of greenery, to the homey, handwoven throw pillows she'd purchased from a tribal craftswoman to cast warmth on what had otherwise been a sterile living area.

He wandered into the kitchen, paused beside a royal-blue mixer on the counter. It was indeed one of the professional models. Quite expensive. Claire used it several times a week, and when she did, the kitchen smelled glorious. Even the memory of the marvelous meals she prepared made his mouth water.

No doubt about it; Claire had turned his house into a home. But it couldn't be a home without her and Lucy.

From the kitchen, he wandered into the dining room and past the expansive oak table, which was usually cluttered with work he'd brought home from the office. It was neat and tidy now, except for a single familiar document, clad in legal blue sheathing.

It was the prenuptial agreement Claire had taken the night before their wedding. In truth, Johnny had forgotten about the document. Now it mocked him. He knew without looking that the final page would bear her signature. And it did.

Trembling, he left the dining room as if distance could erase the reality he'd always feared, the end of a relationship so precious that it was the one thing on earth he couldn't pretend didn't matter. But he'd always known it would end, had always steeled himself for the inevitability of loss. He just hadn't realized how deep the knife would slice this time. Nothing could have prepared him for this agony, this pit of despair.

Nothing.

Absently turning on the stereo and the television, he was comforted by the blast of conflicting sound. Old habits, habits nearly forgotten since Claire and Lucy had entered his life. How easily he slipped on that shroud of loneliness, of pretense.

His hand trembled as he reached for the bottle and poured two fingers of whiskey into his glass. The rhythm of jazz from the stereo pulsed in his brain; a chirpy voice from the TV hawked breakfast cereal. Noise. Lots of noise. Johnny craved it, needed it.

This time the noise couldn't drown the silence of his soul.

His was a soul tormented not by silence, but by sound. The whisper of a tortured mind, the cry of a broken heart. Sounds of sadness, of sorrow, of deep, abiding loss. Sounds Johnny tried to ignore, because to acknowledge them would be too painful.

He sipped his whiskey, felt the comforting sting work its way down his throat. Numbness would follow, the pain would ease.

Or would it?

Ezra Buck's voice whispered at the edge of his mind. *The wisdom to seek lends the courage to find....*

The words haunted Johnny as he studied the amber liquid, turning the glass while the blaze of lamplight penetrated its golden depths. All his life, he'd been disappointed, disillusioned, stricken by loss. He learned to expect it, anticipate it, perhaps even create it, and had developed his own personal pattern of behavior to deal with it.

Every time someone or something hurt him, he shielded himself from the pain by pretending not to care, constructing an illusion that he was in control of his emotions when the opposite was true. Emotions had been running his entire life.

The wisdom to seek lends the courage to find....

Ezra had been right. Johnny had let his people down. He'd let himself down, not by what he had done with his life, but by what he had not done. He'd never shown the courage of conviction, the determination to fight for permanence, to struggle through the pain.

Claire had accused him of having never cared enough about anyone or anything to fight for it. Perhaps that had been true in the past. It wasn't true anymore.

Setting down the glass, Johnny went to the bookcase where his grandfather's mementos were displayed. He touched the beaded bag that had once hung on his grandfather's belt. The wisdom to seek. The courage to find. Johnny had never displayed either. He'd turned his back on his people, turned his back on the callings of his own heart simply because he feared the pain of loss. His grandfather would be shamed.

But no more.

"It wasn't your fault," Megan repeated for the tenth time that evening. "Johnny Winterhawk is not a man who can be forced into anything. He married you because he wanted to."

"He married me so his child would have a mother." Sniffing, Claire discarded a wet tissue into the growing pile, snatched a fresh one from a nearby box. "I was the one determined to turn our relationship into something he never intended it to be."

"A relationship takes two people, hon."

Fresh tears slipped down her cheeks. "I wanted him to love me."

Megan slipped an arm around her friend's shoulders. "Are you so certain that he doesn't?"

Air clogged her throat, nearly choking her. She was grateful when Megan's husband peered into the living room, distracting her friend for a moment. "Are the babies all right, Mac?" she asked.

The man shifted, clearly uneasy. "Lucy is asleep. Tyler is fussing a bit. I thought he might like a bottle of juice or something."

Megan's eyes glowed with love. "You're a good daddy."

Even from a distance of twenty feet, Claire saw his flush of pride at the praise. He cleared his throat, smiled, then slipped quietly away.

Returning her attention to Claire, Megan squeezed her friend's hand. "Did you see the way Mac looked at me? That was love, Claire. I've seen Johnny look at you the same way."

Forcing her lungs to empty, Claire drew a deep, cleansing breath. "How could he love me, Meggie? I was so selfish, so absorbed in my own feelings that I completely ignored what he was going through. I know how dearly he loves Lucy, how devastated he must have been to learn that she wasn't his, but instead of comforting him, all I could do was hurl accusations. I don't deserve him. I don't deserve Lucy, either."

"Don't say that. It's not true." She took Claire's hand, gave it a scolding squeeze. "You were shocked, you were frightened, you reacted normally."

"I was willing to conceal Lucy's true identity from her just to keep from losing her." And to keep from losing Johnny. The enormity of what she'd done, of what she'd been willing to do was shattering. All her life, she'd suffered the heartache of not knowing her own birth parents. She'd been righteously indignant about heritage when it served her purpose, but when it threatened her own happiness, she'd been willing to steal part of Lucy's.

Claire was ashamed of herself for that, and ashamed of herself for having taken advantage of a moment of crisis to force herself into the life of a man who had not wanted her.

"All I have to give Johnny now is his freedom," she murmured. "And I've done that."

"Thank you so much, Doctor." The harried mom scooped her annoyed son from the examining table, hugged the child fiercely. "I don't know how it happened. I mean, I only turned away for a moment."

Claire laid the forceps aside, smiling. This wasn't the first two-year-old to shove a jelly bean up his nose. She doubted it would be the last. "This sort of thing happens all the time." Jotting her final examination notes on the chart, she paused to angle a reassuring smile. "Danny will be fine, just fine."

The examining-room door opened, startling both Claire and Danny's long-suffering mom. "I'm sorry to bother you, Doctor…" Jeri Jansen gulped, slipped a perplexed glance back into the clinic hallway. "I wonder if you could you come to the nurses' station as soon as you're finished here."

Concerned by a peculiar glint of near panic in the usually unflappable nurse's eye, Claire laid the chart on the sink counter, absently retrieved her stethoscope from the breast pocket of her lab coat. "Is there an emergency?"

"Yes… I mean, no…" Jeri took a deep breath, her gaze darting back into the hallway. "It's something that requires your attention."

Expelling air all at once, the young woman stepped back to reveal a hallway crowded with flowers and festive balloon bouquets, along with a crush of bewildered deliverymen searching for someone willing to sign for the myriad items. A riot of color, of vivid blossoms and bows lined the counter of the nurses' station, four huge bouquets each bristling with a balloon on which a single word had been emblazoned. When lined up in the proper order, the balloons spelled Do You Like Surprises?

A giant question mark sprouted from a fifth bouquet, which was set in place by a bustling deliveryman in a blue jacket and baseball cap. His task completed, he spun on his heel to shove a clipboard toward Jeri. "Sign here, please."

"Uh-uh, not me." Tossing up both hands, the nurse backed out of the doorway, and disappeared from sight.

The fellow in the baseball cap gave Claire a glazed glance. "Somebody has to sign for this stuff."

Since he was blocking the examining-room doorway, Claire scrawled a signature, accepted his sigh of relief as he hurried away, then eased out of the room at the same moment that Rose McBride, the clinic administrator, emerged from her office, to gape in stunned silence.

Before Claire could even catch her breath, the main clinic doors opened, revealing a tuxedo-clad Johnny Winterhawk carrying a spray of white roses and baby's breath nestled in greenery and tied with a snowy satin ribbon.

He regarded the pandemonium with an approving gaze, glanced around the gawking onlookers until he spotted Claire, then marched over and laid the roses in her arms.

Astonished, she cradled the fragrant blossoms as if they were an infant. "What—" she coughed away an annoying squeak in her voice "—what are you doing?"

As if on cue, Johnny dropped to one knee and took hold of her left hand, causing her to shift the bouquet to the crook of her right arm. He opened his mouth, closed it and swallowed hard, seeming unaware that an audience had gathered, patients and staff, along with the delivery people, all of whom now bunched around the nurses' station to watch the drama unfold.

Johnny moistened his lips. "You were right about me, Claire. I've never cared about anyone or anything enough to fight for it. Well, I'm fighting now. I'm fighting for you, for Lucy, for our marriage, and I want everyone in this town to know it."

A murmur vibrated through the crowd, but Claire barely heard it. She was speechless, completely stunned by Johnny's pronouncement.

With his free hand, he reached inside his tuxedo to retrieve a folded document, wrapped in legal blue. Claire recognized it as the agreement she'd signed and left on the dining-room table.

"I don't understand... what is this all about?"

"It's about the wisdom to seek love, and courage to find it." He released his grasp on her hand long enough to rip the document into a dozen pieces, flung them into the air like confetti.

Filling his lungs, he held his breath for a beat, exhaled all at once, retrieved something from his pocket and reclaimed her hand. "I love you, Claire, enough to fight for you, to die for you. Most of all, I love you enough to live for you." He deftly snapped open a tiny box in his palm, revealing a twinkling diamond ring. "You are my wife, Claire. Without you, I can exist, but I cannot truly live. You are my heart and my spirit, the breath of my body and the essence of my soul."

The collage of flowers blurred beneath a mist of stunned tears. He slipped the ring onto her finger, a glide of warm gold, a subtle coolness of diamond pressing her knuckle. "Oh, Johnny..." Her heart pounded, a bewildered rhythm of joy tempered with wary confusion. "What about Lucy?"

He stood, his expression quiet, his dark gaze intense and glowing. "She's the child of my heart. I want to raise her, to be a real father to her, a grandfather to her children and a great-grandfather to her children's children. I don't know if that will come to be, but I hope that it will." He lifted her hand to his lips, brushed a sweet kiss across her knuckles, placed a separate kiss on the glittering gemstone that signified their love. "I have spoken with Rodney Frye's parents. They want to be a part of their granddaughter's life, but aren't able to raise her themselves."

Claire clenched her fingers, grasping at Johnny's hand. "They'll let us adopt Lucy?"

"I don't know," he answered honestly. "They wish time to adjust to the knowledge that their son had a child, and to discuss the options with the rest of their family. It'll be a difficult decision for them."

Her heart thudded once, seemed to shrink within

her chest. They could still lose Lucy. She couldn't bear it. "I understand," she whispered, although a part of her could never understand. "She's their flesh and blood." More tears streamed down her cheeks.

Johnny wiped them away with his thumb. "She's also the child of her mother, a daughter of the tribe. It's her birthright, her heritage. I will teach her these things, as Samantha would have wished."

A kernel of hope sprouted deep inside. "The Fryes will allow this?"

"They will. They understand that Lucy is a child of two worlds, and cannot flourish without the nourishment of both."

"But...they may take her away from us?"

"I don't know." He hesitated, brushed his cheek against her finger. "No matter what happens, no matter what occurs, we will love her, protect her, cherish her. We will always be a part of Lucy's life. This I promise you."

And as he spoke, Claire knew that it was true. "I believe you," she whispered.

He closed his eyes, his expression one of utter reverence. When he opened them again, his eyes were beacons of intensity, so sharp and piercing they took her breath away. "Believe this, as well. I love you as I have never loved another. I'll love you until I've taken my final breath on this earth, and beyond. You're everything to me, Claire. I'll cherish you forever, if you'll allow it."

A hush settled over the mesmerized crowd, a silence of anticipation broken only by a muted sob from a deeply touched office worker dabbing her moist eyes.

Claire was vaguely aware of their audience, but

they seemed miles away. The focus of her entire being was on this one man, this precious person whom she loved beyond measure. "Forever," she whispered, "is not nearly enough time for what I have in mind. But it's a start."

A crinkle of relief brightened his eyes, touched the curve of his lips a moment before his mouth took hers in a slow, sweet kiss that warmed her to her toes.

Applause came from what seemed a great distance, a roar of approval that soon filled the flower-filled clinic with a cacophony of cheers. A moment later, Claire and Johnny were mobbed by well-wishers who surrounded them with hugs, handshakes and teary-eyed congratulations.

Life was full of surprises for those with the wisdom to seek and the courage to find. Forever had just begun.

Epilogue

The dishwasher was loaded. Soft music floated from the living-room stereo. Scented candles flickered gently, wafting sweet fragrance throughout a home lush with foliage, warm with love.

Rubbing the small of her back, Claire hung up the telephone, her mother's joyful laughter still ringing in her ears. Regina was thrilled about coming to visit this summer. Claire could hardly wait to see her parents again. She hadn't seen them since the wedding...the real wedding, where Claire had worn Nana's antique lace gown, and Megan had been a beautiful matron of honor bedecked in the cerulean attendant ensembles of Claire's childhood dreams. Johnny had been proud and stoic, waiting at the altar with Spence McBride as his best man and Ezra Buck as an honored groomsman. It had been a glorious ceremony, all that Claire had ever wished for, and more.

Johnny's mother had attended, as well, along with her husband. She was a stately woman, as proud as her son and just as stubborn. But the occasion had heralded the beginning of a new relationship between the estranged mother and the man who was Claire's husband. Both seemed willing to put the pain of the past behind them for the sake of family, and of the cherished child that all adored.

Moving down the hallway, Claire followed the familiar voice of her beloved. At the nursery door, she hesitated, positioning herself to observe the interaction between her husband and their beautiful adopted daughter. Johnny sat in the rocking chair Claire had brought a year ago, when she'd first moved into the house that had become her sanctuary, her haven, her home.

She never tired of watching her husband and child. They were the joy of her life. She particularly enjoyed quietly sharing moments like this one, where father and daughter shared a special bond of their unique heritage.

"Tomorrow is Bear Dance," Johnny whispered to the pajama-clad toddler. "It's a time of great joy and happiness for our people, a time when we remember the stories of the past, and give thanks for the abundance we enjoy."

Gazing up with huge dark eyes, Lucy pulled her thumb from her mouth long enough to emit an indecipherable grunt. At fifteen months of age, the baby had developed a unique personality, insatiable curiosity and unabated delight at every new discovery. To her, the world was a smorgasbord of wonder, a feast for the senses to be savored one miracle at a time. Claire adored her.

So did Johnny, who nodded somberly, as if he understood each of the baby's garbled utterances. "This is true, small one. It is a time for retelling the old tales, remembering those who have gone before us, who have brought the stories from the grandfather of their grandfathers."

Gasping in apparent awe, Lucy jammed her fat fists against her cheeks. "Da-goo-da!" she announced.

Johnny nodded. "It was long ago, when the streams ran clear and creatures of the forest gave their spirits to nourish our people. Two brothers were hunting in the mountains. One became tired, and stopped to rest. The other continued hunting...."

As the familiar story evolved, Claire cupped her swollen belly with one hand, wiped a happy tear from her cheek with the other. Before the day of the Sun Dance, she would bear Johnny's child. Lucy would have a brother, a tiny boy who would grow into a strong and gentle man, just like his father.

"The bear was making noises, and seemed to be dancing with the tree...."

Overcome with emotion, Claire backed away from the doorway and went to retrieve a special gift for her husband. She held it in her hands, stroking it gently with her fingertips. It had taken her many months to create it. Hoping he'd be pleased, she placed the gift on the kitchen table, returned to the nursery just as Johnny completed his story.

"Every spring the people sing the song," he said softly, "and perform the dance to welcome the warmth of spring, and to show respect for the spirit of the bear."

"Eeee-gabadada!" Lucy squeaked, clearly enthralled.

"Yes, it is permitted. You may dance in my arms until you are big enough to enter the circle on your own."

"Gammy-gammy-goo?"

"Of course Grandma and Grampa Frye will be there, as well."

Claire smiled. The Fryes adored their granddaughter and were frequent visitors at the Winterhawk home, as well as treasured friends. Lucy was a child of two worlds, prized by both. She would grow up knowing who she was, and where she belonged. Most important of all, she would grow up loved and cherished.

Standing, Johnny cradled the squirming child in his arms, kissed her cheek and saw Claire in the doorway as he placed the baby in the crib. "Ah, perfect timing. Lucy is ready for her good-night kiss."

"Is she now?" As Claire moved forward, Lucy pulled herself upright on the crib rail, flung her arms out, grunting madly until she'd been thoroughly kissed, hugged, kissed again, then tucked warmly into bed for the night.

As they tiptoed out of the darkened nursery, Johnny slipped his arm around what had once been Claire's waist. "You're particularly fetching this evening," he whispered against her nape. "There's a glow about you."

She shivered at the moist heat created by his lips nuzzling her earlobe. "I glow because I'm happy."

"Are you happy?"

"Very."

Smiling, he stroked her cheek with his thumb. "Perhaps I should call Ezra, and postpone tonight's appearance at the tribal council."

"Don't you dare." It had taken months to convince Johnny to run for a seat on the council, although he'd been doing pro bono legal work for the tribe since the past summer. "I want this weekend's Bear Dance festivities to be your first tribal appearance in an official capacity."

He shrugged, trying for a nonchalant expression that couldn't conceal the pride in his eyes. "If that is what you wish, that is what shall be."

"There is one other thing." Excited, Claire led him toward the kitchen. "Do you like surprises, Johnny Winterhawk?"

He laughed. "You know that I do, wife." Spying the small package on the kitchen table, his eyes lit. "A gift?"

"Yes." Claire could barely contain herself. "Don't just stand there. Open it!"

Grinning madly, Johnny snatched up the present, ripped the ribbon and wrapping off with the exuberance of a child on Christmas morning. He lifted the lid off a rectangular box the size of a small picture frame, then sucked in his breath when he spied the contents.

Claire emptied her lungs all at once. "I know it's not perfect...it's my first time."

"You made this?" He opened his mouth as if to speak, then closed it, as if there were no words. A shimmer brightened his eyes as he reverently unrolled the beaded belt to its full length.

"It's for the Bear Dance," Claire blurted unnecessarily. "Ezra's wife has been instructing me in bead craft. I hoped you would like it."

"It is my most cherished possession," he said simply. "I will wear it with pride, and with love." Still clutching the precious belt, Johnny lifted her chin, gazed deeply into her eyes. "Do you like surprises, wife?"

Her heart hammered at the phrase that had private meaning for them both. "You know that I do, husband."

"In that case, my beloved, the tribal council can wait." With that, he swept her pregnant body into his arms as if she weighed no more than a feather and carried her into the bedroom.

All was as it should be. The ancestors would be pleased.

* * * * *

Devilishly cool, handsome and clever, tycoon Kyle Montgomery always got what he wanted—and right now it was that Emma Valentine and her newborn pose as his wife and child...

* * * * *

Look for the next installment of the miniseries SO MANY BABIES, Millionaire's Instant Baby, by Allison Leigh, on sale March 2000 in Special Edition!

PAMELA TOTH
DIANA WHITNEY
ALLISON LEIGH
LAURIE PAIGE

*bring you four heartwarming stories
in the brand-new series*

So Many Babies

At the Buttonwood Baby Clinic,
babies and romance abound!

On sale January 2000: **THE BABY LEGACY**
by **Pamela Toth**

On sale February 2000: **WHO'S THAT BABY?**
by **Diana Whitney**

On sale March 2000: **MILLIONAIRE'S INSTANT BABY**
by **Allison Leigh**

On sale April 2000: **MAKE WAY FOR BABIES!**
by **Laurie Paige**

***Only from Silhouette* SPECIAL EDITION**
Available at your favorite retail outlet.

Where love comes alive™

Visit us at www.romance.net   SSESMB

If you enjoyed what you just read,
then we've got an offer you can't resist!

Take 2 bestselling
love stories FREE!
Plus get a FREE surprise gift!

Clip this page and mail it to Silhouette Reader Service™

YES! Please send me 2 free Silhouette Special Edition® novels and my free surprise gift. Then send me 6 brand-new novels every month, which I will receive months before they're available in stores. In the U.S.A., bill me at the bargain price of $3.57 plus 25¢ delivery per book and applicable sales tax, if any*. In Canada, bill me at the bargain price of $3.96 plus 25¢ delivery per book and applicable taxes**. That's the complete price and a savings of over 10% off the cover prices—what a great deal! I understand that accepting the 2 free books and gift places me under no obligation ever to buy any books. I can always return a shipment and cancel at any time. Even if I never buy another book from Silhouette, the 2 free books and gift are mine to keep forever. So why not take us up on our invitation. You'll be glad you did!

235 SEN CNFD
335 SEN CNFE

Name	(PLEASE PRINT)	
Address	Apt.#	
City	State/Prov.	Zip/Postal Code

* Terms and prices subject to change without notice. Sales tax applicable in N.Y.
** Canadian residents will be charged applicable provincial taxes and GST.
  All orders subject to approval. Offer limited to one per household.
  ® are registered trademarks of Harlequin Enterprises Limited.

SPED99   ©1998 Harlequin Enterprises Limited

Silhouette Special Edition brings you

by SHERRYL WOODS

Come join the Delacourt family as they all find love—
and parenthood—in the most unexpected ways!

On sale December 1999:
THE COWBOY AND THE NEW YEAR'S BABY (SE#1291)
During one of the worst blizzards in Texas history, a
stranded Trish Delacourt was about to give birth! Luckily,
sexy Hardy Jones rushed to the rescue. Could the no-strings
bachelor and the new mom turn a precious New Year's
miracle into a labor of *love*?

On sale March 2000:
DYLAN AND THE BABY DOCTOR (SE#1309)
Private detective Dylan Delacourt had closed off part of
his heart and wasn't prepared for what Kelsey James stirred
up when she called on him to locate her missing son.

And don't miss Jeb Delacourt's story coming
to Special Edition in July 2000.

Available at your favorite retail outlet.

Visit us at www.romance.net

SSEDEL

SILHOUETTE'S 20ᵀᴴ ANNIVERSARY CONTEST
OFFICIAL RULES
NO PURCHASE NECESSARY TO ENTER

1. To enter, follow directions published in the offer to which you are responding. Contest begins 1/1/00 and ends on 8/24/00 (the "Promotion Period"). Method of entry may vary. Mailed entries must be postmarked by 8/24/00, and received by 8/31/00.

2. During the Promotion Period, the Contest may be presented via the Internet. Entry via the Internet may be restricted to residents of certain geographic areas that are disclosed on the Web site. To enter via the Internet, if you are a resident of a geographic area in which Internet entry is permissible, follow the directions displayed on-line, including typing your essay of 100 words or fewer telling us "Where In The World Your Love Will Come Alive." On-line entries must be received by 11:59 p.m. Eastern Standard time on 8/24/00. Limit one e-mail entry per person, household and e-mail address per day, per presentation. If you are a resident of a geographic area in which entry via the Internet is permissible, you may, in lieu of submitting an entry on-line, enter by mail, by hand-printing your name, address, telephone number and contest number/name on an 8"x 11" plain piece of paper and telling us in 100 words or fewer "Where In The World Your Love Will Come Alive," and mailing via first-class mail to: Silhouette 20ᵗʰ Anniversary Contest, (in the U.S.) P.O. Box 9069, Buffalo, NY 14269-9069; (In Canada) P.O. Box 637, Fort Erie, Ontario, Canada L2A 5X3. Limit one 8"x 11" mailed entry per person, household and e-mail address per day. On-line and/or 8"x 11" mailed entries received from persons residing in geographic areas in which Internet entry is not permissible will be disqualified. No liability is assumed for lost, late, incomplete, inaccurate, nondelivered or misdirected mail, or misdirected e-mail, for technical, hardware or software failures of any kind, lost or unavailable network connection, or failed, incomplete, garbled or delayed computer transmission or any human error which may occur in the receipt or processing of the entries in the contest.

3. Essays will be judged by a panel of members of the Silhouette editorial and marketing staff based on the following criteria:

   > Sincerity (believability, credibility)—50%
   >
   > Originality (freshness, creativity)—30%
   >
   > Aptness (appropriateness to contest ideas)—20%

   Purchase or acceptance of a product offer does not improve your chances of winning. In the event of a tie, duplicate prizes will be awarded.

4. All entries become the property of Harlequin Enterprises Ltd., and will not be returned. Winner will be determined no later than 10/31/00 and will be notified by mail. Grand Prize winner will be required to sign and return Affidavit of Eligibility within 15 days of receipt of notification. Noncompliance within the time period may result in disqualification and an alternative winner may be selected. All municipal, provincial, federal, state and local laws and regulations apply. Contest open only to residents of the U.S. and Canada who are 18 years of age or older, and is void wherever prohibited by law. Internet entry is restricted solely to residents of those geographical areas in which Internet entry is permissible. Employees of Torstar Corp., their affiliates, agents and members of their immediate families are not eligible. Taxes on the prizes are the sole responsibility of winners. Entry and acceptance of any prize offered constitutes permission to use winner's name, photograph or other likeness for the purposes of advertising, trade and promotion on behalf of Torstar Corp. without further compensation to the winner, unless prohibited by law. Torstar Corp and D.L. Blair, Inc., their parents, affiliates and subsidiaries, are not responsible for errors in printing or electronic presentation of contest or entries. In the event of printing or other errors which may result in unintended prize values or duplication of prizes, all affected contest materials or entries shall be null and void. If for any reason the Internet portion of the contest is not capable of running as planned, including infection by computer virus, bugs, tampering, unauthorized intervention, fraud, technical failures, or any other causes beyond the control of Torstar Corp. which corrupt or affect the administration, secrecy, fairness, integrity or proper conduct of the contest, Torstar Corp. reserves the right, at its sole discretion, to disqualify any individual who tampers with the entry process and to cancel, terminate, modify or suspend the contest or the Internet portion thereof. In the event of a dispute regarding an on-line entry, the entry will be deemed submitted by the authorized holder of the e-mail account submitted at the time of entry. Authorized account holder is defined as the natural person who is assigned to an e-mail address by an Internet access provider, on-line service provider or other organization that is responsible for arranging e-mail address for the domain associated with the submitted e-mail address.

5. Prizes: Grand Prize—a $10,000 vacation to anywhere in the world. Travelers (at least one must be 18 years of age or older) or parent or guardian if one traveler is a minor, must sign and return a Release of Liability prior to departure. Travel must be completed by December 31, 2001, and is subject to space and accommodations availability. Two hundred (200) Second Prizes—a two-book limited edition autographed collector set from one of the Silhouette Anniversary authors: Nora Roberts, Diana Palmer, Linda Howard or Annette Broadrick (value $10.00 each set). All prizes are valued in U.S. dollars.

6. For a list of winners (available after 10/31/00) send a self-addressed, stamped envelope to: Harlequin Silhouette 20ᵗʰ Anniversary Winners, P.O. Box 4200, Blair, NE 68009-4200.

Contest sponsored by Torstar Corp., P.O. Box 9042, Buffalo, NY 14269-9042.

ENTER FOR
A CHANCE TO WIN*

Silhouette's 20ᵗʰ Anniversary Contest

Tell Us Where in the World
You Would Like *Your* Love To Come Alive...
And We'll Send the Lucky Winner There!

Silhouette wants to take you wherever
your happy ending can come true.

Here's how to enter: Tell us, in 100 words or less,
where you want to go to make your love come alive!

In addition to the grand prize, there will be 200
runner-up prizes, collector's-edition book sets
autographed by one of the Silhouette anniversary
authors: **Nora Roberts, Diana Palmer,
Linda Howard** or **Annette Broadrick**.

DON'T MISS YOUR CHANCE TO WIN!
ENTER NOW! No Purchase Necessary

Where love comes alive™

Name: _____

Address: _____

City: _____ State/Province: _____

Zip/Postal Code: _____

Mail to Harlequin Books: **In the U.S.**: P.O. Box 9069, Buffalo, NY
14269-9069; **In Canada**: P.O. Box 637, Fort Erie, Ontario, L4A 5X3